GRACELAND ON WHEELS

AND MORE SAM JENKINS MYSTERIES

WAYNE ZURL

GRACELAND ON WHEELS
Copyright © 2017 by Wayne Zurl

ISBN: 978-1-68046-583-9

Melange Books, LLC
White Bear Lake, MN 55110
www.fireandiceya.com

Published in the United States of America.

Cover Design by Lynsee Lauritsen

To Dan Caldwell for adding a story to my Gypsy collection.

To all the good people I met during almost thirty years of gun shows.

To the real Sergeant Mike Fitz for an enlightening look inside a maintenance wing.

To Margaret and George Ling for playing mah-jongg with my wife and feeding me wonderful Chinese food.

To Bob Weir for explaining the mechanics of professional billiards.

To "Inspector Sledge Hammer" who made me think writing about an Elvis impersonator might be fun.

To Luther H. Gillis for making a stop at prospect PD.

And to Mae Wallace for inspiring a description of Roxy.

GYPSIES, TRAMPS & THIEVES

On the way to work one Monday morning, my cell phone sounded off. I didn't expect to hear Horace Colwell on the other end. Not many police chiefs give out their personal phone numbers, but Horace was an old friend and... I really should reassess my practices.

"Sam, we've got a problem."

"Whattaya mean 'we', big man?"

"I mean me and Dwight."

Dwight was Horace's brother and manager of Prospect Marine, a business they owned jointly.

"How can I help?" I asked.

"You kin git yer butt down here, and look at the body we got behind the boat yard." He sounded exasperated.

There are two things I hate in my professional life—catching a major case first thing on a Monday morning and not having a second cup of coffee before starting work. After one phone call, I was two for two.

"Have you called 9-1-1 yet?" I asked.

"Called you first." Horace spoke with a classic east Tennessee accent and a deep voice that would make Sam Elliot jealous.

I sighed. "I'll be right there."

For a day job, Horace Colwell worked as a building contractor. But he had lots of spare cash and invested in the side business because he loved boats, and his younger brother needed a job.

It only took me five minutes before I pulled my unmarked Ford into the parking lot in front of a small showroom building. A mechanic named Butch Sexton met me and pointed toward the repair shop at the back of a large and orderly boat yard where Horace and Dwight stood.

Horace was a big guy, taller than me by an inch—maybe six-one and at least two-sixty. A large mustache set off his thinning, dirty-blond hair. Dwight weighed no more than one-fifty, stood almost as tall and had thick dark hair. Hard to believe they shared parents.

The weather couldn't have been better: clear sky, perfect temperature, birds singing—a day to sell real estate or fall in love.

"What's up, gentlemen?" I said. "You've got a body?"

"Back here," Horace said. "Look fer yerse'f."

He began walking, and I followed, Dwight at my heels. Behind the cement block building, Horace pointed to a male body lying face down on the ground. Blood covered the back of his head, dried and caked in the matted dark hair. In front of the corpse, a section of tall chain link fence had been snipped, leaving a four-foot opening.

"One of you two catch him breaking in here?"

"We did not." Horace sounded vehement, probably thinking I'd be accusing them of murder.

Several flies buzzed around the blood, but I checked for life signs anyway. Finding none, I looked from Horace to Dwight for a reaction when I shook my head.

"We're not supposed to have dead bodies in Prospect," I said. "This is not some sleazy urban crime center."

Neither man commented, but shot looks at each other.

"I think I know this guy," Dwight said.

"Think?"

"Well, I got ta see his face ta be sure. But the long hair and all..."

I took a pair of latex gloves from my sport jacket pocket and snapped them on.

"I really don't like to do this," I said, "but okay. Stay where you are, and I'll turn his face. Don't come any closer. I want the scene as uncluttered from footprints as possible."

Dwight nodded, and I turned the man's head to the right. Even in death, the face was dark-complexioned and desperately needed a shave.

"If you don't know him," I said, "I do."

"That's him, all right. Yeah, I know him," Dwight said.

"Enlighten me."

Horace gritted his teeth and shook his head

"He's one o' the pair that hoo-dooed me outta that Starcraft johnboat rig last week. Yessir, and an older one looked jest like him."

"I remember the complaint," I said. "Not much for us to go on, though. Refresh my memory. He give you a name?"

"Stokes. John Stokes. I damn sure remember," Dwight said.

"That's another alias to add to his jacket. I've dealt with this guy before."

The dead man's name was Yanni Stanko, a Gypsy I had recently arrested for fraud. But in my experience, Gypsies use more names than fishermen have hooks.

"The older one look like a brother or father?" I asked.

"Maybe a father, uncle—somethin' like that," Dwight said.

"When'd you see him last?"

Horace pulled a tin of Redman from his hip pocket and placed a pinch of tobacco under his lip.

"Day he drove outta here with my damn boat," Dwight said.

"As I remember from the report, he gave you a hundred cash and a check for the balance."

Dwight nodded. "Stiffed us fer sixteen-thousand and change."

"You called to verify the balance, but when you tried to cash the check, they said most of the money in the account had recently been withdrawn from the Knoxville branch."

"All but a hunnert dollars."

"It's a classic scam."

Two mocking birds squawked at each other from the branches of a sweet gum tree just beyond the fence.

"Y'all had these no-account flim-flam artists up in New York?" Horace asked.

"They're Gypsies. Scams are what they do. I worked a few cases on them."

Horace closed his eyes for a moment and shook his head.

I wanted to refocus on the job at hand. "I don't remember all the details," I said. "Were the two men alone when they took the boat?"

"No," Dwight said. "They had a young pregnant woman with 'em."

"What did she do?"

"Set in the truck mostly. 'Cept this one," he pointed to the body on the ground, "done so much hagglin' an' took so much time, she asked to use the bathroom. I told her to use the commode in the showroom."

"How'd you know she was pregnant?"

"Had a belly out ta here." He held his hand six inches from his waist.

"I wish I knew they were Gypsies when you called about the boat," I said. "She was probably no more pregnant than me."

The Colwell brothers looked at me like I had two heads.

"Part of the scam," I said. "They wear a false stomach and pretend to need a toilet or a drink of water. Most people feel sorry for a pregnant woman, so no one objects."

Still, I saw no looks of understanding.

"You have cash in the showroom?"

"Sure," Horace said. "Cash, checks, credit card receipts—ever'thin' from bidness the day b'fore yesterday."

"Have you seen the cashbox this morning?"

"Ain't looked," Dwight said.

"I'll bet you a new outboard motor it's gone."

Dwight hung his head. Horace shook his.

Two fish-and-ski boats sat on trailers inside the showroom. Their flashy metal flake paint jobs looked incongruous on a macho sportsman's runabout.

I found the office desk drawer jimmied open, and the metal cash box empty.

"You clean or check the washroom last night?"

"No. Butch was gonna clean it today," Dwight said.

In there, we found the double-hung window unlocked.

"She left the latch open," I said, "hoping you wouldn't find it. And you didn't. Then she or some other burglar came back last night and got through the window. All you have to do is pry open the center desk drawer, and all the others open, too. While she was in here alone, she scoped out your operation. They wanted to screw you twice."

"Gat-dag," Horace said. "Now that y'all know who took the boat, kin ya arrest 'em and git everything back?"

I shrugged. "One of them is dead, and he's not saying much. The big question is why our suspected burglar got killed at the scene of the crime. But this sounds like a package deal to me. If I find the killer, I might locate the other Gypsies and your property. But don't get your hopes up. That boat may have been sold for fifty cents on the dollar an hour after they towed it away."

The brothers did their head-shaking thing again. We walked out of the office and back into the showroom. Several boat manufacturers' posters and a half-dozen mounted fish hung on the walls, offering inspiration to potential buyers.

"Look, guys, I'm assuming you didn't kill him, but I can't swear to that yet."

———

I CALLED PO JUNIOR HUSKEY OFF THE ROAD TO TAKE STATEMENTS from the three men at Prospect Marine. The county sheriff sent two crime scene investigators, Jackie Shuman and David Sparks. Doctor Morris Rappaport and his assistant Earl Ogle represented the medical examiner. While Junior corralled his people in the showroom, I spoke with the evidence technicians.

Three of us stood over the body, while the pathologist and his helper worked their angles.

"Kinda dark skinned. Think he's a Mexican?" Jackie asked.

"Gypsy," I said.

"Gypsy?" David sounded surprised.

"Con men, scam artists, sons-of-bitches." Morris spoke with a New Jersey accent.

"It's an ethnic group called Romani. This one's name is Yanni Stanko," I said. "But he's got at least a dozen AKAs. We arrested him and his brother Aldi a while back for the old driveway sealer scam."

"What's that all about?" Jackie asked.

"Classic Gypsy operation," I said. "They have a legit-looking truck with a pavement sprayer. Late in the day, three or four o'clock, they stop at homes with blacktop driveways. Yani here speaks to the person at home—

usually a housewife or older person—and says they've got a small amount of sealer left from a big job and offer to do the driveway at half price."

Jackie, David and Earl watched intensely, fascinated by my story of exotic Gypsies, people you don't often meet in the Great Smoky Mountains. Morris, who's familiar with the 'Gypos', grinned and shook his head.

"They give a phony sales pitch like the sealer penetrates the blacktop four inches and rejuvenates the pavement," I said, "and guarantee it lasts twenty-four months. If the homeowner balks, Yanni says there's only a short time before the sealer solidifies and they have to get rid of the load quickly at the dump. He drops the price, making the deal even more attractive."

"He's right, you know," Morris said. "These guys are all over the northeast. Right, Sam?"

"You bet, Mo. Ever get approached in Essex County?"

Morris had been an assistant ME in that part of New Jersey.

"Not me, my mother. A male-female pair knocked on her door, selling Amway or some garbage. It was summer, and in the middle of their sales pitch, the girl claimed to feel faint and need water. So, my stupid, trusting mother invites them in, sends the girl upstairs to the bathroom instead of to the kitchen because there are dirty dishes, and she's embarrassed. While the girl's away, the guy continues his spiel. Unbeknownst to my dear sweet mother, the girl was stealing jewelry from Momma's bedroom, not using the bathroom."

"I've heard that one before," I said.

"Lord have mercy." David looked in awe.

"So, what happened with the driveway bidness?" Jackie asked.

"We got a call from an old couple. They said the sealer never dried. Turns out, the Stanko brothers only sprayed waste oil, something that costs next to nothing. Had they used some cut-rate cheap sealer that might get sun bleached away in six months, there would have been no criminal act, just something for civil court. But in this case, they committed a fraud. The old lady was sharp and copied down the plate number. A cop in South Knoxville grabbed them after hearing our alarm."

"What happened?" Sparks asked.

"Plead out to a misdemeanor larceny and paid a fine."

"For life they should go away." Morris was obviously anti-Gypsy.

As our pathologist continued to deal with the body, the crime scene men and I looked over the area.

"See the fence?" I said.

"Yep," said Jackie. "Cut from the outside and pushed in."

"Exactly. And that's strange because Yanni is dead in here, and it doesn't seem like anyone left through the cut in the chain link."

"You think someone was waitin' in here fer him?" David asked.

"It looks that way, but I can't imagine why. They scammed Dwight Colwell Friday morning. He had no reason to believe they'd come back."

"But they did," Jackie said.

"Right. Waited for the weekend sales proceeds to stack up and hit the office Sunday night before someone could go to the bank on Monday."

Jackie removed his BCSO ball cap and scratched his short dark hair. "Pretty slick."

"So why kill Yanni?" I asked. "If one of the Colwell's caught him, why not call us? Even if someone used force to stop Yanni, the average person doesn't know the law and would think cold-cocking an escaping burglar would be legal."

Jackie rearranged the cap on his head. "Uh-huh."

"Here's my problem," I said. "Yanni isn't the biggest guy in the world, but the bathroom window is very small and at least eight feet off the ground. Whoever went through the window would have needed a ladder or a boost from a tall person. There's no ladder here."

"Good thinkin'," Jackie said.

"So, how many others were here? And how did they get out? And who killed Yanni?"

"Questions fer yew, boss man," Jackie said. "Me and David'll do the forensics, but bein' able ta find a killer is why yew git the big bucks."

———

WHEN I WALKED INTO PROSPECT PD, BETTYE LAMBERT, THE loveliest desk sergeant on the planet, greeted me.

"You doin' all right today, Sammy?"

She spun around in her swivel chair, the base station radio and computer gear all around her.

I clenched my teeth. "Grrrrr. I really don't need Gypsies on a Monday morning."

"Gypsies?"

"Same bunch from that driveway scam were the creeps who flim-flammed the boat from Prospect Marine. Now, one of them is the dead body at the boat yard."

"Lord have mercy."

"Exactly."

"What can I do?"

"Fire up the computer. We need everything you can find on Yanni Stanko. Just off the top of my head, he's also known as John Stanko, John Stokes, John Stanley, Juan Storey, Stephen Johnson and God only knows what else."

"Mind writin' those down for me, darlin'?"

She took a pen from the pocket of her khaki uniform shirt and handed it to me.

"Sure. Then look for his older brother Aldi and their father, whose name I can't remember, but it's on the old arrest report. And I need a Gypsy woman who was part of the boat scam. Any other associates you find in the records would be helpful, too."

Bettye smiled. "That's a lot of work. Can I have a raise?"

I shook my head, but noticed how her hazel eyes twinkled.

"No, but I'll take you to lunch."

"Some place nice?"

"The Waldorf Astoria if you can get away for a couple days."

"I think I can get the time. I happen to know the boss is sweet on me."

"Only a fool wouldn't fall head over heels in love with you, Blondie."

"You're my hero."

I used my self-deprecating smile to make her feel good. "And tell Stanley to come in early. I'll need him for some road work."

"Anything you want, Sammy." She batted her eyelashes and returned an even bigger smile, something that could have melted the polar icecap.

"I really like your new haircut," I said.

"It's not new anymore, but thanks. You sure know how to sweet talk a girl."

I winked. "I'm the ultimate supervisor."

"'Course you are, darlin'."

"I'm going to visit Yanni's last known address. Call me when you find the father's name."

"Be careful out there, sugar."

"You got it, momma."

———

THE NEIGHBORHOOD I VISITED IN SOUTH KNOXVILLE DIDN'T APPEAR to be a high-rent district. Years of no zoning brought in a smattering of light industry, junk yards, assorted retail operations and pre-World War Two housing. Number 1869 Vestal Street had seen better days, having long missed its twenty-year reunion with a paint brush. A ten-year-old green Buick sat in the driveway behind a black pickup with a magnetic sign on the door saying Stanko Bros. Driveway Services, but no address or phone number. A man in his fifties answered my knock.

"My name's Jenkins." I held up my badge. "From Prospect Police. Mr. Stanko?"

"He's not here. What's this about?"

The man was short and swarthy with a thick crop of salt-and-pepper hair and a mustache at least four inches wide.

"Let's cut the crap. You look just like your sons. I'm here about Yanni."

"You got me confused with someone else." He ended his lie with a wide grin.

Thanks to Bettye's quick computer work, I had learned all about the elder Stanko before I arrived in South Knoxville.

"No, sir. Your name's Ramon Stanko. You also call yourself Raymond Sharkey, Mike Stanley, Roy Stokes and Marko Lendar. Do you want me to continue?"

He smiled again.

"Please," I said, "you need to hear what I have to say."

"Well, I'll pass the message along." He spoke with only a hint of a foreign accent I couldn't place.

"Okay, I've tried to be kind. Now, try this on for size. Yanni is dead. He's been beaten to death and is lying in a boatyard in Prospect."

I've got to hand it to old Stanko. He tried to maintain his composure, but the color drained from his olive complexion.

"Yanni is dead?"

"I'm sorry."

"Beaten, you say?"

"Can we go inside?"

"Yeah, sure. Come in."

He held the door and ushered me in.

The interior was surprisingly clean and tidy and full of assorted used furniture, none of it matching. But everything seemed to gel—in a European sort of way. We sat in upholstered chairs facing each other.

"Who did this?" he asked. "Yanni was not a violent man."

"I thought you'd be able to help me find out."

"Why would you think that?"

"Let's not dance, Mr. Stanko. I know what you and your sons do for a living. He was on a job last night and probably not alone."

"I don't know what you're talking about."

"Where is Aldi?"

"Haven't seen him in a while."

"How about a young woman?" I recounted Dwight's description. "Small, pretty, dark hair, works with you?"

"Don't know who you mean."

"The girl who accompanied you and Yanni to the boatyard last Friday."

"I was here all day Friday."

"We'll see."

He shrugged. An ornate ormolu mantle clock chimed twelve times.

"I'm trying to find your son's killer," I said. "You want to help or not?"

"I can do that on my own," he said.

"Wonderful."

His grin came back, and the mustache turned upward. "Do we have any more to discuss?"

———

SERGEANT STAN ROSE WALKED INTO MY OFFICE WEARING A TAN blazer, maroon polo shirt and black slacks. He dumped all 235 pounds into one of the guest chairs in front of my desk and stretched out the legs that made up half of his six-foot-four-inch frame.

"Bettye said you needed some detecting. I figured plainclothes would work best."

"You find my killer, you can wear a Speedo to work."

"Let's not get carried away, great white leader."

"What do you know about Gypsies?" I asked.

"They play violins and drive painted wagons."

"Vardos."

"What?" Stan acted like he just heard me speaking in tongues.

"A Gypsy wagon, or caravan, is called a vardo."

He shrugged. "You a wealff o' info-mation, bwana." Stanley occasionally likes to do an Uncle Remus act for me.

"Yes, I am."

"An' y'all know mo' 'bout Gypsies den me."

"Didn't they have gypsies in Los Angeles?"

Stan spent several years with LAPD before bringing his wife and children back to her native state.

He reverted to his usual voice. "We had everything in LA, even Klingons."

"Ever lock up any of those con-artists?"

"Bunko handled that stuff."

"Bunko? I love old-fashioned cop talk."

"Like a Philip Marlowe movie."

"Yeah, but listen, this is what I need you to do..."

I sent Stanley to the Federal building at 710 Locust Street in Knoxville to see Special Agent Ralph Oliveri at the FBI field office. Ralph could expand our nationwide search for information on the Stankos and their associates by accessing FBI confidential intelligence files, which go beyond simple arrests and convictions. Gypsies rarely confine themselves to one area, and the Feds love to get involved with interstate crime.

But because Oliveri needs to receive as much as he gives, I sent my investigator with a gift package of information detailing what we had already learned about our local Gypsy grifters.

———

WHEN IT COMES TO COMPUTERS, I'M BARELY A STEP ABOVE CLUELESS. But while Stan was away, I watched Bettye access a bunch of law enforcement information sites and learned a few things about our data resources and the Stanko family.

The list of cyber places she checked seemed endless. By searching and cross referencing the aliases Yanni Stanko used, Bettye found a few legitimate jobs he held in the metro New York area—New York, New Jersey, Connecticut and even some involvement in Rhode Island.

That gave her additional false names to work with as well as several police departments where Yanni had been collared. I made a few phone calls looking for a sympathetic detective who would invest a little time in my problem.

A sergeant from Bridgeport PD gave me the name Yula Angelo as an associate who posted bail for Yanni after an arrest for driving without a license and criminal impersonation. At the time, he called himself Joseph Smalley.

I called Ralph Oliveri with the new information.

"Stan and I haven't finished with all the stuff we have, and you're adding more?" he said. Ralph always tries to sound overworked.

"If I withheld information you'd have a stroke," I said. "This may be the golden egg, so don't complain. Ready to copy a couple more names?"

STAN WALKED BACK INTO THE OFFICE WITH A BIG GRIN.

"You look pleased with yourself," I said.

Stanley seemed to be in a good mood. He dropped down in a guest chair and resumed his Ebonics act a second time. "Massah, I tink dat las' name y'all give done broke som'fin loose."

"Tell me about it."

"Co-fee foist, boss."

"Does your mother know you talk like this?"

"Uh-huh. But my muddah ain't da one I gots to worry 'bout. Gran'ma hear me talk like I on da plantation, she smack me upside da head."

"You deserve a smack."

"I done bring back da good poop, bossman. Yo cain't smack me fo dat."

He stepped to his left to the cabinet where Mr. Coffee waited.

"It's a fresh pot," I said.

With a cup of light and sweet in hand, he took a spot in front of my desk and again sounded like a Caltech graduate.

"Yula Angelo is another alias," he said. "Ralph connected that name to

Anelka Adamo. Anelka, of course, uses numerous American-sounding names while out scamming, but when cornered by police looking for a true Gypsy identity, she produces a Jersey license for Yula."

"Who's on first?" I asked.

"Exactly. Now, here's the good part. A guy named Josef *Adamo* is married to Tereza *Zurko*. Ramon Stanko was married to the late Likreciya *Zurko*. The Adamo and Stanko families are in-laws. And—a drum roll please—Anelka Adamo and Yanni are cousins—and married."

"Is that legal?" I asked.

"In some states no, but it is here, and they don't seem to care. It's not a real marriage, just a Gypsy ceremony."

"I guess it's not that uncommon for first cousins to marry. Let's hope they don't believe in procreation."

"Then another connection turned up," Stan said. "Anelka's brother Rudi, also known as Rudy Adams, Ronnie Andrews and many other things, ran with Aldi Stanko for a while when the families lived in Rhode Island. They specialized in boosting high-end automobiles from used car dealers who didn't care much about checking credit ratings."

"Get a photo of Anelka?"

"You think you're dealing with an amateur?"

"Certainly not."

He handed me a four-by-five mug shot of a dark, exotic-looking beauty. "Good-looking girl."

"She is," he said.

"Let's see if Dwight Colwell can ID her as the pregnant woman."

"I'm with ya."

———

Dwight Colwell picked Anelka Adamo Stanko out of a six-pack of photos. He affirmed that she was the supposedly pregnant woman who accompanied the two Gypsy men who made off with his new johnboat, Yamaha motor and trailer. After calling Anelka a godless thievin' bitch, he identified a photo of Ramon Stanko as Yanni's partner and called him a hairy-faced bastard.

With all that under my belt, I had enough probable cause to choke a Tennessee plow mule. Stan and I drove back to Prospect PD where I typed up arrest warrant applications for Ramon and Anelka. Because of all the names they used, the paperwork turned out exceedingly long.

Before the end of business that day, I hand carried the warrant applications to Moira Menzies, Chief Assistant District Attorney in Blount County.

Her office, on the second floor of the Justice Center, overlooked the new county jail that, to the casual observer, might appear more like a starship without wings than the local slammer. The receptionist led me into Moira's office, telling me she would be back shortly.

I didn't want to get caught snooping in her desk drawers, so I sat in a plush guest chair and behaved myself.

Ten minutes later Moira, an attractive blonde in her mid-fifties, came storming into her office.

"I've had a miserable day, Jenkins. What in God's name do you want now?" One of her many snits seemed to be peeking through the beautiful exterior.

"Hi, Moira. Good to see you, too. Lovely weather we're having, isn't it?"

"Give it a rest."

"That bad, huh?"

"Worse."

"Buy you a drink?"

"Oh, Lord have mercy, Sam. What the hell do you want?"

I took that as a no. "I'd like two arrest warrants. Got a judge handy?"

"Let me see them."

I handed her the applications.

"You should have more faith in my professional abilities," I said.

She put on a pair of reading glasses and scanned the documents. I love pretty women who wear glasses.

"You're right," she said, "I should. And I hate to admit it, but you write better warrant applications than anyone else in the county."

"Aw shucks, ma'am, I'm gonna blush."

"Yeah, right."

"Must be my New York po-leece trainin'."

She tossed the glasses onto her desk. I liked her white silk blouse and short gray skirt. Moira's got good legs.

"Must be."

"Who's sitting today?" I asked.

"Judge Myers. He hates you, but he'll sign these."

"He hates me?"

"Don't act surprised. Half the people in this building hate you."

"Nonsense."

"Keep dreamin'."

"You love me," I said.

"What have you been smokin'?"

"Let's go see Judge Myers."

"I'm right behind you, big feller."

———

THE NEXT MORNING, TWO PROSPECT COPS AND TWO KNOX COUNTY detectives accompanied me to Ramon Stanko's house hoping to execute at least one of my warrants. But as Bettye once told me, "We live in hope, but die in despair." I think it was something her grandfather used to say.

We found the house locked up tighter than a pair of Spanx. The Buick was gone, and Ramon had obviously taken off for parts unknown. Since he had been my only lead toward Anelka, I stood on the porch of his house feeling like Mighty Casey on the day he struck out.

———

ON THE WAY BACK TO PROSPECT, BETTYE CALLED ME ON THE RADIO. After complying with all the paramilitary network formalities, she gave me a message.

"Stop at the sheriff's office," she said. "See Investigator Shuman. He's waitin' for you."

"10-4. I'm half way there."

The crime scene investigator's room sits next to the CID squad room on the second floor of the Justice Center. Dahlia Owenby, the receptionist at the main desk, gave me a visitor's badge and let me find Jackie on my own.

"This here's one o' those cases like ya see on TV," Jackie said.

"Sounds promising. What have you got?"

"Well, we found what could be the murder weapon."

"Excellent. Keep talking, I'm getting excited."

Uniformed and plainclothes cops walked up and down the hallway outside Jackie's office.

"'Bout twenny yards inta the woods, I found a rock like those around the downspouts on the repair shop. I figger the stain is blood, and guess the lab will match it to the vic."

"How long will that take?"

"Not sure. Couple days. They're pretty busy."

"Ask your boss for a promotion."

"I got no political pull, so he ain't in a givin' mood."

I shrugged. "Anything else?"

"Remember wonderin' how someone coulda got outta the boat yard, the cut in the fence only bein' pushed in?"

"Yeah."

"Well, we found some dirt stuck in the chain link 'bout three feet off the ground and again up on the top."

"Someone scaled the fence."

"Appears so. But after we looked at the photos of the ground outside the fence, we seen narrow strips of grass bent away from the body."

"Like someone crawled out, too."

"Be my guess."

"Pretty small person to get through that cut without pushing the fence out."

"Very small."

"Like a small woman who left her prosthetic belly at home."

"Cain't tell ya what sex, but they weren't even close ta bein' as big as you or me."

While Jackie and I spoke, David Sparks walked in and tossed his baseball cap on a desk ten feet away.

"How'd ya like them pitchers, Chief?" Sparks asked.

"You take them?"

"Yes, sir. Cain't hardly see how the blades o' grass are goin' while yer lookin' straight on with the nekked eye, but I got these by shootin' a flash at right angles ta the lens. Makes a shadow and ya get all kinds o' definition."

"Sherlock Holmes, eat your heart out."

David beamed. "Thank ya. We aim ta please."

———

16

WE SAT IN MY OFFICE, ME WITH A TURKEY, BACON AND SWISS HERO from Quizno's and Bettye with a homemade salad and fat free dressing.

"You think Yanni's wife and father killed him after burglarizing the showroom?" she asked between bites.

"Dwight described the woman as small. He thought no more than 100 pounds. Sounds like Anelka."

"That is small. I can't remember ever being a hundred pounds. She could have gotten through the narrow cut in the fence."

Bettye never weighed over 125 in her life.

"Yeah, but I don't see Ramon bounding over a six-foot fence. He's pushing sixty and not exactly athletic-looking. And why would he kill his son?"

"Sounds like a different third man."

"That's more logical," I said.

"We know anything about Yanni's relationship with Anelka?"

"Not from anyone around here," I said.

"You need to find out."

"From whom, Miss Bettye? From whom?"

She shook her head and sounded like she was trying to explain something simple to a moron. "Why, another Gypsy, o' course."

"Far as I know, the Stankos are the only ones operating in this area."

"There's Madam Mara, the fortune teller. She could be a Gypsy," she said.

A bright light popped on in my head. "That place on Alcoa Highway, just this side of the Knox County line?"

"That's the one. And is it safe to assume the Gypsies are a pretty close-knit group?"

"The Rom is like a separate nation. They're supposed to have their own king, organized territories and all sorts of hierarchy. They all know each other."

"Maybe Madam Mara has the information you need."

"Gypsies are not the most talkative people where us Gadjos are concerned."

"You can be a pretty persuasive Gadjo, darlin'."

———

Madam Mara may have been the only other Gypsy in East Tennessee, but I called a Knox County detective who owed me a favor to check their files for others. After a short wait, Wendell "Windy" Hatmaker picked up a phone.

"I heard ya'll used a couple o' our boys ta serve a warrant t'other day. No luck though, huh?" he said.

"My man wasn't home. That's why I'm calling. What do you know about Gypsies?"

He laughed. "Gypsies? Bless yer heart, but you git involved in some strange stuff."

"Yeah. Lucky me."

I told Windy Hatmaker all about the Stanko murder and where I stood in the investigation.

"I know about those driveway people," he said. "But never took a complaint on them. They seem ta stay jest above the law here in Knox County where they live, but it looks like they wander out and pull their scams in Blount and Anderson Counties."

"How about other Gypsies?"

"Lemme see what we got in our intelligence files. Hang on while I git ta where I need ta be on my computer."

"Branch out a bit, and see if you've got any door-to-door confidence games reported," I said. "These people are dishonest and slick, but generally nonviolent, so forget robberies and assaults."

"Got any names ya want me ta look fer?"

I swung my feet off the desktop and sat upright.

"They change names like you change your socks," I said. "And they all use aliases that sound more American than John Wayne. Look for the type of crime."

I listened to Windy's keyboard click away, while he hummed a few choruses of *Rocky Top*.

"Here ya go," he said. "Got us two complaints in two days 'bout a month ago. One around Millertown and t'other off Washington Pike in North Knoxville. Happened after the big hail storm in early April. Both the same M.O. and description on the subjects. Young man and his grandfather ask about roof work at homes with obvious storm damage. Old man does most o' the talking. Boy asks ta use the bathroom. Both complainants didn't wanna git involved 'cause the swindlers would only take cash and wouldn't work with an insurance company. Also said when the pair left, so did some small expensive stuff that coulda been found near the bathrooms."

"Any description to work with?"

"No, typical witnesses. Didn't know their asses from their elbows. Nothin' good. Both said dark hair, dark complexion. Thought they coulda been Spanish, Jewish or A-rabs."

"Names?"

"One got a business card. George Boswell Home Repair and Improvements. Nothin' on file 'bout the company with the state or county license people. No address, jest a cell phone number that cain't be traced."

"Not much to go on, but it sounds like we've got more Gypsies working the area than I thought. Hey. Thanks for the help. You hear of any more, gimme a whistle."

"Anytime, brother."

———

Since Madam Mara consulted her crystal ball in another jurisdiction, I enlisted help from Blount County Detective Bo Stallins to accompany me and provide the appropriate pressure if needed. I picked him up at the Justice Center and fifteen minutes later pulled into the parking lot of Madam Mara—psychic medium, palmist and master astrologer. The billboard next to her house said:

Psychic Readings ∼ Tarot Cards ∼ Astrology ∼ Numerology
YOUR CONNECTION TO THE OTHER WORLD
Local Checks Only ∼ Credits Cards Accepted

A white Mercedes 550 with gold pin striping, nineteen-inch chrome wheels and the Tennessee vanity plate, MARA 1 sat under a carport.

We found the front door unlocked. Bo and I entered a small waiting room with two couches, a couple of chairs and a huge Glamour-shot photo portrait of the Madam.

We hadn't been there thirty seconds when a curtain stretched across the doorway to the back of the house was swept aside, and Mara made a theatrical entrance.

"Good day, gentlemen. And how may I help you?"

I can't say her accent sounded foreign, but it sure wasn't East Tennessee. I liked what I heard.

The greeting came with a big smile, but her large dark eyes immediately hardened, and I knew she wasn't pleased to see us. Maybe she was psychic, or maybe Bo and I looked enough like cops for her to think the jig was up.

I showed her my badge, made the introductions and returned her smile.

"You said the magic word, Madam—help. We could use a little."

"I've done nothing wrong, witnessed no crimes. I don't see how I can help, unless..."

Mara would never see forty again and could be described as attractive and zaftig—just a little extra in all the right places. She may have been a couple pounds overweight, but it all looked good and the long black wavy hair that surrounded her pretty face made me think Balkans. A large paisley shawl covered an off-white peasant blouse that complimented her full figure.

"I had hoped you could provide a little expert advice," I said.

Her eyes brightened, and the smile returned

"My time is very valuable," she said. "I have clients in need of help arriving quite often."

"I understand, and we certainly don't want to impose upon you."

She bowed her head half an inch and showed me a perfect set of pearly whites.

"Let's start slowly with some basics," I said. "How much would it cost for a tarot card reading or one of the less expensive services?"

"For both of you?"

"Just me, but my colleague would like to watch."

"Of course. The cards are fifty."

"Ouch." I wasn't that interested in my future.

Stallins emitted a barely perceptible growl.

"Well," Mara said, "perhaps for a first-time customer, let's say thirty —cash."

"Let's say twenty, and you'll get my undying gratitude," I said.

""If you weren't so good-looking, I'd say no." Her almost black eyes sparkled. "Come into my parlor."

"Said the spider to the fly?"

Another smile. "Come inside. Come, follow me."

She turned and brushed the curtain aside.

Bo shot me a look and a grin. I scowled, but followed a pair of nicely rounded hips covered by a blue floor-length pleated skirt.

The parlor, or her operations center, looked like Hollywood's version of a fortune teller's inner sanctum. A dozen candles burned on different surfaces around the room. Two lamps with no more than fifteen-watt bulbs glowed beneath dark red shades. Two tables occupied opposite corners of the room, one round with a hooded object sitting off center. The other square, like a large card table.

I pointed to the covered object. "Crystal ball?"

She licked her red lips. "Of course. Perhaps for your second visit?"

"Perhaps."

Mara pointed to the card table. "Here, sit. What was your name again?"

"Sam Jenkins."

"Sit, Sam—across from me."

I took a seat at the table, and Bo spun a chair around and sat with his forearms resting on the back. Mara picked up a deck of large cards and sat in the chair across from me.

"Do you have questions?" she asked. "Or do you want the cards to tell the future?"

"My questions are simple," I said. "I want to know where to find a few other Romani people in the area."

After shuffling the cards, she began to deal them into a line of piles on the tabletop.

"I don't understand."

"A man named Yanni Stanko was murdered. I know at least two others were present at the time. And I believe Yanni's father may try to do something to avenge his son's death that will cause him more trouble than he comprehends."

Mara stopped handling the cards. Her eyes narrowed as she looked at me.

"You speak very well. You are not from here."

"I think you recognize my accent as being from New York."

She gave a slight nod.

"Your gray hair and the lines at the corners of your eyes say you have much experience."

I grinned. "You haven't turned a card, and already you know my inner most secrets."

"I think you like to be humorous."

"If I wasn't a cop, I'd look for a job as a comedian."

"What will you do with the other Rom you're looking for?"

"Ask them who killed Yanni Stanko."

"That's all?"

"For starters."

"Why should I help you?"

"I'm nice?"

"Ha!" She tilted her head and showed us a million-dollar smile.

"You're civic-minded?"

She began stacking the cards back into one deck.

Suddenly her smile faded. "I have a client in ten minutes. Twenty dollars, please."

"Not just yet."

A concerned look covered her face. "What do you mean?"

"We came in like two gentlemen. You can't expect me to leave with nothing for my twenty dollars."

"Whoa, hang on there, mister." The sexy and exotic voice disappeared, and a pure mid-Atlantic accent took over. She looked frightened.

"Take it easy." I spoke softly. "We're not going to harm you."

She loosened up a little.

I continued. "I want to know where to find Ramon Stanko and his son, Aldi, and the daughter-in-law, Anelka."

"How should I know where to find them?"

"You're psychic."

"Oh, for chrissakes."

"Once I get what I need, you get another twenty, and we'll leave you alone."

"And if I don't help?"

"Detective Stallins tells me no one has accused you of any wrongdoing —so far. I don't know if philosophically I agree with your business, but people are going to spend their money anyway, so if you can tell them what they want to hear and make them happy without hurting anyone, I can live with that."

"What's your point?"

"If you stonewall me, I'll make it a point to learn about your past."

I grabbed a card off the top of the deck with two fingers and handed it to Bo, who tucked it into the top pocket of his sport jacket.

"Your prints will tell us who you are and what you did up in New York, New Jersey or wherever you came from."

"Oh, crap." She shifted position and tried to look annoyed.

"I'll bet some police department knows you."

"I've never been arrested."

"A deputy can sit on the street in front of yer shop and take plate numbers," Bo said. "After enough clients get questioned about yer operation, I'm guessin' business'll drop off. And ya'll never know if a new customer is a cop who's gonna ketch ya crossin' the line tryin' ta take 'em on an expensive and dodgy trip communicatin' with dead kinfolks in the great beyond."

"I'm sure you're familiar with the term 'boojo swindle'," I said. "Do we have to explain more?"

"No," she said. "You drive a hard bargain. I'll see what I can find out. Give me your card."

"Thanks," I said and meant it.

Mara looked me square in the eye. "I'll save you some trouble, cutie. My name is Marie Ristik. Now tell your partner to give me that tarot card. Quality decks are not cheap, and I'd like mine to be complete."

Bo smiled and handed back the card. I took a twenty from my pocket, passed her the bill and a business card.

"Remember," I said, "twenty more when I get the 4-1-1."

"Okay. Did you mean what you said about undying friendship?"

"I think it was undying gratitude, but friendship is okay, too—within reason."

She reached across the table and put her hand over mine.

"It's a start. I'll call you."

———

Two days later Mara called and sounded bubbly.

"I've got a lot more than you asked for."

I'd been sitting at my desk calling other PDs who might have information on Gypsy crime in their area.

23

"Great," I said. "I thought you'd forgotten me."

"Hey, tall, dark and handsome, good information doesn't grow on trees. I couldn't get too obvious and ask a lot of questions. I did more listening."

"Sounds like you could be a spy."

"Wasn't Mata Hari a Gypsy?" she asked.

"We never met."

She laughed. "Well, I'm hoping this is worth more than forty dollars."

"I recognize quality when I see it. Let's talk, and maybe I can get you more money."

"How about a teaser before you get here?"

"Put on your Madam Mara voice, and you could tease me by reading the Yellow Pages."

"Wow, you know how to make a girl feel good. How does identity theft sound? A *real big* operation."

"I'll be there in less than half an hour." I stood, ready to leave the minute I hung up the phone.

———

As I HIT THE TOP STEP AT THE FRONT OF HER PLACE, MARA OPENED the door.

"Hi, you're right on time."

She wore her hair pulled back in a ponytail, a black scoop-neck blouse that showed enough cleavage to get me excited and a three-tone tan batik print skirt. Mara oozed sex appeal like a cream-filled doughnut oozes calories. I've never known an informant with a prettier smile.

"I'm anxious to get the big news."

She waved me inside.

"Let's sit down, and I'll tell you."

We used one of the couches in the waiting room. Sunlight streamed in from three windows.

"Would you like something to drink?" She asked.

"Whatever you're having."

"I opened a bottle of Nero D'Avola after we spoke before."

"A nice earthy wine. You're being awfully kind."

"I'm getting there." She stood abruptly. "Be right back."

In two minutes, she returned with a pair of footed glasses half filled with dark ruby liquid.

"Cheers," I said and sipped the wine.

She said something in a language I didn't recognize.

"Where was your family from?" I asked.

"It's Slovenia today. Back then it was part of Austria."

"That was a long time ago."

She nodded, sipped from her glass and crossed her legs.

"So," she said, "what do you think about this big identity theft ring?"

"You have to tell me more, but it sounds impressive. Is Ramon Stanko involved?"

"Not exactly, but he's staying with a family named Grujik. They've organized the scam."

"How about Anelka and Aldi?"

"I'm not sure about Aldi, but Yanni's grieving widow is the talk of the town. They say she's turned her attention to a stud muffin named Spiro Grujik."

"Stud muffin?"

"Spiro is a *good-looking* boy."

"Handsome enough for Anelka to ditch Yanni the permanent way?"

"You're on your own with that one. Just how much do you think forty bucks buys nowadays?" She wrinkled her nose and gave me a coy look over the rim of her glass.

"Where's the Grujik homestead?"

"South Knoxville, off the John Sevier Highway. I wrote out directions."

"Maybe I can get the Knox County DA to kick in a few bucks if we find enough evidence to charge this crew with at least criminal conspiracy."

The idea of additional money caused my Gypsy friend to smile like a girl invited to the senior prom.

"That would be nice."

"I'll do my best."

She tilted her head and showed me a dazzling array of dental hygiene. "A sharp New York boy like you can probably get anything he wants."

———

WINDY HATMAKER ARRANGED FOR A COUPLE OF DETECTIVES TO watch the Grujik house for a day and a half. They took plate numbers, established a pattern of activity beyond the normal comings and goings of a one-family home and confirmed that people fitting my descriptions of Ramon and Anelka were staying there.

Then Windy mobilized a small army of Knox County detectives and deputies to accompany me and the warrants I obtained to a middle-class neighborhood not far from where Governor John Sevier Highway crossed the French Broad River.

We hit the house at 10 a.m. and found nine people, four laptops and a desktop computer surrounded by hundreds of credit card slips, stolen cards, printouts and other technical stuff a cyber-crime expert would have to explain to me. Since a "no knock" clause had been added to my search warrant, the nine occupants were shocked to see us after a burly sergeant kicked in the door.

Ramon Stanko was easy to spot.

"Cuff him," I told a uniformed deputy, "and take him to a separate room."

I had pushed through the front door right behind the sergeant who almost knocked it off the hinges. A beautiful and petite young woman had slammed the cover on the laptop she'd been using and ran to the safety of a tall, dark-haired specimen standing under an archway drinking coffee. He looked like central casting's idea for the title role in the movie *Adonis*. I assumed he was Spiro Grujik, the one Mara called a stud muffin.

"Sorry to break you two apart," I said, "but I've got a warrant for her arrest and want to have a serious talk with you, Mr. Grujik."

Anelka gave me a hateful, smoldering look, and Spiro's eyes popped in surprise. A female deputy cuffed Anelka, and I pushed Spiro toward an unoccupied bedroom.

"Park it," I said.

Grujik sat on the bed.

"Your girlfriend is going away for grand larceny of a boat—that's a done deal. And I'll say the magic words to you. You're under arrest for the murder of Yanni Stanko."

"What?" A look of fright changed his face.

If I read Spiro Grujik right, he looked like a handsome kid who could charm most women out of their cash or clothing with little more than a wink and a smile, but he seemed about as crafty and dangerous as a three-month-old cocker spaniel.

Once I had his attention, I wanted to bluff my way into his heart.

"Don't act stupid, Spiro. Anelka and Yanni were just an arranged marriage. He was too old for her and not near as good-looking as you. So, when the time was right—in the deserted boatyard—you beat him to death."

"Hey, man, you got it all wrong." He began to fidget, and panic showed on his face. "I didn't kill anybody."

The sound of a dozen cops rousting a houseful of Gypsies filtered into the bedroom.

"Says you. I think you did. And I've got more convictions under my belt than I can count. Nobody likes a Gypsy. You're all famous for scamming common people out of hard-earned cash. A jury won't take ten minutes to convict you."

"That's not fair. I didn't kill Yanni."

"Who cares? Life's not fair. Let's go...it's handcuff time."

"Wait, wait, wait." He seemed on the verge of hyperventilating.

The phrase 'gotcha' flashed before my eyes.

"Why should I? I've got my killer and lots of paperwork to do. On your feet."

His handsome face had twisted in fear. Spiro probably figured he was dog chow.

"Let me think. Please, gimme a minute."

"Think about this, pretty boy. Ever see a prison movie?"

He shook his head.

"Too bad. What do you go...160, 170 pounds?"

He looked confused but nodded.

"Prisons are full of tattooed monsters that are six-and-a-half feet tall and weigh 250. They shave their heads and prowl the exercise yard for pretty young guys to get romantic with. Guess who the fresh meat will be."

His eyes bulged, and the corner of his mouth trembled.

"Remember that good ol' boy from *Deliverance*? 'Squeal like a pig.'"

He winced.

"You look dishonest, Spiro, but you're not a tough guy. It'll be a long twenty-five years."

"Twenty-five years for something I didn't do? I want a lawyer."

"That's twenty-five to *life*, moron, and of course you do. I'll get you a public defender who probably hasn't found the court house yet."

For a young guy, Spiro had more furrows on his forehead than an eighty-year-old man.

"Twenty-five to life?" he sputtered. "How much time will Anelka get for the boat?"

"It's the boat and the burglary of the showroom now. And let's not forget her part in Yanni's death. Since you're the killer, she'll make a package deal for maybe fifteen years, but with good behavior, a girl can get out in five."

"Five years? No matter what?"

"Yeah. Think she'll wait for you?" I forced a big grin.

"You have to prove I killed Yanni."

He tried to look tough, but couldn't pull it off.

"How does this sound, nitwit? I'll offer Anelka a deal. Plead guilty to two counts of misdemeanor larceny in exchange for a statement implicating you, and she can do a year in county. One year versus fifteen—what do you think she'll do?"

Spiro was sweating and trying to think at the same time. I could see he lusted after the beautiful Anelka, but didn't quite trust her. I interrupted his thought process.

"Of course, you won't have to worry about those Aryan Nation skinheads if they send you to a state prison around Memphis."

"What?"

"Most of the inmates there are black."

I think that may have pushed him over the top.

"If I only went along with Yanni to do the boatyard job and somebody else killed him, what would I get?"

"You'd have to sign a statement naming the killer. And I'd have to substantiate everything. Just your word is meaningless. Could still be felony murder unless you *didn't* know the third party planned to kill Yanni."

I spotted a spark of hope in his eyes.

"It was all her idea," he squawked. "All I was supposed to do was get her into the window so she could open the door for Yanni. I didn't know anything about murder until she picked up that rock."

"Her?"

"Anelka."

"Why should I believe you?"

"I can tell you how to find the proof."

"Go ahead."

"I threw the rock into the woods after she dropped it. There was blood on it—his and hers, too."

"Why hers?"

"She broke two nails the second time she hit him. Check her hand, you'll see. She was bleeding."

"After you write all this up, I'll get the DA to offer you a sweetheart deal."

———

ANELKA, OF COURSE, WOULDN'T ADMIT ANYTHING AND LAWYERED UP immediately.

Ramon had figured they killed his son, but wasn't sure who actually dealt the blow. He confirmed seeing her injury when she returned from the burglary with a cock and bull story about a night watchman killing Yanni.

Aldi Stanko never participated in the crime.

Spiro Grujik signed the loveliest statement I ever dictated. Moira Menzies looked pleased with my results and promised to prosecute the case herself.

———

WINDY HATMAKER INTRODUCED ME TO FURLAN ATCHLEY, THE Chief Assistant District Attorney in Knox County.

"My informant went out on a limb getting me the poop on the identity theft operation," I said. "I'd like to offer more cash than I've already given."

"Why come to me?"

Atchley looked like an arrogant yuppie who thought he could get a conviction with no help from the police.

"I get one killer. I already knew who did the boatyard larceny. You've got a roomful of defendants and a crime with hundreds of potential victims. Once the Gypsies start naming the clerks who provided the credit card receipts and the pickpockets who snatched the actual cards, you'll have a courtroom full of convictions."

"Hmmm."

Furlan poked one finger into a fifty-dollar hairdo and scratched his head while thinking about the possibilities. He pulled that off without disturbing a follicle.

"And if this goes interstate, I'll get you lots of FBI cooperation."

"I could get that myself."

"Not like I can. And I'll make sure WNXX TV gives you plenty of press on this."

"You can do that?"

Hatmaker grinned and nodded his head. I looked at him and thought he might have picked up his sport jacket on Salvation Army half-price day.

"Guaranteed," I said.

"How much did you plan on giving this informant?" Atchley asked.

I wanted at least three-hundred for Mara, but like any good Tennessee horse trader, I started big.

"The stool mentioned a thousand, and with all the clearances we'll get, the information is worth it."

"You'd have to register the informant with us."

"That's not going to happen. You can register me. If you doubt my honesty, send Detective Hatmaker along when I make the pay off." I tried to sound offended.

"I don't doubt your honesty, but procedure is procedure."

"Sorry, counselor, it's my way or nothing. No FBI, no TV coverage, no further assistance."

Atchley huffed and puffed a little and hooked his thumbs under his suspenders.

"If the snitch wants a thousand, get Blount County to put up half, and I'll get you five-hundred," he said.

I stuck out my hand. "Deal."

Windy Hatmaker laughed. I think he had spotted my act.

———

TWO GLASSES OF RED WINE SAT ON THE CARD TABLE IN MARA'S parlor. A few additional candles had been added to the group I'd seen the other day, and perfume scented the air.

Her hair looked perfect, falling down alongside high cheekbones, and she wore a little extra makeup. I never knew a big girl could look so good in a little black dress.

"Sit down," she said. "Let's have some wine, and I'll read your palm."

She took my left hand and turned it over.

Before Mara commented on my future, I spoke. "I promised to get you something extra if the information panned out. Knox County will be prosecuting the identity theft ring, and we'll deal with Yanni's killer. I couldn't have done it without you and appreciate your help."

She smiled, squeezed my hand and sounded like a little girl. "A little extra would be nice."

I pulled an envelope from an inside pocket and handed it to my mercenary new friend.

"There's a short statement stamped on the front. Fill in the amount and sign on the line."

She opened the flap and took out five bills.

Mara looked and sounded surprised. "This is five-hundred dollars."

"I know."

"My God, I never expected..."

"Then you're not disappointed."

I handed her a pen. She signed the envelope and pushed it across the table.

Mara blinked a couple times. "Wow, let's celebrate. How about an early dinner and then...?"

"I'm afraid I've got to be somewhere else today—police business."

She frowned. "A rain check, then?"

I shrugged. "Look into your crystal ball, and see what happens."

"That doesn't sound encouraging."

"Well," I said, "I've got this thing about not mixing business with pleasure."

"Our business is finished...for now. Let's get on with the pleasure."

"My wife is an understanding woman, but even she would object if I had a beautiful Gypsy girlfriend."

She seemed to ignore the thing about a wife.

"You think I'm beautiful?"

"Drink your wine, Marie. I've got to go catch a few more bad guys."

THE END

HEAVEN'S GATE

Most of the police chiefs I know don't work on weekends. I'm no exception. One warm Saturday in late May, I stood in the driveway washing the pollen off my gorgeous 1967 Austin-Healey 3000 when my equally gorgeous wife, Kate, stuck her head out the door.

"Hey, sweetie, Junior Huskey is on the phone."

"Be right there."

Junior is one of the twelve officers who work at Prospect PD. Prospect is a picturesque little city in the foothills of the Great Smoky Mountains.

I rinsed a coating of suds off the Healey, walked through the garage and answered a wall phone in our kitchen.

"What's up, kid?" I said.

"Sorry ta bother ya, boss, but me an' Bobby's at a gun show in the Jacob Building at Chilhowee Park, an' we need supervision."

Bobby was Officer Bobby John Crockett, another one of Prospect's finest.

"You want me to help you pick out a gun?" I asked.

"No, sir. We got us a po-leece problem."

"Chilhowee Park is in Knoxville—not our area."

"Sam, this looks big," Junior said. "Y'all might need ta git yer Federal friends involved."

"Aren't there any local cops at the show?"

"Yes, sir, two old guys from Knox County who don't look like they can walk and chew t'bacca at the same time."

"And *you* want to get involved?"

"If yew was here, yew would, too."

"What have you got?"

"We had went halfway through the show, and I needed ta go in the men's room. Well, sir, three guys are standin' there, and one opens a briefcase. He showed the other two what looked like a pair o' rocket propelled grenades and an old-fashioned pineapple hand grenade."

"It was live ordnance?"

"Yes, sir. I believe so."

"Why do you think that?"

"While I was takin' a leak, I heard the guy with the briefcase say, 'Yew want other stuff from 'Nam, I kin git ya U.S. or commie—new old stock.'"

"You see any money change hands?"

"The lookers said it was too expensive fer 'em."

"This guy still at the show?"

"He'll be here 'til five o'clock. Got him a dealer's table."

"I'll be there in half an hour."

I grabbed the sport shirt I left hanging on the back of a chair and began putting it on when my wife asked a reasonable question.

"Where are you going now?"

"Knoxville gun show. Junior and Bobby have a problem."

"And only the police chief can help them on a Saturday morning?"

"I'm their fearless leader."

"You were going to help me make pickled ginger."

"Soon as I get home."

The streak of gray that runs through Kate's dark hair fell over her left eye. I brushed it aside and kissed her.

"Hang in there, Kats. I'm off to fight crime and keep East Tennessee safe for democracy."

"You're such a creep."

"But I'm your creep, love. I'll be home soon."

———

CHILHOWEE PARK IS IN THE STATE FAIR GROUNDS ON THE EAST END

of Knoxville. After winding my way through country lanes, I took U.S. 129 north, crossed the Buck Karnes Bridge over the Tennessee River and exited onto Cumberland Avenue. After a short drive through the U.T. campus, I turned north on Broadway and then east on Magnolia. That put me on the poor side of town. In ten minutes, I pulled into Chilhowee Park and found a parking spot next to the duck pond.

I trudged up the half-million steps to the Jacob Building and paid a ridiculous eight-dollar fee to get into the gun show. I found Junior and Bobby standing at the door.

Junior was wearing blue denim overalls over a white T-shirt. At six-one and two-hundred-and-ten pounds, the outfit made him look like a big farm boy. Bobby's an inch shorter, about one-eighty, and looked preppy in a plaid shirt and starched Levis.

We walked to one end of a room with more than 400 tables chock full of guns, knives, militaria and related merchandise.

"Third row up." Junior pointed with his chin. "Then six tables in on the left. Thin guy, medium height, salt-and-pepper crew cut. Got a T-shirt says, 'Peace through Superior Firepower.'"

Half the people at gun shows wear shirts that express similar ideas or something equally sentimental like "Kill 'em All and Let God Sort 'em Out."

"You talk to him yet?" I asked.

"No, sir," Junior said.

"Me neither," Bobby added.

"Okay," I said. "Keep an eye on me. I'll mosey over and see what's up."

I turned the corner and, for appearance's sake, spent a little time at each table in the aisle. When I reached my destination, I looked over eight feet of deactivated ordnance, assorted bayonets and fighting knives, a half-dozen military handguns and bits and pieces of G.I. web gear.

I must have seemed interested because the guy with the salt-and-pepper hair said, "If I kin he'p ya with somthin', lemme know."

"Nice bunch of stuff you've got here," I said. "Brings back memories."

"You in the military?" he asked.

"I was in the Army."

"Look about the right age for 'Nam."

"Among other places."

Then we danced for a few moments establishing my military credentials.

"How about yourself?" I asked after he finished questioning me.

"Marine Corps, '76 ta '80."

"Uh-huh. Got a big collection of militaria yourself?"

"Oh yeah," he said proudly.

"I wish I'd kept some of the things I had back then," I said.

"Never too late ta start a collection."

He wore a name tag pinned to his T-shirt that read Hobart Milby.

"These things are all good, but they're deactivated." I shook my head. "Not much more than paperweights. Kinda like buying a gun without a firing pin."

"Popular items, though, 'cause they's inexpensive."

Two good ol' boys stepped up to the table.

The youngest of the pair said, "These things from Viet-nam?"

Milby said, "Some from 'Nam. Some from I-rack. Some from all over." He picked up a fragmentation grenade. "This here's from World War Two. All gen-u-ine military ordnance."

"Whaddaya do with it?" the boy said.

"Collect it, son," Milby said. "They's pieces o' history."

The other man said, "If ya cain't hunt with it, ain't no reason ta own it. Come on, Hadley, I need ta find me some thirty-ought-six."

They walked off, and I looked at Milby.

"Man's got a point," I said. "If I bought some of these mementos, I'd want them live."

"You're talkin' big money fer live ordnance."

"Yeah, but you only live once," I said. "And right now, I'm living in the past."

"Miss the Army?"

"I didn't think so then, but they probably were the best days of my life."

"I hear that, brother."

"Got any *real* stuff?"

He hesitated for a long moment, still sizing me up.

"Got any *real* money?"

I stuck my hands in my pockets and shrugged.

"I haven't bought a new truck lately and the only big expense I've got is alimony. How much you talking?"

"Depends on what you want."

Three more lookers stopped for a moment. Hobart and I suspended our banter until they moved on.

Milby rekindled the conversation. "You're talkin' about some expensive items. If ya don't mind me askin', what do ya do fer a livin'?"

I hesitated and suppressed a smile. "I run a pest control company."

"Good money in that?"

"We've always got a customer."

"I guess so," he said. "Okay then, tell me what you'd like."

"I always loved those 'bloop' guns," I said. "Got pretty good with one, too. I figure I could put an M-79 round in Charlie's back pocket at 300 meters. Got any 40-milimeter grenade rounds?"

"Shoot, brother, they ain't easy ta come by. You want somethin' dated durin' the 'Nam War?"

"I guess so, but I could live with something later. How about Claymores? Can you get me a whole kit, bag and all?"

"Lord have mercy. You don't want much."

"Just the stuff I lived with."

"Man, I'm gonna have ta do some lookin'. How kin I git in touch with ya?"

"Cell phone's best. Got a piece of paper?"

I gave him a number.

"Call any time," I said. "And while you're looking, how about a Chi-Com B-40?"

"Whooee—rocket-pro-pelled grenade. Okay, I'll look fer ya. By the way, brother, what's yer name?"

I gave him a frown. "I'm not going to write you a check."

"I know, I know. Jest tell me somethin' I kin call ya. I got me a name tag here." He pointed to it. "It's more neighborly ta know yer name."

"Call me Barry," I said. "Barry Sadler."

That seemed to have gone over his head.

"Okay, Barry. I'll be in touch with some news and prices."

"Thank you, sir. I'll look forward to hearing from you."

I found Junior and Bobby standing near the food concession.

Bobby sipped from a bottle of Dr Pepper, and Junior chewed on a chili dog and held a can of Mountain Dew in the other hand.

"That went well," I said. "He's a real entrepreneur. Said he'd look for what I wanted."

"What's that?" Junior asked.

"Couple of grenades and a Claymore."

Junior snickered. "Bless yer heart, boss, ya got right inta this undercover work."

"A Claymore mine?" Bobby said. "Lord have mercy."

———

On Monday morning, I ran Hobart Milby through our data system. He'd never been arrested, and the Department of Safety listed his address in Wildwood, not far from beautiful downtown Prospect. But the driver's license information was four years old so, for all I knew, Hobart could be currently living on the moon.

Three days passed, and Milby hadn't called. Then, while I sat at my desk initialing field reports, my cell phone sounded off. I saw his number and closed the office door so he couldn't hear a radio call come in on the base station.

"I thought you'd forgotten me," I said.

"What yer lookin' fer, bud, don't grow on trees."

"I understand."

"I found one dealer outta state who's got a couple things fer ya. Got him a PG-7 rocket. Just like the B-40, but Russian. Interested?"

Hobart wasn't fooling around. Rocket-propelled grenades were favorites with terrorists all over the world.

I decided to play it cagey. "All depends on price. I remember plenty of RPG-7 launchers over there, so I can live with that."

"Okay, next thing, how about a *pair* of 40-milimeter M-79 rounds? Kin ya use two?"

"Don't need two, but like I said, everything depends on price. Maybe this guy can make me a package deal."

"I kin ask. Everybody likes ta sell in volume. Time we do this deal, he'll have the claymore, too."

After that, he chuckled. I began to feel like a fly approaching the spider's web.

"Appreciate that," I said. "I don't know how many times I'll be adding to my collection, so I might be making a big purchase right off the bat."

"I hear ya, brother. I know, money's tight, but I aim ta please."

"Hope you don't mind the question, but what do you get out of this if you're selling another dealer's goods?"

"I ain't frontin' no money, so I'll be happy with ten percent across the board. You okay with that?"

"Reasonable finder's fee," I said, thinking he had everything sitting in a closet at home and the out-of-state dealer was a figment of his imagination.

"Hoped ya'd say that. Now, how 'bout a couple goodies ya didn't mention?"

"Tempt me, Satan."

He laughed. "He got a fragmentation grenade—good old-fashioned pineapple, dated nineteen-and-sixty-nine. Interested?"

"Holy shit. There are plenty of training aids out there. Is this a factory-loaded grenade?"

"Gar-ron-teed."

"Good. I was there in '69. What's next?"

"Hang onta yer boonie hat, G.I.," he said. "How's about a brand new, in the plastic wrapper, LAWS rocket?"

Milby wasn't peddling lightweight materiel. LAWS stands for light anti-tank weapons system—to the layman, a throwaway bazooka.

"Good Christ almighty," I said. "I never thought I'd see one of those again."

"Gimme enough time an' ya never know what might pop up." He chuckled, obviously proud of himself.

"I'll remember that. What's the bottom line for the collection?"

"Man wants forty-five-hundred."

"Plus your four-fifty?"

"Yes, sir."

My office door opened gently, and Sergeant Bettye Lambert entered carrying two case folders. She's a pretty blonde with a great figure. Every time I see her wearing our khaki and green uniform, I think I should make her a detective sergeant so I could see her civilian wardrobe. But we have no detectives at Prospect P.D, and I'd have to keep on dreaming.

Bettye sat in one of the guest chairs and looked at me over the tops of her little granny glasses.

"Sounds like a lot," I told Milby. "If I take the whole bunch, he should cut me some slack. Offer thirty-five-hundred and see what he says. You square that away, and I'll give you five-hundred commission, the extra one-fifty under the table."

He took a long moment to answer. I noticed Bettye was wearing a little green eye shadow. It complimented her hazel eyes and the uniform. I pointed to my eyes and gave a thumbs-up. She smiled.

Hobart finally spoke. "Have ta git back ta ya on that."

"Sure. And while you're asking, see if he deals in guns, too."

"I know that already—he does. Whatcha need?"

"How about an M-2 carbine. I carried one when I was advisor to a Vietnamese airborne unit."

"That's full auto, man. We all could get inta big trouble handlin' one of those. The risk makes the price go up."

"We can get into boo-coo trouble for having any of the things you just mentioned. I know the price will be high. Hey, look, I can buy a nice M-1 at any gun show. I want that selector switch and the pot-bellied stock. See what you can do."

"I'll tell ya rot now, that one's popular with collectors and won't be cheap."

"A good pizza ain't cheap, Hobart. I'm committed here. You've made a collector out of me."

He laughed, probably happy to have a fish on the hook.

"Okay, I'll call ya." He hung up without waiting for my response.

Bettye shook her head, and her hair swayed from side to side.

"And just what are you doing now, Sammy?"

It sounded like she was scolding me.

"You act like my mother."

She screwed up her nose and stuck out her tongue.

I filled her in on the new developments.

A CHECK WITH THE SOCIAL SECURITY ADMINISTRATION REVEALED

that Milby hadn't paid FICA in many years. So, I assumed he earned a living exclusively as an unlicensed weapons dealer. Bettye checked with BATF when I asked nicely and verified that he had no Federal firearms license.

Hobart's ability to locate destructive devices had me excited and nearly foaming at the mouth. Nonetheless, my case originated in another jurisdiction, and I wondered if he would deliver the goods to Prospect or take me outside my geographic area of employment.

I doubted Mayor Ronnie Shields would front more than five-thousand dollars for me to make a case in someone else's backyard.

But Federal agents are famous for having all the flash money you can shake a nightstick at. I called Ned the Fed at the Bureau of Alcohol, Tobacco, Firearms and Explosives in Knoxville.

"How the hell'd you get a deal from him?" Special Agent Edward Greznik asked. "We've been keeping an eye on Hobart Milby for a couple years."

"He likes me."

Greznik was a short man with dark hair and glasses who looked more like a watchmaker than a Federal cop.

"Yeah, right," he said. "Milby's a sleazy weasel. Into everything from profiting on gun sales without a license to suspected trafficking in restricted weapons."

"If you've got the money, honey, I'll get the grenades."

"And you think this is going down when?" Greznik spoke with an Upper Peninsula, Michigan accent.

"As soon as you come up with the cash."

"Lucky me. How much and exactly what are you getting for our money?"

I described the illegal items I had ordered.

"He wanted forty-five-hundred for the lot," I said, "but I offered thirty-five and a bigger commission. See, I've already saved you a grand."

"You're all heart."

"And I asked him to find an M-2 carbine."

"You're hot shit. He's ready to do business, and you act cheap. Very nice. You think he'll call back about the M-2? That baby will up the cost considerably."

"Count on it. Can you get that much cash?"

"Of course. Your tax dollars at work. We'll even wire you up as part of the package."

"No, thanks. These guys tend toward paranoia. I don't want a friendly pat down to jeopardize the operation. Just stick close to me, and I'll be okay."

———

Two days later, Hobart Milby called back at 8 p.m., while I was home watching a rerun of NCIS.

"Okay, bud," he said. "I got all ya wanted. Found me another guy with an M-2, but I gotta be honest, it's a parts gun. Rockola receiver and Inland barrel. Don't know who made the trigger group."

"Doesn't matter," I said. "A military armorer would make sure the parts fit and the gun functioned. They didn't care about collectors wanting guns with matching parts. Long as it's full auto, I'm happy."

"Oh, it's an M-2 all right. And he's gonna throw in a bayonet and a half-dozen thirty-round magazines."

"Whoopee. How much is he asking?"

"Okay, here's the deal," he said. "Original dealer said he'll take thirty-five for the ordnance ya wanted, and this new guy wants another twenty-five for the carbine. That's a damn good price on that M-2. Sorta a gesture o' good will fer a new customer."

"Good job," I said. "You get the Claymore package, too?"

"Got it. Even the remote detonator. Bag an' all, jest like ya ordered."

"Then six-thousand sounds good for the package." I didn't want to haggle anymore, so I set the hook this time.

"How about seven-hundred for me? I done made lotsa phone calls to git all this t'gether."

"Done. Where do I meet you?"

"I live in Prospect now," he said. "Know where that is?"

———

Ned Greznik accompanied six ATF agents, and I brought four Prospect cops who looked like they needed a little O.T.

We shaped up about a quarter mile away from Hobart Milby's place on

Hickory Creek Road. I tried to dress the part of a budding military munitions collector by wearing blue jeans and a T-shirt I bought when Kate and I visited the new Infantry Museum at Fort Benning, Georgia.

I parked my truck in Hobart's driveway next to a red Ford Ranger with Blount County plates and carried the cash, stuffed into a battered 'AWOL' bag, to the front door.

"Hey, you're rot on time," he said.

A pretty brown and white English setter stood behind him, four feet away.

"Boof," the dog said.

I looked past Milby and locked eyes with the setter.

"Hello, dog," I said.

She wagged her tail and walked over. I scratched her on the chin. I relate well to animals, but have problems with people.

"Whaddaya say, Hobart? Hell of a watchdog you got here."

"Don't pay no attention ta her. She's a pussy cat."

I put down the AWOL bag and bent over. Using two hands to hold the dog's face, I kissed her on the nose, and her tail spun at two-thousand RPMs.

"Nice old girl," I said.

The dog wiggled.

"Kin I git ya a beer?" Hobart asked.

"Gimme a beer, and I'll give you a bunch of money."

"Sounds good ta me," he said.

I picked up the satchel and followed Milby through his house. The digs impressed me—post and beam construction, quality trim work. I could live in a house like that.

"Nice place you got here," I said.

"Thanks," he said. "Been here 'bout a year an' a half. College teacher got him a job down ta Jackson and needed ta sell quick-like. I low-balled an offer, an' he bit. I'm happy as hell."

He handed me a Bud in a longneck.

"Thanks," I said. "You got something to show me?"

"You bet, brother. Foller me."

We left the kitchen and entered the dining room. On the table, Hobart had laid out an array of very illegal military ordnance. I was impressed.

"Yahoo," I said and picked up the M-2 carbine.

I worked the bolt and checked that the chamber was empty. I stuck my thumb into the breech, caught the light from an overhead fixture and looked down the barrel.

"Clean and shiny bore," I said.

"Only the best."

I fondled the gun and looked it over carefully, all the while smiling like an enthused collector.

"I love it," I said. "Hobart, ya done good."

He smiled. I thought I saw dollar signs register in his eyes.

"Look at the other stuff, soldier," he said and handed me the rocket launcher.

I heard a toilet flush in another part of the house and wondered if Milby had a live-in girlfriend. Public records showed him as divorced.

"Damn, son," I said, "you're bringing back memories."

I shouldered the LAWS rocket launcher and flipped up the hinged sight.

"Look out, Charlie," I said, "this one's for you."

"Careful now. That's one hunnert p'cent armed and dangerous."

I nodded and placed it back on the table and took a long pull on the Budweiser.

"Seen much action over there?" he asked.

"Enough to get me three Purple Hearts and just as many Bronze Stars."

"Lord have mercy, a gen-u-ine war hero."

"After getting hit three times, the Army said I was accident prone."

"Still, nice to have them medals."

"Yeah. That and two-fifty will get you a New York subway ride."

"Speakin' o' money," he said. "Mind if I see what ya brung?"

I handed him the AWOL bag.

"Mind if I count it?"

"I assumed you would."

As Hobart thumbed through the cash, a guy about forty, short and borderline skinny appeared in the doorway. Immediately, I didn't like having company and didn't like the looks of the man who I assumed drove the red pickup. The S&W Chief's Special in my ankle holster seemed a long way off.

I'd been juggling the fragmentation grenade while Hobart counted the money. When Skinny appeared, I gripped the metal and hooked a finger into the ring attached to the pin.

"You didn't say we'd be having company, Hobart," I said.

"Oh, sorry," he said. "This here's Dickie, a friend o' mine. Dickie, meet Barry. Like I tol' ya, he's startin' a collection o' 'Nam souvenirs."

"Whaddaya say?" Dickie spoke without smiling.

"Hey, yourself."

He looked grubby, needed a shave or was trying to grow a beard and couldn't pull it off.

"Hobart tells me you's in the military," he said.

"Yeah, long ago and far away."

"Me, too. 101st Airborne. First Gulf War."

I wanted to see how truthful Dickie was.

"Made a combat jump then, didn't you? What was the name of the place?"

"I wasn't in the brigade who jumped."

"Uh-huh." I figured as much. "You collect this stuff, too?"

"Jest guns."

"Right."

When Milby finished counting the cash, I wanted to have a word in private.

"Hobart, show me where your bathroom is."

"Through the kitchen, first door on the left."

"Show me." I sounded insistent.

Hobart frowned.

"Excuse us," I told Dickie.

Milby followed me. Once out of earshot, I spoke, "Who is this guy?"

"A friend. Name's Dickie Cooper. He's part o' the bunch I shoot with."

A guy in my position would have had two concerns and figured I'd better start voicing them.

"How well do you know him?"

"Good enough."

"You sure he's not a cop?"

"Dickie Cooper a cop? No way."

I grabbed a handful of his shirt and pulled Hobart close.

"Then I'd hate to think you two were planning to gang up and rip me off for the cash. I do not plan on going home without my new collectibles."

Hobart looked upset at my suggestion.

"No way, friend. No way. I ain't like that. Remember what I said 'bout wantin' satisfied, repeat customers?"

"Yeah, I remember." I let my eyes widen and began breathing heavily. "Now you remember this. If I find out you set me up in any way, I'll hunt you down like a dog. I'll cut off your ears, and then I'll kill you. We understand each other?"

I wanted Hobart to think I was crazy.

His eyes widened, and he looked frightened. Hobart nodded and looked down at how I held the grenade.

"Sure thing, brother. Don't go gettin' excited now. I'll vouch fer Cooper. Don't yew worry. I'm jest doin' bidness, not settin' ya up."

I took in a deep breath. "I hope so."

We returned to the dining room to find Cooper teasing the dog by slapping her ears.

I let my annoyance show. "Get away from the dog."

"I'm jest playin', and she ain't yer dog."

"Touch her again and I'll stick this grenade up your ass and pull the pin."

"Y'all cain't talk ta me like that."

I stepped close to him. "Sure I can. I'm still not sure who you are and why you're here. Who do you work for?"

"Who do *I* work for?" He sounded surprised.

"That's what I said."

"Yew got a lot ta say, an' I'm wonderin' who you are. I think I seen you somewhere b'fore. Why would I know yew?"

I didn't like the sound of that. I'd been on television a number of times, smiling for the Knoxville press corps, and maybe this numbskull watched the news. I thought about the old strategy of a best defense being an offense.

"I must have given you an estimate for our termite control system. If someone asked me to exterminate you, we wouldn't be having this conversation. Any more questions, little feller?"

Dickie didn't comment. Sometimes acting like a bully works just dandy.

"Hobart," I said, "you and I were supposed to do business. I don't want him here. If he's not a cop, who is he? The other dealer you got these things from? Your supervisor?"

"I done tol' ya, jest a friend. We don't want no trouble here. Dickie, maybe you oughta go."

"Take care o' yerse'f, Hobart," Dickie said. "This dude's crazy."

Cooper snatched his beer from the table and stormed out. I wondered if he had a gun and was stupid enough to wait for me outside.

"Can we wrap up this deal?" I asked Milby.

"'Course we kin. We're cool, rot? Don't want no hard feelins."

"Yeah, we're cool. And keep me in mind if you pick up something I'd like. You've got my number."

"Will do."

———

Hobart Milby kept the money, and I packed all the small items in the AWOL bag, slung the carbine over my right shoulder and carried the rocket launcher to my truck. Cooper's Ranger was no longer parked in the driveway.

When I hit the blacktop of Hickory Creek Road, I turned left and blinked the headlights twice. Two unmarked ATF sedans and two marked Prospect PD cruisers took off. I let them pass and made a U-turn, following the procession.

Greznik's agents confiscated the marked money and, during a search of Milby's home, found an impressive collection of illegal military weapons, my favorite being an M-60 light machine gun. Not something the average deer hunter or target shooter needed.

I returned to Milby's house and found Officer Johnny Rutledge standing on the front porch assigned to maintain a log of who entered the premises and keep unwanted visitors out.

"Hey, boss," he said.

I put my hand on his shoulder. "Do me a favor, and get Greznik out here. I want a word before I speak to Milby."

A minute later, Rutledge returned, and Greznik followed.

"You see the red pickup leave before me?" I asked.

"Couldn't miss it."

"Milby IDed the owner as Dickie Cooper. You get a plate number?"

"Think you're dealing with an amateur?"

"Heaven forbid."

"Ready to talk with our big-time arms dealer?" he asked.

"Lead the way."

Hobart, Greznik and I sat in the living room. The dog leaned against my right leg as I scratched her neck.

"What's the dog's name?" I asked.

"Queenie," Hobart said, sulking.

"Why?"

"Was my mother's name."

I shook my head. "It'll be a shame. When you go to the slammer, Animal Control will take Queenie. If no one adopts her in thirty days, they'll put her down."

"That ain't right," he said, scowling.

"That's life," I said. "Tell us something that'll get you out of this big mess, and you don't have to lose her—or your freedom."

Milby shook his head. "I ain't no traitor."

"Think you're Gordon Liddy?"

He didn't answer.

"Only an idiot falls on his sword nowadays," I said. "Tell us where you got all this good stuff, and the Assistant U.S. Attorney can offer you a deal."

"No, sir, I ain't that way."

It felt like I was dealing with a cretin.

"Don't be a nitwit. We've got enough to keep you in jail until you die."

"I ain't sayin' nuthin'."

"Well, think about it while you become intimate with Special Agent Greznik from the Bureau of Alcohol, Tobacco, and Firearms."

"And Explosives," Greznik added.

"Of course," I said. "Can't forget the new addition to their title. Came with nine-eleven."

Milby slouched on the sofa and crossed his arms across his chest.

"With all this weaponry, Ned, you think Mr. Milby is a homegrown terrorist? Gonna send his ass to Git-mo?"

"I ain't no damn terrorist," Hobart said. "I'm a patriot."

"Then maybe he'll appreciate the powers we derive from the Patriot Act," Greznik said.

Hobart snorted. "When the Muslims and Mexicans and other godless heathens try an' take over this country, y'all will be happy folks like me are willin' to fight to keep us free."

"Excuse me, Edward. Mr. Milby is a true patriot and former Marine."

"Far as I'm concerned," Greznik said, "he's cat meat, and he's going away for a long time. Let's send him to Guantanamo to sit in a cell with an Arab terrorist or two."

Milby sighed. "I know how this works. Ya threaten ta bring smoke on me an' use yer damn Patriot Act ta take away my freedom. Jest how much do ya want?"

It seemed as if our true patriot now thought a tactical withdrawal might be in his best interest and softened his hard stance.

Greznik picked up the conversation. "You didn't find these weapons in a landfill, mister. After you give us names and details, you're going to introduce us to your suppliers so we can make a few purchases."

Milby laughed and shook his head. "You wanna git me kilt?"

"Give us enough to work on and he'll give you a new identity and protect you and Queenie," I said.

He paused and did the head-shaking thing again. "I ain't no snitch."

"Too bad," Greznik said.

Milby had annoyed me, and I let it show. "You'll get out on bail. And while you're free, maybe a few well-placed words from us might make your patriotic friends think you are."

Milby frowned. I smiled.

———

HUBBELL WELCHANCE, AN ATTORNEY FAMOUS FOR REPRESENTING right-wing neo-fascist defendants, miraculously appeared to represent Hobart Milby at his arraignment. We ran into each other in the hallway of the Justice Center.

"Well, hello, Chief Jenkins." He had a slight overbite and an oily smile. "We seem ta meet ever' time you deprive a patriotic Amurican of his civil rights."

The overbite made him speak with a slight lisp.

"Counselor, I'd ask how can you sleep at night, but they'd be wasted words."

He grinned. "I'm surprised a decorated soldier and lifelong po-leeceman like ya'se'f would have a problem with Amuricans willin' to defend their country."

I had no intention of debating philosophy with Welchance. Instead, I gave him the finger.

"See you in court, Hub, old buddy."

I left the building and headed back to Prospect.

———

THAT AFTERNOON, MAYOR RONNIE SHIELDS HELD A PRESS conference to tell East Tennessee about my success and Hobart Milby's misfortune. I hate when he does things like that, but he's a publicity junkie, and I've learned to tolerate his need to jump in front of a camera as often as snakes eat mice. Moreover, I saw my time with the Knoxville reporters as an opportunity to increase the pressure on poor old patriotic Hobart.

At four o'clock, the TV and newspaper crews began wandering in. While most of them milled around the lobby of the Municipal Building waiting for the mayor to make a grand entrance on the marble staircase, Rachel Williamson, senior news anchor and most beautiful woman on Knoxville television, walked into my office. Cameraman John Leckmanski followed.

After a kiss on the cheek from Rachel and a handshake from John, I asked her a stupid question.

"What's different about your hair?"

She smiled. "I had highlights put in. Glad you noticed."

"Why?"

"Why did I have it highlighted?"

"Yeah, it looked lovely the way it was."

"You don't like it."

Leckmanski shook his head and turned. "Jeez, I'm getting a cup o' coffee."

John is a rugged-looking ex-war photographer who dressed the part in an old Willie Nelson T-shirt, desert camouflage field pants and an Atlanta Braves ball cap.

He turned abruptly and walked to the counter at the far end of my room and poured himself a cup.

"I do not want to be part of this conversation," he said. "I'll be outside talking to Bettye."

"I can't believe you don't like my hair," Rachel said.

"I didn't say that."

"No, but—"

"No buts. I like everything about you. I just thought your dark chocolate-colored hair looked stunning next to your almost black, almond-shaped eyes. All very sexy."

"Oh." She offered a little smile.

I seemed to be gaining ground.

"And for someone your age, you have a figure like...well, since you're a married woman, I won't elaborate."

"My age?"

"You'll never see forty again, but you look *much* younger."

"Thank you." The little smile turned into something worth a million dollars. "You certainly know how to save your ass."

"That's why you love me."

"Ha. Wait until the conference starts, I'll make mincemeat out of you."

"Fat chance, Shorty. Hey listen, if no one else asks, here's a question you can use..." I gave her a loaded suggestion.

Before the mayor's press release had gone public, I called Rachel and told her about the big arrest. I knew she'd be able to formulate plenty of questions of her own, but I wanted to ensure that someone fed me a lead on a point I wanted covered. She agreed, but I'm not sure she liked the possibility the question might have generated.

Ronnie kicked off the festivities with his usual politician's smile and greeting. I stepped behind the podium when he finished schmoozing the reporters.

After I summarized my exciting undercover operation and the subsequent search and arrest of the dastardly Hobart Milby, most of the reporter's questions sounded redundant. But they needed a photo-op for the filmed segments on their six o'clock news reports, and I aimed to accommodate.

Allen Peters, a big, sandy-haired anchorman from a major network affiliate wearing an expensive-looking pearl gray suit, beat Rachel to the punch and asked the question I wanted to answer.

"Chief," he said, "this resident of Prospect is obviously not an international arms dealer. Where did he get those automatic weapons and explosives?"

Ned Greznik sat one chair to my left. I looked at him and winked.

"Our investigation has only begun, Mr. Peters," I said. "I expect to have an answer for you shortly."

"You mean the defendant is interested in cooperating?" Peters said.

"The defendant wasn't charged with resisting arrest. He's been cooperative all along."

Rachel put her hand up, and I pointed to her, but Allen Peters remained standing and shot another question at me.

"Does that mean he's willing to provide you with the names of his suppliers?"

"Surely you don't think I'm going to answer that question."

Peters smiled and took his seat. A few other reporters snickered. I looked at Rachel who had lowered her hand. She shook her head.

"Now," I said. "I think we've covered every aspect of the case, and I'll turn the program back to Mayor Shields. Thanks for coming."

As the crowd broke up, I walked back into the reception area of the PD, and Ed Greznik followed.

"Are you trying to get Milby killed?" he asked.

"Who? Me?"

"If he's in with some really bad guys and they heard you, it won't take them long to find Milby. Part of his bail restriction is staying within Blount County."

"Maybe not, but suppose they don't watch TV?"

"Yeah, sure."

Bettye Lambert listened and frowned at my answers.

"Milby wasn't smart enough to recognize me as the Prospect police chief. His cohorts probably aren't any brighter. But Hub Welchance is, and he may pressure his client to accept your big deal of the day."

Greznik shrugged. "Like I said, you're hot shit."

I think Bettye was about to scold me, but Rachel stepped in and took my arm. She led me to my office and closed the door.

"You're trying to set up that man." she said.

"Milby was arrogant, and his attorney is worse. I want him to come back and ask for protection and a deal."

"Suppose he gets hurt?"

"It's essential that we find the source of those very destructive weapons. The risk is worth it."

"Can you live with the results if this goes south?"

"I've lived with worse."

She shook her head. "No wonder you drink."

————

TWO DAYS LATER, AT EIGHT O'CLOCK ON A BALMY EVENING, MY phone rang.

"You are not going to believe this," Sergeant Stan Rose said.

"Stanley, you know I hate surprises. Just tell me."

"It sounds like a war zone over here on Hickory Creek Road."

In the background, I heard noise similar to a busy afternoon in Manhattan.

"I can hardly hear you. Yell," I shouted into the phone.

"Hang on, I've got to move."

I waited a few moments, and Stan spoke again. "This isn't much better, but can you hear me?"

"Are you standing next to a big truck?"

"We've got fire trucks all over," he yelled. "There was an explosion, and your man Milby's house went up. It's still burning."

"I'll be right there."

I hung up and found Kate standing behind me in the kitchen.

"Must you shout?" she asked.

"Stanley was outnumbered by fire trucks. Hard to hear him."

"Can I assume you're leaving our happy home?"

"Sorry about this, but I assume I'll be awhile. Don't wait up."

"If they paid you overtime for all the extra work you do, we'd be listed in the Fortune 500."

"You're so clever," I said.

"While you're gone, I'm going to make myself a drink...or two. By the time you get home, I may be in a romantic mood and not mad because you've abandoned me."

"What woman could get mad at me?"

"Got a pencil?"

———

I MET STANLEY AND PO WILL SPARKS A HUNDRED YARDS NORTH OF the opening to Hobart Milby's steep driveway. Another man in his mid-sixties leaned against Stan's white-and-blue cruiser with his arms folded across his chest. The acrid smell of gunpowder hung in the still air, and a small army of firemen crowded the roadway. A heavy pumper from the Blount County Fire District honked its horn, and I moved to the side of the narrow blacktop. As that truck disappeared, another drove past us in the opposite direction.

"How many fire trucks are here?" I asked.

"That makes the eleventh hose truck," Stan said. "There's a bunch of other vehicles down past the driveway."

I nodded.

"This is a real horror show," he continued. "The first tanker tried to get up the steep hill and broke its universal joint halfway to the house. It rolled down, and they had to get a heavy-duty wrecker to pull it out. Then they used a small four-wheel-drive hose truck to get near the house."

"Are they keeping the water tankers down here and stretching the hoses all the way up the hill to the all-wheel-drive pumper?"

"Yes, but that's only part of the big problem."

"I can hardly wait."

"When they started deploying the hoses to fight the house fire, the ammo started exploding, and they evacuated and let the place burn."

"Exploding ammo?"

"Haven't heard anything for a while, but rounds were still popping when Will and I got here."

Stan went on to explain that according to Milby, he and his dog returned home and once inside the garage, his truck caught fire. The fire spread quickly, the wood-framed home became fully involved, and approximately 2,000 rounds of small arms ammunition he stored in the garage created a big bang. Milby's story sounded like rubbish.

The middle-aged man spoke for the first time. "Sounded like more than 2,000 rounds to me. All different calibers, too."

"How do you know that?" I asked.

He stuck out a hand for me to shake.

"Sergeant Rudy Starnberg, Detroit PD, retired. I spent eighteen months in Vietnam and twenty-five years as a cop. Here's what I heard..."

Starnberg explained that he'd been sitting on his porch about 400 yards from Milby's house. He first heard what sounded like a half-dozen high-caliber rifle rounds go off. Just as he complained to his wife about someone shooting within the subdivision, dozens of smaller caliber handgun rounds discharged rapidly.

"Sounded like a few people with nine millimeter pistols returning fire at the guy with the .30 caliber rifle," he said. "Then three more rifle shots went off in rapid succession. After that, all hell broke loose. Sounded like at least two reinforced platoons were in a firefight: .223, .30 caliber, and bigger stuff—you name it. That lasted about ninety seconds, maybe two minutes."

"Then I heard a single explosion. It shook the windows. I'm guessing either a pound of black powder or some big-ass destructive device. A cloud of black smoke rose above those tall pines." He pointed to the trees in front of us. "Then sporadic mixed-caliber stuff continued to go off. That stretched out...hell, I don't know. The firefighters got here. Trucks were moving around. Sirens were wailing, I lost track." He paused for a moment. "But I heard four more big explosions."

"Hell of a mess," I said.

"Worst I've seen in this country," he said.

I thanked the retired cop, and Stan and I picked our way between the fire apparatus to find Hobart Milby sitting on the tailgate of a heavy rescue truck, his dog on the end of a leash tied to his left leg. Milby removed an oxygen mask from his face and looked at me.

"You did this to me," he said.

He reeked of bourbon. His eyes looked glassy, and his speech was slurred.

"And you're shit-faced, partner," I said. "You know damn well I had nothing to do with this. While you were out getting a toot on, your patriotic friends planted an incendiary device, and you triggered it. Nobody's truck just goes up in flames. The story you told Sergeant Rose was a lie."

He sneered. "Go fuck ya'se'f."

I stared off into space, amazed that Milby would still protect the people who tried to kill him.

The noise of the firemen and the trucks' diesel engines covered the usual night sounds normally heard in the sparsely populated neighborhood. Nonetheless, hundreds of fireflies blinked continuously in the surrounding woodland. Everything around us seemed incongruous.

I looked back at Milby. "I'm not the guy whose house is burning out of control. You're the one here who's screwed."

He said nothing. I knelt down and rubbed my hand on the dog's back. She whimpered slightly.

"Be a shame if your patriotic comrades hurt Queenie," I said.

Milby shook his head and looked about ready to crack.

"Let the Feds protect you, for chrissakes," I said. "So far, your radical politics has gotten you into hot water. Start over. Be safe."

As if on cue, Queenie lifted a paw and placed it on Milby's knee. I think it influenced him.

He looked at me and then at Stan Rose.

"I might talk ta you," Milby said, "but I don't want yer black friend here while we do it."

"The man's six inches taller than you and outweighs you by more than fifty pounds. You think it's a good time to crack wise?"

"You lookin' fer information or wanna be a social worker?" Milby asked.

"Well y'all mus' 'cuse me," Stanley said, using his Uncle Remus accent. "But I gots me no reason ta stay here with yo white folk."

I rolled my eyes.

"Personally," Stan said, again using his normal voice, "I'd let his neo-Nazi friends kill him. But you're the boss."

"Call Greznik for me?" I said. "We need an arson/bomb technician to work the scene."

Stan nodded and walked away.

"Hobart, that guy's ten times the man any of your friends are. You really need to identify your priorities."

He shook his head. "Buulll-shit."

"I'll give you sixty seconds to tell me who did this and what their story is."

He waited a long moment with his head hung and finally began nodding.

"Do I need my lawyer here?"

"How did you meet Hub Welchance?"

"People told me about him. A friend called him for me."

"You got the money to pay his fee?"

"I figger I'll get a little he'p from my friends."

"Are you a moron? Your friends arranged for your lawyer. They've got him on retainer. You want him here when you rat them out?"

He looked at me with a blank stare. I could have gotten more sense from the dog.

"They just tried to kill you," I reminded him.

"I sure hope you don't screw me again."

"You screwed yourself, numb nuts, so let's not debate that. I'll keep my part of the bargain, and so will the Feds."

Hobart nodded slowly.

"The sergeant was right," I said. "We should let your Nazi friends kill you, but for some reason I'll help because I think this dog needs you."

I hugged the dog, and she pressed against me.

"A few members live 'round here," he said, "but most of 'em are down around Tellico Plains."

"Members of what?"

"Patriots at the Gate."

"What gate?"

"I don't know...the gate o' heaven."

"Oh, wonderful, self-styled soldiers of the Lord. I can just see it, amateur militiamen target shooting with Saint Peter. And you're one of them?"

"I ain't a regular. I only go ta meetings ta drum up bidness."

"More convenient than a gun show?"

"I can buy and sell. These guys change guns like I change my dirty britches. Some of 'em need cash."

"Fascinating. And I suppose you also know more dealers like you who help provide guys like me with our illegal weapon needs?"

He nodded. "Most of 'em aren't bad guys."

"I'm sure. Keep talking."

Ned Greznik and I got together with Ralph Oliveri at the FBI field office in Knoxville to gather intelligence on the Patriots at the Gate.

No one seemed to know much about the group, other than they considered themselves patriots in the most traditional sense and planned on defending American ideals to the last member when the apocalypse they envisioned—minorities, women and Democrats forcing their ways on society—kicked into high gear.

Many times, when information is at a premium and it seems like all the sophisticated law enforcement resources can't help you learn more, it's best to go back to basics and look for something right out in the open. Back when I was a young cop, the telephone book helped me many times. As we sat around Ralph's desk, I took a more modern approach.

"See if they have a website," I said.

On the third try, Ralph hit pay dirt. Patriotsatthegate.org brought up a snazzy website which not only provided us with the group's full manifesto, but photos of the members shooting what looked like everything from M-16s to AK-47s at a makeshift rifle range.

I pointed to one figure among the crowd holding an assault rifle. "This is the one Milby called Dickie Cooper."

"Dickson Cooper, according to motor vehicle records," Greznik said. "Couldn't find anything else on him."

After a few more clicks, we found additional shots of the membership, all dressed in surplus woodland cammo, sucking down suds at their patriotically decorated clubhouse.

An American flag hung on one wall, flanked by a poster-sized copy of the U.S. Constitution. Elsewhere, framed photos of several Founding Fathers shared wall space with plaques from every military service and a few nationally known organizations that remain close to the hearts of conservative gun owners. I didn't see a portrait of John Birch.

"Quite a group," Ralph said. "Maybe we should try and infiltrate them."

"Are they suspected of doing anything?" Greznik asked. "Other than trying to kill Hobart Milby?"

"Claimed responsibility for any act of domestic terrorism?" I asked. "Burned any crosses? Hung any enemies of the state?"

"Hang on," Ralph said.

He clicked his computer keys, looking for information in the Bureau's database.

"I can't find anything."

"So you infiltrate them and do what?" I said. "So far we've only got a reasonable suspicion they bombed Milby's house. Probably not even enough to get a wiretap warrant to see if they talk about it. Unless you can stretch the Patriot Act and consider them terrorists."

"The last vice president would allow us to tap the phones of old women who criticized the government during their quilting bees, but not this administration."

"So what would the undercover man do?" I asked. "Burn up ammunition and then drink beer and read *Soldier of Fortune* magazine on the weekends?"

Oliveri shrugged.

"Let's match these pictures with the driver's license photos for the names Milby gave us," Greznik said.

"Maybe we'll find a weak link and get him to flip on the guys who planted the bomb," Ralph suggested.

"The bomb wasn't very sophisticated," Greznik said. "Just something out of the *Anarchist's Cookbook* or what you find on the Internet. I doubt we'll be dealing with rocket scientists."

With Hobart Milby's statement and public videos of the lunatics at the gate rattling off machine guns, we had enough probable cause to obtain warrants to search and confiscate their weapons. Those members with the least involvement and the most to lose might be ready to talk in exchange for leniency. The Patriots at the Gate seemed more like a group of zealous idiots than a threat to national security.

"They all should be this easy," I said.

Greznik and Oliveri nodded.

Hobart Milby had provided names, places and detailed information on group members who were stockpiling ammunition and weapons, many of those weapons being on the Feds' list of restricted items. In addition, he tossed in a half-dozen out-of-town people who provided him with assorted munitions and other illegal military collectibles subject to the restrictions of the Federal Gun Control Act of 1968.

Ralph volunteered to prepare the information for a friendly assistant U.S. attorney and work on obtaining search warrants.

As Ned Greznick and I took the elevator in the Federal building at 710 Locust Street down from the FBI's penthouse suite, we discussed a little embarrassing and unfinished business.

"How the hell did we miss Milby's stash of ammo?" I asked.

"Beats the by-jesus outta me. I thought we snooped in every corner of that house."

"Let's go take a look."

We drove back to Prospect, and even the V-8 in my Crown Victoria strained getting up the hill to Milby's house, which looked like a charred skeleton. Less than two-thirds of the structure remained after the fire.

The evidence technicians had left yellow crime scene tape stretched and tied everywhere. As soon as we opened the car doors, the unmistakable stench of a burned building assaulted us.

A curious squirrel ran away from the car and poked his head into the garage looking for a safe haven, only to be repelled by the pungent smell. As the animal scurried away, two crows sitting on the branch of a scorched maple tree screeched at us. The place felt ominous. I wouldn't have been surprised if we found Edgar Allen Poe sitting on the porch.

The mostly melted overhead garage door looked like grotesque, synthetic stalactites. Milby's once-silver Dodge pickup sat in its usual spot, the exploded tires melted to the concrete floor, the truck blackened and its paint blistered by the intense heat.

We carefully looked around the garage, trying not to get any of the wet ash on our clothing.

Soggy ash from the floor began coating my loafers. "Shit. I wish I brought boots."

Greznik nodded. "I hate this smell."

I wondered how many post-explosion scenes he had investigated.

"Then you're in the wrong business," I said.

"You investigate murders. You like the stink of a week-old corpse?"

"I see your point."

It was easy to spot the point of origin of the incendiary bomb. The center unit of a group of three wall-hung cabinets had been charred terribly and the door completely burned away.

"How do you figure they detonated the device? I asked.

"Probably something simple like a trip line of monofilament stretched across the floor. When he drove in, the line set off the trigger mechanism. The technicians will tell us soon enough.

After a few minutes of retracing our steps through the garage, I looked up and then at Ned and shrugged. "Must be."

"Yeah. These rafters and plywood look blown up rather than burned out," he said.

"I guess Hobart stored his ammo above the garage. The rising fire and heat detonated everything."

"I looked over the room's perimeter and didn't see any doors or staircase going to the attic space."

He pointed to the exposed area above. Only three roof beams remained over our heads in the two-car garage.

"Nothing else fell down." I said. "I guess he only kept ammo up there."

I spent a few moments looking around the walls surrounding us and, after seeing nothing else, I pointed to a spot behind the door opening into the kitchen.

"That small section of wall extends three feet into the garage. Let's see what's on the inside," I said.

I pulled on latex gloves to keep the char from my hands and opened the kitchen door. The brass knob still felt warm—or was it my imagination?

Greznik followed, and we found no setback along the wall adjacent to the door.

"That's funny," I said. "This is a straight wall with no alcove."

"So, what's behind that wall?" Greznik asked, jerking a thumb toward the garage.

"Let's find out."

We went back into the garage where I found a three-foot pry bar hanging over a workbench.

"Stand back," I said.

I swung the steel bar against the sheetrock, striking it four times. Using the crooked end, I pulled much of the soggy plasterboard inward.

"I'll be damned," he said. "A hidden staircase."

"We know it leads to the attic space. Let's see how Hobart gained access to it."

I ripped down more sheetrock, carefully stepped into the stairwell, and used a flashlight to find a narrow door against the kitchen wall. It opened inward, revealing a plywood barrier. I pushed and found a wall-mounted ironing board covered by a raised panel door—all part of the kitchen cabinet scheme.

"Crafty bastard," I said.

"Paranoid son of a bitch."

"Certainly was."

"So now we know," Ned said.

"Hard to spot something like this." I pointed to the false wall.

"Thanks for the rationalization."

"Chalk it up to education," I said.

"Yeah, when this prick wants Witness Protection to relocate him, I'll ask the Marshal's Service to get him a single-wide in North Dakota. Let him shovel a little snow every year."

"You're vindictive."

"You ain't seen nothin' yet."

———

LED BY RALPH OLIVERI AND HIS MERRY MEN, A FEDERAL AND LOCAL task force executed search warrants in three Tennessee counties and four locations out of state. Eighteen members of The Patriots at the Gate were arrested, and dozens of automatic weapons, explosives, ammunition and other more conventional gear and weapons were confiscated. Four other individuals who provided Milby with hard-to-find illegal weapons by mail were also arrested. I was happy to have started the ball rolling.

———

WE ALL SAT IN MY OFFICE: JUNIOR HUSKEY, BOBBY CROCKETT, Rachel Williamson and me.

"You know Officers Huskey and Crockett," I said.

Rachel nodded and smiled at the boys. "I do. Hi, guys."

"Hey, Miss Rachel," Junior said.

The suave Bobby John lowered his voice and said, "Hello, Ms. Williamson."

"If it wasn't for these two," I said, "we wouldn't have made that case against The Patriots at the Gate."

The two cops beamed as I continued to detail what happened, from the Saturday at the gun show through the culmination of the multi-agency operation.

"So," I said, "these two whippersnappers deserve the credit."

"Whippersnappers?" Junior said.

Bobby reached over and punched him on the arm. "Shut up, stupid."

"You just got your fifteen minutes of fame," I said. "Now, the pair of you, get out of here."

The two young cops grinned and left.

"They made all this happen?" Rachel asked.

"Sure. I was sitting at home on my day off, minding my own business, when they called."

"I'll be sure to mention them in my story," she said.

"Thanks."

"I wish I worked for you, Sammy."

I smiled. "You could be a detective—as long as there was no height requirement."

"Hey, watch it, big feller."

"I guess calling you Shorty can get me in trouble. What's politically correct—height-challenged?"

"I think you should take me to lunch," she said.

"I gave you an exclusive on the biggest case of the year and I buy lunch, too?"

"Of course. You're a gentleman."

"What's wrong with this picture?"

THE END

NOTHING FITZ

On a rainy Thursday morning, I stood in my office pouring a cup of coffee, knowing I'd have to attack the monthly vehicle report I'd been avoiding. Just as I sat behind my desk, the intercom buzzed, and I spoke to Sergeant Bettye Lambert.

"Change your mind and want a second cup of coffee?" I asked.

"No, you have a visitor."

"To whom will I be speaking?"

She laughed at my attempt at grammatical correctness. "Special Agent Wallace from the Air Force Office of Special Investigations."

"What's so *special* about him?"

"Darlin', I'm gonna let y'all see fer yer own se'f." Bettye's delightful Smoky Mountain accent took on a decidedly more country sound.

"What does it say on my door?"

She chuckled. "Chief."

"And I believe the nameplate on your desk says 'sergeant.' Is it proper for you to speak to your fearless leader like that in front of a total stranger?"

"And you have a pleasant day, too, sir." She hung up.

I took a sip of black coffee and moments later looked up at a gorgeous African-American woman wearing a tan suit with a skirt all of three inches above her knees. She held a khaki raincoat draped over her left arm, and a five-hundred-dollar leather bag hung from her right shoulder.

My visitor stepped up to the edge of my desk and extended a hand.

"Hi, I'm Roxanne Wallace, resident OSI agent at McGhee Tyson."

I stood and shook her hand. "Nice to meet you, Ms. Wallace. I'm Sam Jenkins."

"I know." Her smile lit up the room. "Call me Roxy."

I nodded. "Please sit down."

She did, and so did I, after watching her skirt slide up another two inches. Nothing gets past a trained investigator.

"What can I do for you, Roxy?"

She tilted her head and fluttered a pair of the longest eyelashes I'd seen in years. Her almost full lips parted in a perfect smile.

"I want to ask a favor."

Then she turned up the smile another 500 watts.

"I thought you might," I said.

"Word is you're the best homicide investigator in this part of the world."

I flashed my own dazzling but modest smile. "That's a statement of fact. You spoke about a favor."

"Yes, it is, and so I did."

She tilted her head again. This one could give Halle Berry a run for her money in a beauty pageant for girls over thirty.

"Have you heard about the captain who was murdered on the air base?"

"Sure. Beaten to death with a foot-long crescent wrench."

Flutter, flutter. "I need your assistance."

I shrugged. "I have no jurisdiction on your air base."

"I know. I just thought I might enlist your help. You know, from one professional to another, you having so much experience and being so good at your job. That's all."

She smiled again, blinked a few times and waited. I needed to get to the bottom line.

"Roxy, you are a beautiful woman, and I love flattery as much as the next guy, but why are you asking me to help with an investigation on the air base when you must have a chain of command that can provide all the assistance you could possibly use?"

Her smile faded a little, but the eyelashes remained in motion. She tapped the long acrylic nails of her right hand on a lovely knee. The candy apple red paint job on her nails looked like something you'd see on a restored, chopped and channeled '49 Mercury coupe.

"I really need some help," she said. "I've been with OSI for ten years and never handled a murder before. My boss wants results, and I hate to admit I've got nothing and don't know where to look next. I just don't want to appear inept."

"I thought the security police arrested someone at the scene."

"They did, but he isn't confessing. They don't have much of a case on him, and I can't find any evidence that definitively links him to the murder. Nothing fits."

"Who processed the crime scene?"

"I did."

"Are you a technician?"

"I learned in criminal investigation school. We often do our own work."

"On a homicide?"

She shrugged.

"Where's your regular forensics team?" I asked.

"Seymour Johnson air base."

"That's in North Carolina."

"Yes, and I've got another problem."

"What?"

"I don't think the defendant killed him."

"Why do you think I can find your killer?"

She crossed her left leg over the right and resurrected the smile. "Because you're Sam Jenkins."

I flipped my hands in the air. "I give up," I said. "If I wasn't an old married man, I'd say I'm in love. But I have a job here. How long do you think this'll take before you call in your big guns?"

"Why don't you come over to McGhee Tyson and look at the crime scene. I'm sure you'll know after you look things over."

"May I hear your version of the incident first?"

"Of course you can."

I've spent a lifetime getting bamboozled by good-looking women, but this one was a crackerjack—a real pro at interpersonal manipulation.

"The SPs responded to an anonymous call about a dead body in a maintenance hangar," she said. "They found Captain Norwood Brower dead and a crew chief present. The guy is Master Sergeant Michael Fitzgerald. But I don't buy him as the killer."

"Why did the SPs lock him up?"

"He was standing over the body."

"Hmmm."

"Holding a bloody wrench."

"Yikes."

"I know."

"Any info on the phone call?"

"Prepaid cell."

"Think that's odd?"

"A little. It was early morning. There are usually some people out and about. Perhaps someone just didn't want to get more involved."

"Not great, but sounds possible. I'm not sure I can do more than you."

"But you'll help me?" She sounded like a little girl who lost her puppy.

"All I have to do is point you in the right direction for a good arrest and conviction?"

She did the head tilt thing again. "Uh-huh."

"And if I work this magic for you, you'll owe me a favor?"

The lashes went into motion. "You bet." And she flashed a set of priceless pearly whites.

"Your car or mine?" I said.

———

Fifteen minutes later, Roxy Wallace pulled her unmarked, gold Impala up to the security police kiosk at the main gate of the McGhee Tyson air base in Alcoa, Tennessee. To the right, on a nicely landscaped quarter acre of land, a decommissioned Korean War vintage F-86 Saber Jet rested on a giant pedestal fifteen feet off the ground, pointing upward at a forty-five degree angle, simulating a radical takeoff. Two Air Force cops dressed in cammies stood on either side of the booth. A tall man wearing senior airman's chevrons on his sleeve looked into the car. The name tape over his right pocket said "Tallant."

He smiled. "Hello there, Miss Roxy. What kin I do for y'all today?"

"Hi, Justin. Got a visitor's badge for Chief Jenkins?"

He looked me over. I grinned. He didn't smile for me.

"Mornin'," I said.

He nodded. "Sir." The response sounded more businesslike than friendly. He switched his eyes back to my partner and rested a right hand on the butt of a holstered Beretta automatic attached to his shiny Sam Browne belt. "Sure thing, Miss Roxy."

Airman Tallant stepped into the kiosk and picked up a clipboard and laminated card. We waited for him to walk around to my side of the car.

"May I see yer ID, please?"

I handed him my Prospect PD identification card. He filled in a few spaces on the visitor's log and handed me the pass.

"Wear this at all times, sir. And turn it in when ya leave."

I nodded. "Will do."

"You wearin' a weapon, sir?"

"I am."

He looked past me. "Not supposed ta do that, Roxy."

"It's official business, Justin. I'll take responsibility."

He sighed. "Okay, jest don't go gettin' inta no shootouts."

I said, "I hope not."

"Thanks, Justin," Roxy said and dropped the gearshift lever into Drive.

———

WE WALKED INTO A HANGAR WITH AN INTERIOR LARGE ENOUGH TO play a decent game of touch football. Yellow crime scene tape still marked the spot of a brutal murder. Narrow white tape outlined where the body fell onto the concrete floor—old-fashioned, but effective. A dozen mechanics dressed in the current pattern of sage-green camouflage fatigues worked on a large midair refueling jet.

I did a three-sixty, taking in all the sights and sounds of the workplace. There were giant roll-arounds holding simple and sophisticated tools, workbenches, storage cabinets, racks of large, expensive-looking tires and things I couldn't identify a use for. Against the wall at the far side of the building, a stocky NCO with a sleeve full of stripes picked up a wall phone and made a call.

"Quite a set-up," I said.

"Your tax dollars at work," Roxy said.

"Tell me about the vic."

"Captain Norwood Brower, CO of the maintenance wing. In charge of about a hundred and eighty people, the three hangars along this runway and the motor pool."

"Regular Air Force or fulltime guard employee?"

"Fulltime guard. Been nine-to-five military about twenty years."

"What do his subordinates say about him?"

"Not much. He was just here and not particularly friendly with the NCO or enlisted personnel. The four lieutenants in the unit said he was okay."

"How about his bosses?"

"Like I said, he was just here. No problems. He ran a clean unit, but no ball of fire."

"And how about the arrested Sergeant Fitz...?" I had forgotten his name. "Fitz-whatchamacallit?"

Roxy smiled. "Fitzgerald, Michael, no middle initial, Master Sergeant, one each."

I laughed at her proper use of classic military nomenclature. "That's the one."

"It's an eighty-twenty split of likes and dislikes. Major Fancy is in charge of all the support wings on base. He thinks Fitzgerald is a hard worker, good leader and an asset to his unit. His immediate supervisor, Lieutenant Girty, says Fitzgerald isn't a team player. The senior NCOs and most of the EM like him. A couple others cast aspersions on his character."

"Aspersions?"

"There's been an ongoing loss of equipment—truck tires, some aircraft tires and parts, some other items. It gets complicated. Some things were written off as unaccounted for expendables, while others were listed in the inventory as missing, but *not* reported as stolen. They would rather admit to sloppy bookkeeping than not stopping thefts of government property."

"Stolen equipment and supplies would make the unit look bad."

Roxy nodded. "It would impact on all the supervisor's efficiency reports. After Captain Brower put out a few internal memos asking for tighter inventory control, the disappearances didn't stop. Everyone looked at the losses as thefts."

"Can't report that. No unit CO wants a bunch of pesky cops looking around his shop."

"Most personnel look at us as necessary evils."

"You don't look evil to me."

She smiled.

"Explain those aspersions."

"A few people said they wouldn't be surprised if Fitzgerald wasn't behind the thefts. Sort of hinted that he's not only the killer, but the thief or the leader of a team of thieves."

"What do you think about that?"

"He had the opportunity to steal anything here, but there's no evidence or reason for me to believe he's the thief or the ringleader. His financials look normal. He lives in a modest house, married with 2.4 children, wife drives a small and financed car—Mister Middle America."

I laughed again. "And if he's the crafty *ringleader,* who are his evil minions?"

She grinned. "Beats the stuffin's outta me, sweetheart."

I puttered around the crime scene for a few more minutes, not seeing a damn thing. Roxy followed.

"This is useless," I said. "You had a body, a bloody weapon and a suspect present. I can see why the SPs made an arrest. Sergeant Fitzgerald did it in the hangar with the wrench."

"Maybe it was Colonel Mustard," she said.

"Is he stationed here?"

"You gonna help or make jokes?"

"Nothing in this hangar is going to help. Can we speak with Fitzgerald?"

"That could be a problem."

"Lawyered up?"

"Yes and no," Roxy said.

"I love a straight answer."

"The base CO arranged for an officer to represent him."

"A JAG lawyer?"

"No, an admin officer. A captain who works in base ops."

"The guy's charged with murder, and he doesn't get a real lawyer?"

"They've applied to the district judge advocate's office. The next guy on call is going to come from Seymour Johnson."

"More from North Carolina. Hell of a commute."

"Afraid so. Came with the budget cuts and reorganization. We can't talk with Fitz until his counsel is present."

I shook my head. "This Constitution gets in the way at times."

"Don't it just?"

"Where is Sergeant Fitz being held?"

"I borrowed some space from the Blount County Sheriff."

"Close enough. Let's talk with Captain Clarence Darrow at base ops and tell him we won't question Fitz, just talk at him."

Roxy frowned. "The captain's name is Clarke. I can try."

"You got an office nearby?"

"Do I ever."

As we began to leave, an old, Air-Force-blue staff car pulled up next to Roxy's Impala. Two officers got out, a first lieutenant in cammies and a captain wearing a blue raincoat over his class As.

"Oh, crap," Roxy said.

"Enemy troops?" I asked.

"Maybe."

"Still investigating, Agent Wallace?" the captain asked. Neatly trimmed blond hair peeked out from beneath his overseas cap. He looked to be approaching middle-age—a little old for a captain, but he still had his boyish good looks, just not a very friendly smile.

"We're looking things over again, sir," Roxy said.

"They send you some help?" he asked.

Roxy didn't respond immediately. I had nothing to lose, so I answered.

"I'm just a professional friend offering a second opinion."

"And you are?"

I hate when people say that.

"Sam Jenkins, police chief from Prospect."

The lieutenant spoke for the first time, "You have no jurisdiction here."

He was almost medium height, but wiry and dark with eyebrows that looked like two caterpillars crawling over almost black and shifty eyes. His name tape said "Girty".

"I know that, Lieutenant. Perhaps you didn't hear me. I'm only offering a second opinion." *So there, you little twerp.*

I guess Roxy sensed a potential problem with the flow of testosterone and intervened.

"I should make the introductions. You gentlemen know the chief. Sam, this is Captain Lance Hamilton, the base Provost Marshal and CO of the security police company. And this is Lieutenant Darnell Girty, now acting CO of the maintenance wing."

I nodded. "Gentlemen."

The captain extended his hand. "Good to meet you, Chief."

Girty sulked and remained silent.

"See anything here that could help Agent Wallace?" Hamilton asked.

"I'm afraid not. It's a pretty uncomplicated crime scene."

"My thoughts exactly," Hamilton said.

"Y'all still thinkin' Fitz didn't do it, Mizz Wallace?" Girty made 'mizz' sound dreadfully demeaning. I really didn't like him.

"Special Agent Wallace is doing what all good investigators do, Lootenant." I made sure my words dripped with sarcasm. "She's keeping an open mind and avoiding what many amateurs have—tunnel vision."

Darnell Girty tensed up. I guess he didn't like me either.

"Of course," Captain Hamilton said. "Good way to look at this. But when all's said and done, I think Fitzgerald will still be our man."

"Yes, sir, could be," Roxy said.

I glared at Lieutenant Shit-for-brains and remembered Justin the gate guard worrying about me getting into a shootout. He must have known I'd meet Girty.

"Captain, we were just leaving," Roxy said.

"Okay, us, too," he said. "Nice meeting you, Chief."

"Same here," I said.

Girty made an about face and walked toward the captain's sedan. Hamilton followed.

I looked at Roxy. "Nice guys."

"Oh, yeah."

"When we walked in here, I watched a senior sergeant make a phone call, and then this pair showed up. I wonder if he dropped a dime on Hamilton or Girty."

"Be good to know."

I nodded. "Your office in the PMO?"

"Afraid so. I'd rather be tucked away on my own, but the Air Guard thinks I should be a fixture in the Provost Marshall's office."

"I don't want to see Hamilton again. Mind transacting business in a restaurant?"

"It's almost lunchtime," she said.

"You pick it. I'm buying."

"Eat Chinese?"

"Like a native."

"Ming Tree?"

"Haven't been there in years. Still good?"

"I think so."

"Lead the way, Mizz Wallace."

———

OUR WAITRESS PLACED AN ORDER OF SWEET-AND-SOUR SHRIMP IN front of Roxy and slid a plate of chicken with cashews on my side of the table. A bus boy set down a stainless steel, footed bowl of steamed rice between us.

"Can I top off your tea?" I asked.

"Thanks."

I poured, and Roxy helped herself to the rice.

"Who are the enlisted men who didn't like Fitzgerald?" I asked.

"You're going to love these names. Two NCOs in particular. One named Alvin York Grindstaff. He's also a crew chief like Fitzgerald. Same hangar, but a different crew. The other's a material control specialist—an inventory clerk—a staff sergeant named Arlo Bordwine."

I shook my head and put on an East Tennessee accent. "Lord have mercy. I guess they's local boys."

Roxy laughed loud enough to get looks from two men at a nearby table. Both were young officers wearing flight suits. One went back to his lunch, and the other spent a long moment devouring Roxy with his eyes.

"What do these two say specifically?" I asked.

"Conjecture mostly. Grindstaff is the one who suggested Fitz was behind the thefts. He sounded rather vehement about that. He thinks Captain Brower caught Fitz in the act, and Fitz silenced him—permanently. Bordwine did a lot of agreeing. He thinks he can tie Fitz in with the missing goods."

"Anyone know of any conflict between Fitzgerald and those two?"

"Fitz must be a neat freak or something. He made two formal complaints about Grindstaff's crew not returning tools or equipment to the proper places."

"Does Lieutenant Darnell Dipstick know if Fitzgerald tried to resolve those situations informally before writing up Team Grindstaff?"

"I asked, but he didn't know. Grindstaff says no." Roxy smiled and popped a shrimp into her mouth.

I glanced at the table where Roxy's admirer sat and noticed he was again looking her over as if she was scheduled to go on an auction block.

I cleared my throat loudly. He shifted his eyes to me.

"Lose something? I asked.

He looked back at his egg foo yong.

"What was that about?" Roxy asked.

"Orville Wright there was wondering what you look like without your clothes on."

She smiled again. "We've just met, and you're already my hero."

———

Roxy and I were ushered into a small conference room at base operations by a uniformed female clerk. She closed the door, and we sat. Roxy pulled a yellow, lined pad from a zippered case and dropped it on the table.

"Where are you from, Roxy?"

"Originally, Arkansas."

"Sorry to hear that."

She chuckled. "It's not as bad as you think."

"They should put that on their license plates."

"Don't be mean. Little Rock was nice."

"Ever been to Toad Suck?"

She raised her eyebrows. "I see your point."

The door opened, and a thin man with thinning, sandy hair stepped into the room. The furrows on his forehead looked like something a plow left, and he seemed to have the weight of the world on his shoulders. Dark captain's rank slip-ons decorated the epaulettes of his pale-blue shirt.

"Hello, I'm Captain Christian Clarke, and I represent Sergeant Fitzgerald." He sounded almost out of breath.

He sat, and we introduced ourselves.

"If you don't mind me asking, Chief...why is a civil policeman investigating a crime on an air base?"

He sounded like someone bewildered by stress. If it wasn't an act, he'd have a peptic ulcer before he turned forty.

"I'm strictly helping a friend. The OSI detachment doesn't have the personnel available to send assistance right now, so Agent Wallace asked me to offer a second opinion."

"Pardon me again, but I believe you said you're from Prospect?"

"Correct."

"That's not exactly a high-crime area. Why would you be qualified to offer an opinion on a homicide?"

Maybe this non-attorney isn't a bad choice to represent Sergeant Fitz.

"I've only been in Prospect a few years. I retired from a large police department in New York."

"And you've investigated murders before?"

"I've investigated the suspicious deaths of more people than you've got on your Christmas card list, Captain."

"Well."

"Captain," Roxy said, "I think if you listen to what I have to say, you'll see why we're not totally convinced your client is the killer."

"Oh."

Roxy explained a lot, but not everything to Captain Clarke. When she finished, I asked a big question.

"Do you have a few minutes to sit down with us and the sergeant and listen to what we have to offer him?"

He answered too quickly. "Actually, I don't."

That one shocked me. I looked at Roxy. Her eyes had widened like saucers, and her mouth was slightly open, showing her surprise.

"Captain, I know you've got other duties," I said, "but this is a man's career and possibly a big chunk of his life hanging in the balance. We're not sure when a regular JAG officer will get here. The sheriff's detention facility is just ten minutes down the road. So, how about it?"

"I don't know. I'm not a lawyer, and maybe Fitzgerald shouldn't answer any questions."

"We want him to listen," Roxy said. "He doesn't have to answer anything."

"I don't know."

Clarke was beginning to annoy me.

"Captain, listen carefully, and I'll help you make the right decision," I said. "I'm here to assist Special Agent Wallace, and in doing so, I'm only interested in learning the truth. She gets paid once a month no matter what happens to Sergeant Fitzgerald and has no vested interest in convicting an innocent man. We both think he may not be the killer." I turned my palms up in frustration. "Surely you can spare an hour of your time."

He thought for a long moment. He wiggled his nose, frowned and relaxed his brow and did an annoying act of pushing his lips in and out. I looked at Roxy. She looked at me. We looked back at Clarke.

I really shouldn't talk to someone like him without first having a drink.

Finally, he answered. "Okay, can you arrange it for tomorrow morning? Shall we say 0800?"

"Works for us," I said.

On our way through the parking lot, Roxy said, "You're cutting into my beauty sleep. I usually start work at nine."

"You're beautiful enough. Meet me at Starbucks on Alcoa Highway about seven-thirty. I'll buy the coffee."

"Aren't you just the sweetest man?"

TEN MINUTES AFTER LEAVING CLARKE AT BASE OPERATIONS, WE SAT in Captain Hamilton's office at the PMO.

"Lieutenant Girty seems to have left base, Captain," Roxy said. "So I left word of my intentions on his voice mail. I need Sergeants Grindstaff and Bordwine in here tomorrow at noon."

"Shouldn't you wait for Girty to arrange that? It would follow proper chain of command."

"Sir, I don't have time to wait for Girty."

The Provost Marshal showed her a look of displeasure.

"Although the lieutenant isn't exactly trying to obstruct my investigation," she said, "he's made it perfectly clear that he doesn't agree with me and has no intention of helping unless I insist."

"I'd rather follow protocol. Is it necessary to conduct these interviews tomorrow? Grindstaff and Bordwine aren't going anywhere."

Roxy was doing fine on her own, but I thought being the bad cop to her respectful, good cop might speed things up.

"Captain, Agent Wallace is regular Air Force and detached from your SP company. She answers to her boss, who's getting impatient for a wrap-up. I think Girty is going to have to live with a little short circuiting here."

A look of annoyance once more marred Hamilton's baby face. "With respect, Chief, do you know how we do things in the military?"

"I'm quite familiar, yes."

"And how is that?"

Try this on for size, sport. "Before I retired from the Army reserves, I was on general staff at the New York State Division of Military and Naval Affairs as deputy chief of intelligence for special operations. I spent twenty-one years in the system."

He raised his eyebrows. "I see."

Roxy picked up the ball as Hamilton undoubtedly thought about how he'd like me off his air base.

"Sir, Bordwine is working days, so he's no problem. Grindstaff will have finished a four-to-one tour. He'll have to be here on his off-time. I'll authorize the overtime voucher."

Hamilton sulked for a moment about her overriding his preferences. "If it's necessary and you have the authority to grant the overtime, so be it."

"Thank you, sir. I'll make the phone calls."

A CORRECTIONS SERGEANT NAMED CHARLIE WHITTAKER LED Michael Fitzgerald into the private interview room at the Blount County pretrial detention facility.

Roxy Wallace sat between Captain Christian Clarke on her left and me on her right. Clarke was again in dress blues, and Roxy wore a pale-yellow suit. I looked snazzy in a navy-blue blazer and tan slacks.

Sergeant Fitzgerald wore a set of wrinkled cammies. He was in his mid-forties, stocky and had a recent crew cut. Even after a few days in the local slammer and a half-defeated look about him, Fitz appeared clean cut and not like the kind of guy responsible for repeated thefts from the maintenance wing supply system.

Of the three people there to see Sergeant Fitzgerald, Charlie Whittaker knew only me.

"Hey, Chief," he said, "you doin' aw rot today?"

"Whaddaya say, Charlie? Thanks for bringing Sergeant Fitzgerald. We won't keep him long."

"Yessir, take yer time. I'll be waitin' outside."

Whittaker left, and Fitzgerald stood across the table from us.

"Sit down, Sergeant," Roxy said. "In case you don't remember, I'm Special Agent Wallace from OSI. This is Chief Jenkins, my colleague. You know Captain Clarke."

Fitzgerald nodded and looked from Roxy to me with a face full of doubt.

"Sit down, Sarge," I said. "We're not here to hurt you. Your counsel is here. We just want to talk for a few minutes."

Fitzgerald's hands were cuffed in front. He sat and laid both hands on the table.

"This all okay with you, Captain?" he asked.

"It is," Clarke said. "If I think you shouldn't comment, I'll let you know."

Roxy started her interview with a smile. "Michael, are you doing all right in here?"

He shrugged and tried to act manly, but it seemed clear he wasn't doing very well.

"Would you mind listening to what Chief Jenkins has to say and perhaps answer a few questions?" Roxy asked. Fitzgerald didn't speak, but looked to Clarke for an answer. The captain nodded.

"Okay," Fitzgerald said.

"You understand that the security police placed you under apprehension and turned you over to OSI because you're being charged with a felony?" I used the military term for arrest.

"Yes."

"Agent Wallace and I aren't one hundred percent sure you're the killer."

That grabbed his attention. His eyes widened, and he looked intently at my face.

"Sir?"

"You're surprised?"

"Yes, sir. What's this all mean?" Fitzgerald spoke with a neutral accent, sounding unlike any specific area of the country.

"To me, it means I'm not happy with the amount of probable cause the uniformed cops had to lock you up. When I send a person to jail for a lifetime, I want to be sure he's guilty...not reasonably suspicious. Understand?"

"Yes, sir. I mean, no, sir."

"I'll explain if you answer a few simple questions. No answers and I'll be wasting my time."

"I didn't do this, sir."

"What were you doing in the hangar?"

He sat forward in his chair. The cuffs jingled. "I was scheduled to start work at 0700. I got in a little early—about 6:15. I'm always the first one there."

"Why were you stupid enough to pick up the bloody wrench?"

"Sir?"

"That's as simple as it gets, Sarge. Why did you pick up something a nitwit would recognize as a murder weapon?"

"Sir, I don't know. I've never seen a murdered person before."

"Costly mistake."

"Michael," Roxy said, "With Captain Clarke's permission, will you tell us again what you know so far?"

He looked at Clarke who nodded. I thought the captain was having fun acting like F. Lee Bailey. Fitzgerald recounted the basic story Roxy had already told me.

Hearing nothing new or even interesting, I sighed before speaking. "You formally complained about a guy named Grindstaff. I've looked at your file, Sarge. You're a team player, and I think there's more to that complaint than what the form says."

He looked quickly at Clarke and back to me.

"By reading between the lines," I said, "it sounds like you think Grindstaff is the one stealing the tires and equipment that have been written off as missing."

"I can't prove anything, sir."

"And I can't fix an airplane. Who asked you to prove anything? That's our job. What do you *think*?"

"I can't say, sir. I won't accuse someone without proof."

I felt a frustration headache building. "I'm sure you also believe in death before dishonor, but I'm offering you an opportunity to lead me to something new...something that might be a light at the end of your tunnel."

"It would be wrong to accuse Sergeant Grindstaff of something I'm just guessing about."

We spoke for another twenty minutes. I asked good questions, and Fitzgerald offered frustrating, childlike answers. It was too early, but I felt the need for a drink.

"You seem like a nice guy, Fitz," I said, "but you're no damn help. Talk to Captain Clarke. It may be a while before your real lawyer gets here. When you're ready to stop this Boy Scout crap, give Ms. Wallace a call."

Roxy and I walked out of the Justice Center to the parking lot near the detention facility. "What do you think?" she asked.

"Ever try to have a rational conversation with a tsunami?"

She laughed.

"I've seen ethical people, but this guy is unstoppable. Maybe he's from outer space."

"Same question," she said. "What do you think?"

"I think he's innocent of everything except naiveté, and I still want to strangle him."

"You're a tough man."

"Who would keep up an act like that?"

"That's why I brought in the big gun, sugar."

"If I knew the zip code for Mars, I'd send Fitzgerald a post card."

"So, what are we going to do?"

"Let's get a beer and sing a few choruses of 'Wild Blue Yonder'."

———

At quarter to twelve, the PMO desk sergeant buzzed Roxy's phone, announcing Staff Sergeant Bordwine's arrival. But we wanted to see Grindstaff first, so Roxy told the desk man to let Arlo cool his heels.

At 11:59, the desk sergeant told Roxy that Master Sergeant Grindstaff had arrived, and someone ushered him to an interview room.

"Let this guy sit for ten minutes," I said. "It looks like he wants to play the time game."

"You're bad."

"You ain't seen nuthin' yet, baby."

The only similarity between Alvin York Grindstaff and Michael Fitzgerald came with the sage-green camouflage fatigues and the chevrons on their sleeves. Fitz looked like a clean-cut gentleman. He was well-spoken and polite. Grindstaff looked like a street hoodlum more suited to be an infantry grunt than an aircraft technician. Alvin stood about five-nine and was stocky, but solidly built like a power lifter. He had a wide face, a mottled drinker's nose and only a little fuzz atop his head. What hair he had left was cut close to his scalp. Grindstaff didn't look happy about returning to the air base on his off time, but he looked suspiciously like the man I saw making that phone call as soon as Roxy and I walked into the maintenance hangar.

After the introductions by Roxy, Grindstaff broke the ice. "What do ya need me here for?"

"I have a few questions," I said.

"She called you 'Chief'." Grindstaff jabbed a finger at Roxy. "You a chief master sergeant? Chief warrant officer? What?"

"I'm police chief at Prospect PD. Special Agent Wallace is a friend. I'm helping out until more OSI agents get involved. You have a problem with that?"

"I gotta talk with you?"

"You don't *gotta* talk with either of us, but we thought you might want to."

"Why's that?"

"You said Fitzgerald might be responsible for the thefts at your workplace. We'd like to hear why. If he's guilty of murder, why not charge him with misappropriation of government property, too? You might help OSI put this guy away forever."

A nasty and vindictive smile crossed his not-so-handsome face. "Simple," he said. "Look at the facts. Each time Fitz finished working a four-to-one tour, things went missin'. You do the math."

"The time or date when things went missing has never been established. They haven't even been officially declared stolen...just missing from inventory. You tell Captain Brower your theory?"

"I got no proof. 'Sides, the captain's got his own ideas. Ain't my job ta ketch a thief. I jest make sure these C-135s keep flyin'."

"Fitzgerald wrote a complaint about you. Why not tell us the reason you suspected him?"

"I jest did."

"Being the last guy out of a building isn't much hard evidence. He could say the same about you. If you have anything else, let us know. Even something circumstantial would help."

"Look at what was stolen," he said. "High-end tools, aircraft parts for hydraulic systems, truck tars. Lord have mercy, even a couple o' aircraft tars. Ya steal stuff like that and ya need a ve-hickle ta transport 'em in. Fitz got him the biggest van I ever seen, a GMC longer than a stretch van with a big injun. He's the only one coulda hauled the stuff away."

After we let Grindstaff split, Roxy retrieved Staff Sergeant Arlo Bordwine.

I've seen nervous and jerky individuals in my time as a cop, but this guy immediately found a spot in my top ten. Bordwine took a seat and began picking imaginary bits of lint off his fatigue jacket, shifting in his seat and generally staying just this side of performing Saint Vitus' dance. He was a slight man whose fatigues looked like they were meant for a larger person. His short, brown hair needed a wash, and his pasty complexion could have used a few days in the sun.

"Something wrong, Sarge?" I asked.

"No, sir, its jest I gotta git back ta my job."

"Agent Wallace squared everything. You're here on official business. Your bosses know that."

"Yes, sir, but I don't like ta be away from my desk too long."

I didn't try to hide my annoyance. "That is just goddamn admirable, Sergeant. I hope they recommend you for an Air Force Commendation Medal."

He looked like I just suggested he was a pedophile.

"We'd like you to elaborate on your thoughts about why Fitzgerald is responsible for the thefts at the maintenance hangar." Roxy said.

Bordwine shrugged, and his demeanor changed. He looked smug. "Well, I s'pose it's obvious. The missin' items are traced back ta the time when Fitzgerald worked."

I hated to rain on his parade, but ... "Why Fitzgerald? Why not someone else in his crew? Why not someone who came in after they closed up shop at 1:00 a.m.?"

"Well, uh, I jest, uh ... Fitz was in charge. He'd be the one ta look at."

"How many larcenies have you investigated, Sergeant?"

"Do what?"

"Are you a police officer in civilian life?"

"Huh? Me?"

He shifted his fidgeting into fourth gear.

"Who traced the goods and thinks Fitzgerald engineered the thefts?" I asked.

"Uh, I guess it musta been Captain Brower."

"Not Lieutenant Girty?" Roxy asked.

"I think Captain Brower, ma'am."

"Brower is dead," I said. "He can't confirm these suspicions. Were you the inventory clerk who noted the loss in the books?"

Bordwine got flustered and looked like he wanted to take his bat and ball and go home. "Well, uh, yes, sir. I was."

"So why would Captain Brower think Sergeant Fitz was the thief? You accounted for the missing goods. Did you point out any evidence that Fitzgerald might be guilty?"

"Uh, no sir. Uh, I don't know, sir. I come here and all, tryin' ta he'p y'all. Maybe ya oughta be beatin' a confession outta Fitzgerald. Do it right, and he'll talk."

Not much of an answer—nitwit.

"We don't beat suspects, Sergeant," Roxy said.

I stepped close to Bordwine and looked down at him. "Maybe she doesn't, but I'm not above beating someone who I think lied to me."

His head flicked back and forth between me and Roxy and back to me. He settled on Roxy as the only possible ally.

"Kin I git back ta work now, ma'am?"

"If you have nothing to add, Sergeant, you may."

I didn't move when Arlo stood. He grabbed his fatigue cap from the table and almost tripped over the chair in which he had been sitting.

"'Cuse me, sir." Bordwine scurried out, and I looked at Roxy. "That's a lying sack of ... he's got something to do with this. Pencil pusher. Inventory clerk. Pfui."

Roxy laughed.

———

CAPTAIN CLARKE AND I WAITED IN THE SAME ROOM AT THE BLOUNT County jail where we had spoken to Michael Fitzgerald before. Roxy decided to handle a new and unrelated investigation of criminal mischief to an Air Force vehicle.

Clarke blinked when a corrections officer opened the door, and Fitz walked in. The stress of confinement showed even more on the sergeant's face.

"You look like you're having a tough time," I said.

"I'm doing okay, sir."

"Why don't you cut the crap, Mike? Jail isn't a place for a guy like you. What do you think it's going to be like living in the general population of a hardcore penitentiary?"

He stared at me, but had no answer.

"I hope you're not planning to take a shower for the rest of your life."

"Chief, is that necessary?" Clarke asked.

"Just something for him to think about, Captain. By the way, when is his regular JAG officer supposed to get here?"

"I'm afraid there's been a delay. OSI has made an arrest of an airman for a series of rapes on the post over there, and the man assigned to Michael's case will be delayed with hearings."

I looked at Fitzgerald. "Looks like the regular Air Force gets priority over you guardsmen."

"Should I hire an attorney, sir?" Then he looked over at Clarke. "Sorry, Captain. I mean a real civilian lawyer."

I didn't give Clarke a chance to speak. "If you don't start speaking up for yourself, Mike, you may have to. And if they're any good, they don't come cheap."

Fitzgerald slumped into the chair; his shoulders dropped three inches. "What do you want, sir?"

"Go back to my question of the other day. What do you know about Grindstaff and Bordwine?"

Fitzgerald shook his head. He looked as if I asked him to betray his savior. "I said I've got no proof of any theft, sir, but I think Grindstaff and his crew are unorganized and sloppy workers. Bordwine follows him around like a little puppy."

I shook my head. "I'm not looking for an efficiency evaluation, Fitz. Yesterday I thought you were a space cadet. Today I want to knock your head against the cement block wall—not to make you confess, but to get information that may help clear you."

He just sat there looking at me. His lawyer was no better.

"Let me give you a hint, Sarge. You didn't write those complaints because you thought Grindstaff and Bordwine were sloppy. You thought they were stealing tires and equipment, and you wanted Captain Brower to start taking inventory after Grindstaff's shift and before Bordwine could monkey with the records, right?" I almost spat out the last word.

"I told you, sir. I don't want to accuse those men unless I have proof."

"Goddamnit! How do you expect to get proof, Sherlock, while you're sitting behind bars?"

Finally, Captain Clarke decided to speak. "Perhaps, Sergeant, you can just relay your conjectures to the Chief."

Fitzgerald didn't speak immediately.

"This is your last chance, Fitz," I said. "Speak now, or I'm outta here. Major Purvis at the district OSI headquarters wants this wrapped up pronto. He thinks Ms. Wallace is wasting time with you. My boss is going to start wanting me back in Prospect where they pay me. So, knock off this disgustingly moral act, and give me something."

Fitzgerald took a deep breath and ran a hand over his reddish-brown crew cut. "It just seemed that each time we came in after Grindstaff's crew worked a night shift and started looking for things—tools, equipment, parts, all sorts of stuff—we couldn't find them, or we found them misplaced, I mean in really strange places. Then when we asked for a material control clerk to record missing items, Bordwine always showed up, and the missing goods were written off as expendables."

"So you think the misplaced items that could be found were a smoke screen to confuse the issue and make you think the stolen items were misplaced also?"

"Yes, sir."

"And if you reported items actually missing, the inventory was doctored up so a theft wasn't reported to the SP's?"

"Correct."

"But when an item was classified as missing rather than unaccounted for, the record showed it was lost after you saw it last?"

"Yes, sir."

I took a deep breath and expelled a large puff of air. "Thank you. That wasn't so hard, was it?"

"No, sir."

"Have you ever heard the expression, 'sounds like someone is trying to frame you'?"

"Yes, sir."

"Excuse my ignorance, but aren't aircraft parts hard to get rid of? You said even a couple of airplane tires went missing. I mean, you can't set up at the Highway 321 flea market trying to peddle that stuff."

"No, sir, but old C-135s are sold all the time to small independent cargo airlines. One thirty-fives are nothing more than hollowed out Boeing 707s. Legitimate parts are expensive. And everybody knows truck tires cost a lot. Black market aircraft parts bring big money even when sold at fifty cents on the dollar."

"So all you need is a list of not-so-honest cargo carriers who want cheap parts to keep their planes flying or truck shop owners looking for extra profits."

"Exactly, sir."

"Let's look at more of that missing equipment. How can you write off a stolen aircraft part?"

"This is what I think...little parts would be easy. Just blame sloppy recordkeeping. Big items are another story. Sometimes the part that's malfunctioning can be rebuilt to work properly. Same as with your car. But it's our policy to replace parts because it's quicker. Someone could check out a new part, steal it and doctor up the old part and reuse it. Then they say they installed the new part and provide the aircraft ID number for the record."

"And this rebuilding could be done on the late tours when an officer wasn't present to ask questions?"

"No, sir. Most of the late tours were covered by one of the lieutenants."

"Like Lieutenant Girty, but not Captain Brower?"

"Yes, sir. I never saw the Captain work nights."

"Interesting. How about the tires? If you steal a good tire, you can't leave a bad one on the vehicle and say it's new."

"No, sir, not exactly. Most of the base trucks never get high mileage. They really never go on trips, but stay in use. Policy is you don't replace a vehicle until it reaches a certain mileage. But for safety, the motor pool has to replace tires that have been in use too long."

"Makes sense. And I'm seeing the possibility for a scam."

"Sir, most of the replaced tires still looked good—had plenty of tread.

Someone from the motor pool repair shop could sign out a set of new tires, say they're destined for a certain vehicle and then put them aside and clean the old set, apply a coat of tire dressing, and they'd look like new."

"And no one questions a senior NCO who signs off on the work order."

"No, sir. We all have security clearances."

I shook my head. "No wonder this country is in trouble."

"Yes, sir."

I sighed, waited a long moment and shook my head again. "Quite educational. Why didn't you tell us all this before?"

"Because I couldn't—"

I cut him off in mid-sentence. "If you say, 'I couldn't prove it' one more time, I'll smack you."

Fitzgerald wrinkled his forehead and squinted at me.

"Well, maybe not," I said. "Your lawyer would only turn me in for police brutality."

That actually got a smile from the defendant and his legal counsel.

"Chief," Captain Clarke said, "if these two sergeants are guilty of systematic thefts, isn't it possible they may have killed Captain Brower if he caught them in the act?"

"Now you're thinking like a defense attorney, Captain. You're getting dangerously close to establishing a reasonable doubt that your client didn't kill anyone. But who said there are only two thieves? I've met other people who look like possible players, too."

Clarke looked even more interested.

"What happens next, sir?" Fitzgerald asked.

"First, tell me about Lieutenant Darnell Girty. Why does he have a grudge against you?"

"Didn't know he did, sir. I had no problems with Captain Brower or Lieutenant Girty."

I wondered why Girty was so keen to see Fitzgerald charged and convicted. "Someone told me you've got a van big enough to haul away airplane tires," I said. "They suspected you as not only a killer, but a thief. Why do you need an oversized van?"

"I never stole anything, sir. I swear."

"Okay, let's say I believe you. Why do you own a van big enough to hold two sticks of paratroopers?"

A smile crossed his face. "You're not far from wrong, sir. I belong to a

World War Two reenacting group. We portray a company from the 2nd Ranger Battalion. We need lots of equipment and weapons to set up our camp and displays. I'm the guy who hauls it to and from reenactments."

"Who else owns a vehicle large enough to get these tires and other stolen goods off base?"

"Beats me, sir."

———

"ROXY, BABY, I THINK WE'VE GOT THIEVES WHO GOT CAUGHT IN THE act and turned into killers. Well, one of them did. Here's what I think..."

I sat in the side chair next to Roxy's desk, put my feet up and told her what I had learned from Mike Fitzgerald.

"I can check base vehicle registrations for any privately owned truck big enough to hide and transport stolen tires," she said.

"Beauty and brains. What more could a man want? Find me a big POV, and I'll find you a killer. If you ever want to quit OSI, I'll hire you at Prospect PD."

"If I don't clear this case, I may need a new job."

———

WHILE ROXY WORKED ON CLERICAL MATTERS, I DROVE BACK TO Prospect to see if I had a functioning police department.

"Hey, darlin'," Bettye said, "you doin' all right today?" She didn't wait for an answer. "The mayor called down lookin' for you. I didn't say specifically what you're doin', but he said he hadn't seen much of you in two days and... well, you know the mayor."

"Yeah, I do. I'll go see His Highness and smooth him out."

"I thought you might."

Trudy Connor, Mayor Ronnie Shield's secretary, was in her mid-fifties and every bit a proper southern lady—except she smoked. I'd never caught her sneaking a butt out by the dumpster, but I had a pretty good nose and could smell nicotine on her clothes.

"Hi, Ms. Connor. Ronald McDonald in his office?"

She gave an abbreviated shiver of her head to express her disapproval of my irreverence. "Oh, Mr. Jenkins, you shouldn't call the mayor that."

"If you let me walk in unannounced and surprise him, I'll promise not to."

"You know I can't do that."

"Okay, maybe we'll work on a Plan B."

She smiled, buzzed the intercom and told the boss his errant police chief had requested an audience. "Yes, sir, I'll tell him," she said and then turned her attention to me. "Y'all can go in now."

I found the mayor sitting behind his desk, a mahogany specimen just slightly smaller than the flight deck of the USS Coral Sea, but shinier. After explaining my recent role as advisor to Air Force OSI, and all the details of the Captain Norwood Brower murder, he looked concerned.

"Is it legal for y'all ta enforce Air Force laws?"

"I'm not exactly enforcing the Uniform Code of Military Justice. I'm just helping an associated law enforcement agency. Look at it as my civic action project. I'm only doing something to help the community at large."

"Have you spoken to the base commander?"

"I spoke to the Provost Marshal. He's like the base police chief."

"And he says it doesn't violate any law?"

"I don't think he knows. He doesn't seem like much of a cop. But you can take this one to the bank. The Posse Comitatus Act of 1878 prohibits Federal troops from enforcing civil laws. It doesn't say anything about civilian cops not dealing with Federal law."

"You know all this?" He looked surprised.

"I'm a police chief. I know everything."

Ronnie shook his head. "Sam, could this backfire on us if ya don't find the real killer?"

"You mean like bad publicity?"

He nodded and looked even more concerned.

"Can't see how. And we're not one-hundred-percent sure Fitzgerald isn't the killer, but I'll find out. I just think the SPs jumped the gun locking him up."

"This is very complicated."

"That's why you pay me the big bucks, boss."

———

WHEN I RETURNED TO ROXY'S OFFICE AT THE PMO, I FOUND HER smiling.

"You have any luck with those vehicle registrations, or are you just glad to see me?"

"Both," she said.

"Lucky me."

"Lucky us. When I searched the base records, look who popped up as owning a heavy duty F-350."

She showed me a printout with vehicle and owner information. One line had been highlighted.

"And," she said, "I took a short walk and found the truck. It's a huge thing with dual, rear wheels, blackout windows and a tall camper cap over the bed—plenty of room to haul off all kinds of contraband."

"We spoke to this guy the other day."

"We did."

"And he's a guard employee, not regular Air Force?"

"Correct."

"Let's see if he was working around the time of the murder."

"I'm crushed. You think I wouldn't check that?"

"I'm sadly remiss."

"You are. And...are you ready for this? He worked a midnight tour during the time Brower would have been murdered."

"Hot dog! You've got us heading for an arrest at Mach one."

"I *am* in the Air Force, you know."

"I wonder if he'd talk if we pressured him."

"Don't have anything else on him except his work schedule and the size of his truck. He's not stupid."

I shrugged. "Even by military standards, not enough to search his vehicle for trace evidence."

"Even if we found something, he could argue that it came from legitimate personal use. I mean rubber and metal isn't like blood."

"True. He may not be the weak link in this conspiracy, but I know who is."

She smiled like I just told her where to get cheap Loubitin shoes. "Bordwine."

"You betcha. With the right push, you could crack him with a plastic spoon."

"Let's give it a try," Roxy said.

———

ARLO BORDWINE COULDN'T STOP FIDGETING AS HE SAT IN AN ARMLESS chair behind a small utility table in Roxy's interview room. Prior to his arrival, I loosened the screws holding the chair legs together to deprive him of a solid, comfortable seat. The more he wiggled, the more the chair wobbled and the less secure Arlo felt. I've been told it's unnerving. Interrogating him would be almost like shooting fish in a barrel.

Roxy leaned against the wall to my left; she'd be the good cop. I didn't want to waste time with a soft start, so I dropped a full complement of verbal bombs hoping to scare the shaky Bordwine half to death.

I slapped down an eight by ten, glossy close-up of Captain Brower and his bloody scalp in front of Arlo. "Remember him, Sarge?"

He recoiled from the photo.

"Well?"

"Yes, sir, that's Captain Brower."

"That's his dead body. See the amount of blood that comes from a head wound?"

He appeared squeamish, but stared at the photo again. "Yes, sir."

I pointed twice at the picture. "See there. Two gashes, one deeper than the other. I'm guessing the deepest one was the second blow. What do you think?"

"Don't know, sir."

"Had to be, Arlo. The first contact wasn't as efficient. The second one occurred when Brower was stunned. The killer had a moment to get a good grip and swing harder—more accurately. That shows determination and malice."

Bordwine remained silent.

"You know the various subdivisions to the murder sections in almost all the criminal laws of this country?"

"Me, sir? No, sir."

"Invariably, one of them is called *felony murder*. You get charged with that if, during the commission of a felony class crime, you cause the death of a non-participant in the crime. Ever hear of that?"

He became really agitated. "Uh, no, sir. Why are you tellin' me this?"

"You need to know, Sergeant. And there's more. Even if you didn't do the killing yourself, if you were just along for the ride and part of the crime, you're as guilty of murder as the guy who swung the wrench."

"You sayin' I murdered Captain Brower, sir?"

"Hypothetical *you*." I leaned closer. "But look at it personally."

Arlo let his emotions run away with him. He gasped, "Lord have mercy, that's not fair."

"Sort of takes you from being a simple thief into the unenviable position of a killer. In effect, a person innocent of murder could get life in jail, or...wait a minute." I looked over at Roxy and continued my act. "This is the military, isn't it?" She kept a straight face and nodded. "They have the death penalty. Do they still use a firing squad to execute murderers, Special Agent Wallace?"

Roxy shook her head. "Lethal injection."

Bordwine's eyes bugged out.

"Too bad. A firing squad has panache." I shrugged. "But, what the hell? Dead is dead."

Bordwine's shoulders were shaking. He acted like a man wearing a T-shirt in seventy-below-zero weather.

"Hell of a thing, isn't it Sarge?" I asked. "But that simple thief, the guy whose only intent was to steal a little government property, might be able to save his life by cooperating with the police. Sounds good, doesn't it, Arlo?"

"Don't know what ya mean, sir."

"You don't? I'm disappointed. I thought you were an intelligent man. Maybe not. Now, tell me, what do these three people have in common?"

I took three more photos from a folder. Roxy had copied several base ID card pictures and created mug shots from that file for me. I laid down Darnell Girty, Alvin Grindstaff and Bordwine's own picture.

He shivered even more, but mustered up the courage to speak. "Lieutenant Girty, he's the XO. Master Sergeant Grindstaff, he's a maintenance crew chief, and that's me, sir."

I hoped to hell I was right, because if my next trick failed, even this numbskull wouldn't be fooled by my final ace in the hole. I moved my face to within six inches of his ear.

"Do you think I'm stupid, Sergeant?"

"Sir?"

"You heard me, you little weasel. You're involved with the thefts, not Fitzgerald."

He stammered. "Uh...uh, no, sir."

I mocked him. "Uh, uh, yes, sir. Arlo, you had better start talking now, or I'm going to throw one more photo on the table. That will show you how much we know, and then let's make a deal time is over. Start thinking about that death penalty, sport."

I turned and spoke to Roxy. "This guy is pissing me off. Another minute with him, and I'm done. I need a drink, or I'll start hitting him."

Roxy, the good cop, took over. "Sergeant, everything the Chief said is true. We know who did this. We just need to know why Captain Brower had to be killed." She turned two palms up and shrugged. "I can't help you if you don't help me."

"I, uh, I want a lawyer, ma'am."

"Sure." She spoke in a soothing tone. "I'll put in a request for a lawyer. But JAG personnel are in short supply right now. Fitzgerald got an Admin captain from base ops. I guess there's someone out there who might be available to speak up for you."

"Uh, what about Lieutenant Girty?" Bordwine asked.

I broke in. "Girty is going to need his own attorney, moron."

Roxy rolled her eyes. "Unless you hire your own counsel, Sergeant, you don't get to pick who we appoint. But why let it go that far? Do you want to face charges of misappropriation of government property *and* murder?"

"What? You want to charge me with murder? I didn't kill nobody."

Roxy sat on the edge of the table, her knee only inches away from Bordwine. Her short skirt showed a little thigh, and he looked on the verge of a coronary.

"If you explain everything to us, and we're sure you didn't know that someone planned to kill Captain Brower, we can offer you a special deal. You probably didn't know anyone wanted to kill Brower, did you?"

That thought stopped him cold. He couldn't bring himself to deny it.

"We don't have to charge you with murder, Arlo." She spoke in a soft, sexy voice that was getting me excited. I could only guess how it made Bordwine feel. "But to get that big favor, I'd need a detailed statement telling the truth about your accomplices and the thefts. If you cooperate, I can let you plead guilty to misdemeanor larceny in satisfaction of all charges."

Bordwine labored to breathe. He had started blinking a mile a minute, and he couldn't keep from shivering. I took another shot at him. "Look, stupid, she's offering you the moon. You may lose your job, but a misdemeanor only carries a maximum of a year in jail—and you cretin, if you give us a statement, she can recommend Federal probation rather than hard time. How much more do you want?"

He pulled away from me and looked at Roxy. "I don't know what to do, ma'am."

I slammed the last photo on the desk. Roxy hadn't seen it coming, and she flinched. Arlo almost fell off the chair.

He looked at the picture. "Oh, Lord have mercy, you do know."

"Of course we know, Arlo." Roxy continued using her smooth, sexy voice. "We've known all along. Now why don't you save yourself all that grief, and tell the truth. Believe me, it will feel good to get it off your chest." She leaned closer and placed a hand over his forearm.

Bordwine hung his head for a long moment, tried to control a shiver and then looked into Roxy's eyes. "Yes, ma'am."

———

"I can't believe this," Captain Hamilton said. "I felt certain Fitzgerald was guilty."

"Sometimes, sir, what looks apparent isn't the truth," Roxy said.

"Lieutenant Girty and Sergeant Grindstaff being guilty of the thefts is bad enough, but this one," Hamilton tapped a copy of the report Roxy had given him, "as your killer? I'd never have guessed. He's a good man."

"Captain," I said, "I have no doubt we'll get statements from Grindstaff and Girty. We have them in custody now, and it's their only option. As you can see, Bordwine named three additional NCOs as being involved, and he told us where they sold the stolen goods. The locations are all off post and involve civilians receiving the stolen property. My friend from the FBI will handle those arrests. Special Agent Wallace is prepared to offer Girty and all the sergeants a slide on the felony murder if they plead guilty to the larcenies and if those who were present implicate Airman Tallant as the killer."

Hamilton winced when I mentioned one of his security policemen as the killer.

"Tallant was a good SP," he said. "I'm ashamed that he involved himself with these others and then killed Captain Brower. It's unbelievable."

"Bordwine said Tallant was on motor patrol that night," I explained. "When he took a meal break, he brought his truck to the hangar to pick up a new load of goods. Grindstaff helped with the loading, while Bordwine took down inventory numbers so he could fix the books. Girty supervised and made the anonymous phone call as they drove away and saw Fitzgerald approaching the hangar. Apparently Captain Brower decided to check up on things that night. When he caught that foursome in the act and told them to report to him in the morning for charges, Tallant grabbed the closest wrench and eliminated the possibility of facing a court martial."

"I placed him under apprehension earlier today," Roxy said. "He's being held for questioning. JAG has promised to send someone quickly this time."

"But why kill someone over that?" Hamilton asked.

"I did a quick background on Tallant," Roxy said, "and found that he scored high on the state police exam and was reachable off the current list. I guess he didn't want to lose his job. Brower's criminal charges would have crushed his future plans."

Hamilton tossed the pencil he had been nervously tapping against his left hand on the desktop. "Thank you, Agent Wallace. Please keep me in the loop."

It was after five o'clock. Bettye had closed up shop and turned the phones and dispatch duty over to the county 9-1-1 center. I had been in the middle of telling her all about my adventure at the air base when Mike Fitzgerald walked into the lobby of Prospect PD.

He needed a shave, still wore the same wrinkled camo fatigues he had lived in for several days, but compared to the last time we spoke, he looked greatly relieved. I made the introductions.

"Nice to meet you, Sergeant Fitzgerald," Bettye said. "I'll leave you gentlemen alone. It's time I went home."

"I'll call you later and finish our conversation," I said.

"Thanks," she said.

Bettye left, and I turned my attention to Fitzgerald. "Come inside,

Mike." I pointed to my office. "I can make a fresh pot of coffee if you'd like a cup."

"No, thank you, sir. My wife's waiting in the car. I just wanted to tell you how much I appreciate what you did for me."

"No sweat. All part of the job." Sometimes I'm so modest, I make myself sick.

He smiled and nodded.

"I'm just glad you didn't stick with that 'I can't accuse anyone without proof' thing."

"I know what you mean," he said.

I pointed to a chair, and he sat. I dropped into Bettye's swivel chair. "I don't think you do."

He wrinkled up his brow and looked confused.

"In this case, there was no evidence...no proof. We came up with those arrests out of our asses."

He still looked doubtful.

"Contrary to what you see on television, most felonies are not solved by forensic science. Most serious crimes are cleared by informants or by one participant ratting out another to save their butts." I shrugged. "Sometimes really bad guys are picked up for piddly little things like expired license plates, being drunk and disorderly or tossing litter from a car. Then a cop finds the proceeds of another crime or a weapon or who knows what? If you waited for proof, you'd still be enjoying prison chow."

"I guess I'd better stick to being an aircraft mechanic."

"Nothing wrong with that. I wouldn't know where to begin to fix a plane."

———

SEVERAL DAYS LATER, ROXY WALLACE AND I AGAIN WERE EATING lunch at the Ming Tree across Alcoa Highway from the air base. This time she wanted sesame chicken, and I ordered beef curry.

Roxy topped off my cup with a splash of hot tea. "Thanks again, Sam. You worked a little magic with Sergeant Bordwine."

"Maybe it was your short skirt?"

She smiled. "I don't think so."

"I guess you just needed someone to play the nasty thug."

"Well, you're my favorite tough guy."

"Nice of you to say so, but you dug up some good information on your own. The crucial clue, so to speak."

"I guess we make a good team."

"We do. Your detachment CO happy with the results?"

"I think so. Major Purvis called yesterday to say he obtained a time-in-grade waiver that will allow me to be promoted to senior master sergeant. The board meets at the end of the month. I owe my new stripe to you, sugar."

"Congratulations. I guess this means you don't need a job at Prospect PD?"

THE END

THE SWAN TATTOO

At 12:30, Kate and I waited inside the doorway of the Magic Panda, a new Chinese restaurant in Prospect. Every table was occupied, five people stood in front of the sushi bar, and more than a dozen hungry souls circled the two long buffet islands like buzzards over a dead cow, each holding a large white plate. One heavyweight cracked his head on the glass canopy when he reached to the opposite side of the steam table and grabbed the last egg roll before a young girl could take it.

"I told you to meet me here at 11:30," I said. "A new restaurant always creates a feeding frenzy. Look at these people...they're animals."

"I only finished my program at Prospect Pines a little after noon. I couldn't get here any earlier."

Four sumo-size customers sitting at a table looked like they'd finished eating, but continued to shoot the bull, caring nothing for the local police chief and his wife who needed a seat. I hate when people do that, and I envisioned more steam escaping from my ears than what circulated beneath the buffet trays. If my wife wasn't so good-looking, I'd have gotten mad at her.

Then a bloodcurdling scream from the kitchen grabbed everyone's attention. Being the only man of action in the building, I pulled out my badge and trotted toward the noise.

"Call 9-1-1," I said to Kate who followed me.

We pushed through the double-swinging doors and found a middle-aged man holding a bloody apron around his left hand. The color had drained from his face as quickly as his blood soaked the apron.

"Bettye, this is Kate," she said into her cell phone. "Sam needs a car and an ambulance at the Magic Panda, the new place in the strip mall across from the Foothills View Motel. A man's bleeding."

Several cooks, waitresses and a few unidentified men stood in the kitchen watching the injured man bouncing around and squealing in what I thought sounded like the Foochow or Hokkien dialect I once heard in Singapore, but no one helped him.

When I got near the victim, I noticed a foot-long kitchen knife and a little finger lying on a wooden cutting board in the middle of a stainless-steel table.

"Hold still," I said. "Let me see your hand."

I unwrapped a not very hygienic apron from around his hand and saw a short stub where the severed pinkie had once been.

"Someone hand me a clean towel or apron quick," I barked at the onlookers.

Blood drizzled out of the wound, and still no one moved. My Chinese is limited to getting around Hong Kong in a taxi, so I tried a little pigeon lingo, pointing at the bloody apron. "Che um che clean? Quick! Kuai, Kuai!"

The calmest man in the room, a thin, young guy with a ponytail and a brightly-colored sport shirt pulled a clean apron from a nearby shelf and handed it to me with as much emotion as a two-toed sloth. I rewrapped the hand, but in only moments, the oozing blood soaked the white cloth. Pressing the veins on the underside of the man's wrist helped, but not much.

"I can't stop the bleeding," I told Kate. "Tell Bettye I'll transport, but have her get clearance to Blount Memorial. Adult male, severed finger. You come with me."

As Kate and I pushed through the kitchen, I grabbed a plastic bag and stuck his bundled-up hand inside.

"I don't want blood all over my car," I said. "Sit in the back with him, and keep this elevated."

As we hustled through the dining room, most of the customers gave us their undivided attention, but a resolute segment of the starving masses kept gobbling their pepper steak or gnawing on their chicken sticks.

With Kate and my victim snuggling in the back seat, I fired up the Crown Vic, turned on the flashing grill lights and flipped a switch for the siren. Once I hit the blacktop and nailed the accelerator, I grabbed the microphone.

"Headquarters, this is Prospect-one. Have the man responding to the Magic Panda get names from everyone in the kitchen who witnessed this, then find someone at the restaurant who speaks good English and bring them to the ER in case we need an interpreter. Also, have medics wrap the severed finger in a clean cloth soaked in a saline solution and put it in a closed container. With luck, a surgeon can sew it back on."

"Ten-four, Prospect-one. Five-zero-one is ten-three-six now," Bettye said calmly—she never gets rattled. "He'll meet you at BMH as soon as possible."

"Ten-four, Headquarters," I said. "Five-oh-one, switch to channel two."

I flipped a toggle on my radio console and heard, "Five-oh-one on."

"Junior, pick up the big knife on the kitchen table, and preserve it for prints."

"Ya mean this ain't an accident?"

"Not certain yet. Be sure to get names for the three men in the kitchen wearing sports clothing. If they're still around."

"Ten-four," he said.

I looked in the rearview mirror at the Asian man who was still moaning, mumbling and gently rocking back and forth as Kate held his crudely-bandaged hand.

———

KATE AND I STOOD IN FRONT OF THE TRIAGE AREA ONLY A FEW FEET from the entrance to the emergency room.

"Sometimes this police work gets in the way," I said. "I'm starving."

"You're always hungry, sweetie, but how often do you get to save a life?"

"Do-gooder."

"We can eat when you're finished here."

"If I don't eat soon, I'll faint."

Kate smiled and was about to tell me to shut up when the Chinese woman that PO Junior Huskey brought to the hospital walked out of the ER. She looked pale and thin and wore her black hair pinned back with barrettes. I stepped over to meet her.

"I'm Sam Jenkins, police chief in Prospect."

"I am Agnes Lee. Someone from the restaurant called me at home. It was my husband Jerome who had the accident. We own the Magic Panda." She spoke with a slight accent and appeared concerned, but not too upset.

"How is he doing?"

She shrugged. "They say he lost much blood and gave him a transfusion. Nurses have taken him to surgery. The doctors think they can attach his finger. He may get feeling back, but maybe not."

"How did it happen?"

Her eyes flashed between Kate and me. She looked like I had just asked the $64,000 question, and she didn't know the answer.

"It was an accident."

I thought about that and wondered how a right-handed man using a kitchen knife could slip and cut off his left pinkie. Why not the thumb or index finger? They're closer.

"I'd like to speak to him about that," I said. "Will they keep him overnight?"

She frowned. "He will be ready to leave later this evening."

"Then I'll come back. I won't bother you much more, but can I have your husband's information for the report?"

"What report? It was an accident." She sounded surprised.

"All accidents get what we call a field report. It just accounts for our time."

She didn't look happy with my answer. "All right."

I found a scrap of paper in my jacket pocket and wrote down a pedigree on Jerome Lee. "If you're going to wait, can I call someone to stay with you?"

"Not necessary, thank you. I have a cell phone."

Kate toned down her usual dazzling smile to low wattage and said, "We hope Mr. Lee recovers quickly."

Agnes Lee mumbled something, turned and walked a few yards to the waiting area. Kate and I left the building.

"Notice anything odd back in the kitchen?" I asked.

"There were two mah-jongg sets on the shelf where they kept the clean aprons."

"That's odd?"

"Who plays mah-jongg in a commercial kitchen?"

"I'll bet when they close the restaurant, they break out the mah-jongg sets and play in the dining room all night. The Chinese are great gamblers."

"They always play mah-jongg for money," she said.

"They play everything for money. I meant, did you see anything odd— about the whole scene?"

"I'm not sure. Things happened pretty fast."

"There were no vegetables on the cutting board where he lost his finger. That long knife is used to cut carrots and things."

"Very observant, Inspector Charlie Chan." Kate spoke with a theatrical Chinese accent.

"Right, number one wife. Also, he would have to reach across hand to cut off pinkie when three other fingers and thumb were closer to blade." *Two can do Asian accents, doll-face.*

"'Number one wife?' Who's number two?"

"What about my theory on access to the pinkie," I growled.

She thought for a moment. "Sounds about right. I'd hold what I was cutting with my thumb, middle and index fingers. My pinkie would be too far away."

I reactivated Charlie Chan. "Exactly, grasshopper. I think we have oriental mystery."

"You're so clever...and sarcastic. How can anyone stand to work with you?"

"They look at working with me as the ultimate education."

"Oh, pa-leeze. Go live with number two wife."

I ignored her juvenile statement. "Did you look at the thin young guy wearing the loud Indonesian print shirt? The guy with the ponytail."

"Briefly."

"No one in the kitchen would move before he did. When he handed me the clean apron, his arm stretched out of the shirtsleeve, and I saw a swan tattoo. I've never seen one like it before."

"Everyone gets tattoos nowadays."

"But he looked like a gangster, and these Asian hoods are very into macho. They usually get dragons or tigers or snake tattoos. A swan seems a little tame."

"Why is that strange? Maybe the swan has some meaning to him."

"I think his presence was strange. The waitresses and kitchen help were dressed appropriately for their jobs. Jerome Lee, one of the owners, wore a white shirt and black slacks. Also appropriate for his role. Mr. Ponytail and the two other clowns didn't fit."

"Maybe they sell things to restaurants. Or maybe they just stopped in to see Mr. Lee."

"And Lee played with a big knife while he had company?"

"You've got a point."

"Maybe they sell protection to restaurants. Or maybe they make loans or who knows what."

"You think they're loan sharks?"

"If Jerome Lee is a big mah-jongg loser, maybe he needs extra cash to settle his debts. Maybe he makes bigger wagers on other things, sports betting perhaps. There's lots of money in that. Maybe he was late with his payments, and Ponytail wanted to express his displeasure. All possibilities."

"Who is Mr. Ponytail?"

"No idea yet, but I'll ask."

"Who?"

"The man with the severed finger for starters."

Kate snapped her seatbelt in place, and I switched on the ignition in the big Ford.

"Are we going back to the Magic Panda?" she asked.

"Hard to maintain my mystique as the Charlie Chan of Prospect, while I'm nibbling on dim sum dumplings. Let's go see Mr. Lum."

———

I FOUND A PARKING SPOT ON THE TOWN SQUARE, AND WE WALKED across the street to Wah Lum, which, prior to the opening of the Magic Panda, had been the only Chinese restaurant in beautiful downtown Prospect. When we entered, the owner, Mr. Lum, an elderly man who looks suspiciously like the actor James Hong, welcomed us by combining his accented English and the traditional East Tennessee greeting.

"Mr. Sam. Missy Kate. Good to see you. You doin' all right today?"

We responded with our own hellos, and Mr. Lum showed us to one of the dozen tables in the back room. He placed two bundles of silverware wrapped in spotless white napkins and two menus on the table.

"I bring you hot tea," he said. "Be right back."

In a few moments, our host came shuffling back carrying a covered teapot and two small cups.

"You know what you want to eat?" he asked.

"Not yet, Mr. Lum," I said. "Can you sit for a minute? I need to ask you something."

"Yes, yes. Not busy now. I can stay." He sat and looked at me intensely, perhaps waiting for me to tell him he won the lottery.

"We just saw the new Chinese restaurant in town. Very crowded. You think they'll take business from you?"

He made a face and shrugged. "Maybe at first. But they are buffet only. Buffet food is not so good as my food. You know. You eat here long time."

"You're right. Your food is good. Very authentic."

The old codger smiled. "You see?"

"What do you know about the owners of the Magic Panda?"

"Not Chinese."

"Excuse me? The Lees aren't Chinese?"

"Yes and no, Mr. Sam."

I was getting the inscrutable oriental treatment. I frowned.

"Yes, owners are Chinese," he elaborated, "but not from China."

"From where?"

"Malaysia."

"Ethnic Chinese who lived in Malaysia?"

"Yes. I think maybe from Sibu. Many Chinese people live in Sibu."

"Know anything else?"

"I think Sibu is bad place. Everyone say, 'Be careful in Sibu.'"

Old Lum left us to ponder his assessment of Sibu and sip our tea.

"Isn't your Chinese friend Margaret from Malaysia?" I asked.

"She is," Kate said. "And Sibu rings a bell. She and George used to own a restaurant—in Atlanta—and later in Maryville."

"I remember. I may want to talk with her about this."

"She may ask you to play mah-jongg."

I made a face. "Ugh. The things I do for king and country."

"But George will feed you."

105

"Good."

A few minutes later, Mr. Lum returned, not with new information on the Magic Panda or the Lees, but with an order of happy family for Kate and sa sha chicken for me.

———

A NURSE FROM BMH CALLED ME AT 8:00 P.M., STATING THAT JEROME Lee would be released within the hour.

"Want to take a ride back to the hospital, partner?" I asked Kate.

"Are you putting me on the payroll?"

"I'll take you back to the Magic Panda after they clean up the blood."

"Such a sport."

During the drive to the hospital in nearby Maryville, I asked, "Can Margaret give me a lesson on the current state of affairs in Sibu?"

"I would think so. She and George go back every other year. And she likes you."

"Smart girl. All the Chinese people from Sibu seem to have anglicized first names."

"They're Catholics, so they get a saint's name."

"They're all Catholics?"

"Back in 1900, Sir Charles Brooke, the last rajah of Sarawak gave a group of Chinese mainlanders a piece of real estate and guaranteed them religious freedom. China wasn't so liberal to those who converted to Catholicism."

"You knew that?"

"I Googled Sibu about an hour ago."

"You're a smart girl, too."

"Thank you."

"Now, let's see what Mr. Lee has to say for himself. Then I can run a few things by Margaret and George Wing and see if Lee speaks with straight tongue."

———

AT 9:15, A NURSE USHERED US INTO THE PRIVATE ROOM WHERE Jerome Lee had spent his post-operative time. We found him sitting in the visitor's chair with his hand wrapped up, looking like one end of a pugil-stick. His wife stood ten feet away staring out the window.

"Mr. Lee," I said, "I'm Sam Jenkins, police chief in Prospect. This is Detective Kate Wisniewski." I use Kate's maiden name when I exaggerate her job title.

Lee nodded, but didn't speak. His eyes were glassy, I assumed from medication, and he still hadn't regained a normal color. I noticed for the first time, his dark hair was liberally sprinkled with gray. His wife looked in our direction and scowled.

"Hello, Mrs. Lee," I said.

She also nodded, but didn't speak. I was the guy who kept Jerome from bleeding to death, and they made me feel as popular as a root canal. I focused on Mr. Lee.

"What happened in the kitchen?"

He answered with a heavy accent. "It was accident."

"What were you cutting?"

"Vegetable." He looked almost as shifty as Mr. Ponytail.

"There was nothing on the table except the knife and your finger."

Mrs. Lee answered, "Someone cleaned up."

I ignored her. "I arrived in the kitchen no more than thirty seconds after you screamed, Mr. Lee. Who cleaned things up so quickly?"

"Mr. Wu, my number one cook."

"Mr. Wu must be a very fast worker."

"He is good man."

"Who were the other people in the kitchen?"

"Kitchen help and two waitress."

"How about the young man with the ponytail and two men in sports clothes?"

Lee took a long moment to think. "Friends from Atlanta. They stop to see new business."

Mrs. Lee decided to stick in her two cents again. "My husband had accident. Why do you ask so many questions? He is in pain. Please leave him alone."

I ignored her again. "I can leave you for now, Mr. Lee, but we must talk again soon. Things are not clear in my mind." Then I asked a question that would allow him to save face and get closer to the truth. "Is it possible that one of the men from Atlanta *distracted* you and caused you to have the accident? Bumped into you, perhaps?"

Agnes interceded again. "Men from Atlanta did nothing. Please leave us alone."

I didn't believe her story and gave her the evil eye. "Okay. For now. But I need the names of those men from Atlanta. The ones who left quickly... before the policeman could speak with them."

She said, "Friend from Atlanta is Jimmy Fong. You ask Jimmy other men's names. His friends, too."

Then Kate took a turn. "I saw two mah-jongg sets in the kitchen."

Agnes frowned.

Jerome's eyes widened. "You know mah-jongg?"

"Do you play often in the restaurant?" Kate asked.

Agnes answered. "Mah-jongg is popular game with Chinese people."

"I know that," Kate said. "Do you play often? Do you play with the cooks and waitresses?"

"Yes," Jerome said. "Play with restaurant people."

I picked up the ball. "Do you invite other players? Do you play for money?"

Agnes sounded louder and agitated. "We play with all people. Why do you ask? It is nothing. Now, I say again. Please leave. My husband is very tired. Very hurting."

Her voice must have carried into the hall. A nurse stepped into the room. "Is anything wrong?" she asked.

"No," I said. "We were just leaving."

―――――

THE NEXT MORNING AFTER I SETTLED INTO MY OVERSTUFFED SWIVEL chair, I called Ralph Oliveri at the FBI field office in Knoxville.

"You know anything about a Chinese or Malaysian hood named Jimmy Fong from Atlanta?" I asked.

"I'm not familiar with all the players down there, but Atlanta has quite an Asian community with plenty of hoods. Actually, it's outside Atlanta in Duluth."

"Duluth is in Minnesota, Ralphie. Ask Bob Dylan."

"Georgia has one, too, smartass."

"Who can I call about this guy Fong? I think he's responsible for chopping off the little finger of a local restaurant owner."

"Sounds like something a gang member would do. There's an agent in Atlanta named Rosie Kwan who deals with the Asian gangs. The girl really knows her onions. She'll be able to tell you if this Jimmy Fong is one of their wise guys."

"Does Rosie make house calls?"

———

Special Agent Rosanne Kwan did in fact leave her office in Atlanta to assist local police departments. As she sat in one of the guest chairs in front of my desk next to Sergeant Bettye Lambert, both of them sipping from cups of Oolong tea, I noticed that Rosie looked more Amerasian than one hundred percent Chinese. Her hair was as black as a crow's feather and had it not been tied up in a French twist, I'd bet it would have cascaded half way down her back. She stood as tall as Bettye, about five six, looked pretty enough to do commercials for Cathay Pacific Airlines and was built like a bamboo outhouse. Ralph told me she was a lawyer, and after she spoke for a few minutes, I had no doubt she passed her bar exam on the first try.

"Does young Jimmy Fong deserve a spot in your book of Asian gangsters?" I asked.

Rosie smiled and set her cup on the edge of my desk. She reached into the open briefcase on the floor next to her chair, fished out a dossier on Fong and held it in my direction. Chivalrous bugger that I am, I stood and reached across the desk to take it.

"Jimmy Fong has been in the metro Atlanta area for almost three years," she said. "In that time, he's made quite a name for himself. He's ambitious, and it seems like he wants to fast track to the upper echelon of the local triad through brutality and wholesale ruthlessness. Jimmy may be a small man, but he's a genuine bad guy."

"I'm impressed." I said. "We have our own little triad here in beautiful downtown Prospect."

Rosie tucked a few loose strands of hair behind her right ear. "There may be some triad presence in any small town with an Asian business," she said. "The Lees are, as you suggested, Chinese from Malaysia—Sibu on

Sarawak." She picked up her tea cup again and sipped. "So, you may ask, 'How does a run-of-the-mill couple get involved with these thugs?'" She paused and sipped more tea.

I smiled. "I know you'll tell me."

And she did. "They didn't have the start-up capital or mainstream credit line to finance a big restaurant like the Magic Panda. So, they petitioned a Sibu gang leader to allow them into their circle of restaurants in the southeast US."

"And the Sibu hoods hand off the action to their representatives in Atlanta?"

Rosie sipped more tea and nodded.

"I love it," I said. "A gang from Malaysia controls business in East Tennessee."

Bettye shook her head. "Lord have mercy."

"It's the same with most ethnic restaurants," Rosie said. "You work through a cooperative group to get a franchise, so to speak. In this case, people who take their lineage from the old Ah Hing gang from Sibu control the co-op. Restaurants and other businesses are only part of their operation. Toss in drugs, prostitution, loan sharking, selling women into slavery, corruption of politicians and the police, even illegal logging."

"Busy people."

"The same as any modern diversified business," she said. "These Malaysian gangs are strictly economic. They don't stand on old world ceremony like the Hong Kong triads."

"A good mix of proven methods and modern technology."

Rosie nodded.

"But one technique never goes out of fashion," I said. "It's easy to get compliance through fear."

"Exactly. That flying swan tattoo you saw was a dead giveaway. The swan is the symbol of Sibu city. Jimmy Fong wants everyone to know where he's from and how bad he is."

"His campaign ribbon?"

"Yes, so to speak. The way the restaurant game works is after you're accepted into the co-op, you don't pay a dime of your start-up cost. The rest of the members pick up the freight. Then, when a new member wants to open a new business, you contribute a share of the cost to set them up. After you're open, and for the rest of your professional life, you use only approved suppliers for food stuffs, supplies and equipment, furniture, employees, waste disposal—you name it."

"Same as the goombahs back in New York."

Rosie smiled again and added a little old world accent to her next comment. "There is nothing new under sun."

"Was Fong shaking the Lees down for protection money?"

"Hard to say. Fong's boss, Martin Kee, is also a loan shark and gets a kick back from all the people with whom the Lees are supposed to do business. Maybe Jerome Lee strayed from his agreement or was late paying vig or principal. That would be a simple answer."

"What price can you put on your little finger?" Bettye asked.

"It's an effective teaching tool," I said.

"What might Mr. Lee expect next?" Bettye said.

"Difficult to say," Rosie said. "It depends on what precipitated Fong's action."

I ventured a guess. "If Lee rolls over to Fong's satisfaction, perhaps nothing. If he doesn't, our imagination is the limit."

"With Jimmy Fong involved, you'd need a vivid and evil imagination."

"I can hardly wait," Bettye said.

Rosie drank the last of her tea. "I've seen it all."

———

FOR THREE DAYS, I WORKED ON THE CASE, BUT WITHOUT A VICTIM willing to make a complaint, I got nowhere. Then, as I sat in Howell's Pub gobbling a barbeque pork sandwich the size of half a soccer ball, Bettye took a phone call on the 9-1-1 line. Moments later, she dispatched two cars to the home of Agnes and Jerome Lee, at their daughter's request. While POs Junior Huskey and Johnny Rutledge drove blue light and siren to the Lee's home, Bettye called me at the pub.

"Sammy darlin', I hate to interrupt your lunch, but you'll be needed at Mr. and Mrs. Lee's home. I've got Junior and Johnny headin' there."

I placed my sandwich back on the plate and wiped a spot of barbeque sauce from my thumb while I juggled the cell phone. "I'm afraid to ask why we're going to the Lee's place."

"The daughter came home and found him hangin' from the second floor railin'. She said he left a suicide note."

————

JEROME LEE WASN'T A LARGE MAN, SO HIS WEIGHT DIDN'T STRAIN THE lathe turned spindle in the railing that overlooked the spacious entryway of his two-and-a-half story home. His feet dangled less than a yard above the floor with a length of half-inch nylon rope tied to the base of the spindle and a simple noose looped around his neck. Again, he wore a white shirt and pair of black slacks. A pair of silk slippers lay on the polished floor beneath his bare feet. Lee already had turned blue, and his tongue protruded from the left side of his mouth. The unmistakable smell of a violent death tainted the air in the foyer. PO Johnny Rutledge stood ten feet away in the living room holding a clipboard.

"Hey, Johnny," I said, "What's this I hear about a suicide note?"

"We left it where it was, over yonder on the cocktail table."

He pointed to a four-foot-square, carved teak table that might have cost more than one of the shack-like homes from the slums of Hong Kong where the table may have originated. I read the note without touching it.

"Have you called crime scene and the ME?"

"Yessir, first thing."

"Bettye said the daughter called this in."

Rutledge stuck the back end of a ballpoint pen into his brown hair to scratch an itch. "Yep, I feel sorry fer her findin' her daddy like this. I mean, killin' himse'f and soilin' himse'f and all."

"Yeah, if daddy decided to end his troubles like this, he's a real prince. No one ever thinks about who they leave behind to find them. This image won't get erased from the girl's memory card. She saw it and it's there —permanently."

"You said *if* he killed himse'f?"

"We'll see. Where's Junior and the daughter?"

"In the kitchen. I think he made her a cuppa tea."

————

JUNIOR HUSKEY IS A FRACTION OVER SIX FEET TALL AND WEIGHS more than two-hundred pounds. He's a good-looking kid in his early thirties, but will forever look like a high school linebacker. Lucy Lee may have been a foot shorter and perhaps half his weight. She was twenty-eight years old, employed as a pediatric nurse at Children's Hospital in Knoxville and wore a print-on-white uniform top and pair of bright-blue scrub pants.

I offered Ms. Lee my condolences and asked all the necessary questions, which she answered without much emotion—until I came to this. "Why would your father want to commit suicide?"

She snapped at me. "He wouldn't!"

"What do you think happened?"

She hesitated. "I don't know. He was sort of traditional, but not the kind of man who'd kill himself because he lost face. He just wasn't that old school."

"What do you think he referred to in the note?"

"May I see it again?"

"The evidence technicians have to photograph it first. It simply said, 'I have shamed you. I am sorry.'"

"What does that mean?" she sounded a little miffed. "Who doesn't get embarrassed over something and suffer shame? If everyone in that boat killed themselves, there'd be no one left."

"You think someone killed your father?"

She shrugged. "You need to ask my mother."

"I will, but what do you think?"

"My father gambled and usually lost. That may have been his shame. But he borrowed money to pay his debts. He didn't make a big deal out of that. It seemed like using a credit card after the fact."

"Who did he borrow from?"

"I don't know, but even if he didn't pay the money back on time, why would a lender kill him? You can't collect money from a dead man."

"You're right. Generally, loan sharks don't kill clients. They break a leg or perhaps cut off a pinkie."

Lucy gave me a hard stare.

"Was Jimmy Fong more than a loan shark to your father?"

"I don't know Jimmy Fong."

"How about Martin Kee?"

"Don't know him either."

"Jimmy Fong is a very bad guy from Atlanta. Martin Kee is his boss, the man who would actually supply the money your father borrowed. Fong is his collector and hired thug."

"I'm sorry, I don't know those people."

I explained what I knew about the cooperative system of restaurants.

"You know more about the business than I do," she said.

"Did your father comply with whatever stipulations the triad people made? Did he use all their vendors, or did he try to save money by going outside the system?"

"Chief, I work four ten-hour shifts and usually some overtime every week at the hospital. I haven't gotten involved with the restaurant business. Please, ask my mother."

By the time I finished with Lucy Lee, crime scene investigators Jackie Shuman and David Sparks from the Blount County Sheriff's Office had arrived and begun processing the scene. Two minutes after I left the kitchen, Agnes Lee pulled up behind the deputy medical examiner, Doctor Morris Rappaport, and his assistant, Earl Ogle. Mrs. Lee pushed her way into the house.

"My God," she said. "Why haven't you taken him down?"

"I'm sorry you have to see this, Mrs. Lee, but the medical examiner has to do that. Your daughter is in the kitchen. Will you come in there with me?"

"You leave my husband hanging in the air, and you want me to go to my kitchen?" The faster she spoke, the more her accent thickened.

"I'm sorry, Mrs. Lee." I said. "But perhaps someone killed your husband. We have to treat this as a crime scene until we know for sure."

She threw her purse on a chair in the foyer. "That is stupid. Someone want to kill my husband, they shoot him—stab him. Who would hang him?"

I tend to have patience with grieving widows, but Agnes Lee's personality had worn very thin days ago. I took a breath and mustered up a little more bedside manner.

"We don't know yet. Please go, and see your daughter. She's upset and needs you."

I escorted Mrs. Lee into the kitchen and exchanged her for

Junior Huskey who I wanted to assist in carefully easing the deceased down to earth. Junior and Johnny Rutledge would do the heavy work, and Mo Rappaport and Earl would take over once Jerome Lee was lying on the floor.

"Jackie," I said to the senior crime scene investigator, "Grab a chair and your sharpest knife and cut Mr. Lee down."

After he placed a dining room chair next to the dangling corpse, Jackie Shuman took a sturdy switchblade knife out of his pocket, snapped it open and cut the rope six inches above Lee's neck. As the dead weight fell, the two cops grunted and eased the body to the floor.

"Gat-dag," Rutledge said. "I hate that smell."

"You got that right," Junior added.

"Thanks, guys," I said, while the ME began looking over the corpse.

"Were you a sailor, Sam?" the doctor asked.

"I was a soldier, Morris."

"Well, anyway, you may be interested in this knot. It looks sort of complicated."

I took a look. "Obviously you weren't a Navy doctor."

"I was on a cruise ship once. What do I know about knots?"

"I've been around boats all my life," I said. "Remember, I'm from Long Island? You either get stuck in traffic on the Expressway or you take a boat."

"Ah, a weekend sailor."

I ignored his observation. "The knot's called a bowline. It's not complicated, and it's a good knot. Ever hear, 'The rabbit comes out of the hole, around the tree and back in the hole?'"

"Rabbits, trees, holes. What are you talking, Samilah?"

"It's a way to remember how to tie a bowline. Most people wouldn't know."

"Interesting."

———

THAT AFTERNOON, AFTER I INTERVIEWED THE EMPLOYEES AT THE Magic Panda again, it rained like hell. For two hours, it appeared like Mother Nature opened a fire hose on the Smoky Mountains. In that short time, the runoff sought all the low spots. Crystal Creek looked like a raging stream of chocolate milk about to overflow its banks.

I ran from the parking lot to the back door, tapped in my four-digit code while drips from the building overhang landed on my neck. I cursed profusely and finally ducked inside.

When I got up front, I shook like a soaked dog, tossed my Prospect PD baseball cap on a coat tree hook behind Bettye's desk and stripped off my hooded rain jacket.

"You can land your hat on a hook just like he did in the James Bond movies, darlin'," Bettye said.

Taking advantage of the perfect opportunity to do my Sean Connery impersonation, I said, "And you're my favorite secretary, Mish Moneypenny. Let's have vodka martinis—shaken, not stirred—and make love in the evidence closet."

"In case you haven't noticed, Double-oh-Seven, your secretary wears a gun and no sex for you, mister."

"Gee, I should go back into the rain."

Bettye took off her reading glasses and tossed them onto the desktop. "Sit down, and tell me what you learned at the Chinese restaurant."

I grabbed a hanger from the hook on my office door and hung my soggy jacket. That done, I dropped into the chair next to Bettye's desk like a paratrooper hitting a drop zone.

"Waste of time," I said. "I talked myself blue in the face, and those workers wouldn't budge. They're all scared of Agnes Lee and petrified of Jimmy Fong and his hoods from Atlanta."

"Well, that's not good."

"Tell me about it. Expecting frightened workers to help me catch a killer is stupid. Time for Plan B."

"Oh, Lord have mercy. What do you mean 'killer'? And what is Plan B?"

I shifted in my chair, looked intently at the lovely Mrs. Lambert and crossed my legs—right over left.

"I no more believe Jerome Lee hung himself than pigs can fly. The only thing I can establish is that Lee was a gambler and a big loser. My best guess is that Martin Kee got tired of waiting for his vig or full payment and dispatched Jimmy Fong to make an example out of poor old Jerome—and scare the hell out of his other clients. Cheap advertising. Pay on time or die."

"That's a grisly thought."

"These guys are genuine thugs. And he can always collect from Agnes, or maybe her daughter will be next. It's what I'd do."

Bettye frowned. "Sometimes you scare me."

I smiled and shrugged, thinking that was a compliment.

"So, what's Plan B?" she asked. "I assume it's how you'll get evidence on Jimmy Fong."

"It's how I'll try. Contact every one of the cops. Tell them to forget about writing traffic tickets or routine patrol until further notice. If they're not handling a 9-1-1 call, hang out near the Magic Panda—especially at closing time. Stop every worker who comes out and hassle them. Get ID. Run everyone for warrants. Question them, and write a field interrogation card. Invade their privacy. If they find someone dirty, call me. I'll squeeze the truth out of somebody."

"Have you forgotten about that annoying little thing called the US Constitution?"

"A minor inconvenience. Maybe someone doesn't have a green card, and I can threaten to call INS or ICE or whatever the immigration agents are calling themselves this week."

"Are you going to bully a little, five-foot-tall waitress?"

"It's a lot easier than trying to intimidate a six-foot-four construction worker."

———

A DAY AND A HALF LATER, AT 10:30 P.M., I RECEIVED A CALL FROM Sergeant Stan Rose. After the Magic Panda closed, he stopped a young man named Leon Chow driving a twenty-year-old Toyota Corolla with only one taillight and an expired registration. A half hour later, I showed up at the PD.

Chow was short and thin. The black shirt and jeans he wore made him look even smaller. His grown out, almost black, crew cut looked like the bristles on an old shoe brush, and his long sideburns had ragged, uneven bottoms. I doubted that Leon had ever needed to shave.

"You're the greeter and cashier at the Magic Panda," I said.

He raised his eyes to look at me. "Yes."

"Before we secured Leon's unregistered car," Stanley said, "Will Sparks took a quick inventory and came up with this." He dangled a plastic bag holding dull green, dried plant matter. I doubted it was oregano.

"Yikes," I said. "Looks like the evil weed."

"Be my guess," Stan said. "And I'll give you odds it's more than an ounce. Using the right scale, we could get a felony out of this."

"I'll bet we could," I said. "Does Mr. Chow have a green card?"

"He does. And says he wants to become a citizen."

Leon Chow's eyes darted back and forth between Stan and me. He blinked rapidly at the mention of a felony.

"I guess that citizenship thing is going down the toilet," I said. "Uncle Sam doesn't make felons a citizen. He deports them."

"Deport?" Leon sounded shocked. "You can't deport me."

The slightest accent told me that English was his second language, but he spoke it well, much better than I can speak Chinese or Malay or Iban.

"Of course, I can't," I said. "I'm just a local cop. I'd have to call my friend at Homeland Security who investigates immigration problems. He does the deporting."

"I hear the weather in China is nice this time of year," Stan said and exaggerated a Cheshire-cat smile.

"Leon might be Chinese, "I said, "but I'll bet he came from Malaysia."

"I'll be damned," Stan said. "What's it like in Malaysia?"

"Probably hot and humid," I said. "And it would get even hotter if we sent him back home and made a guy like Jimmy Fong think our new friend, Leon, gave us information about the Sibu triad that works the area between Atlanta and Knoxville."

"I have told you nothing," Chow said.

"Says you. Why should I tell the truth if you won't do me a favor?"

"Favor?" He sounded confused.

"Favor," I repeated. "You do us a favor, and we may forget about the broken taillight and the unregistered vehicle. I'll bet your insurance is expired, too. That's a misdemeanor."

Leon spent some quality time checking out the condition of his cuticles.

"Then we have the felony-weight marijuana, which looks like enough to charge you with possession with intent to sell."

"I do not sell drugs!" Leon was getting excited.

"That's your story. For all I know, you work for Jimmy Fong selling marijuana."

"I work for Magic Panda, not Jimmy Fong."

"Why should I believe you?"

"It is truth."

"Then you shouldn't care what happens to Jimmy Fong."

"What do you mean?"

"Your boss Mr. Lee just died, and before that, Jimmy Fong cut off his finger. I think Fong may have killed him. I want to arrest Fong, and you can get me the information I need."

"How can I do that? I know nothing about Jimmy Fong and Mr. Lee."

"Too bad. If you did, you might not go to jail or be deported...and some day you might become a US citizen."

Leon began an intensive thought process, going through elaborate facial gyrations to make me believe he was dreadfully concerned. Then he made a superfluous statement obviously meant to enlighten Stanley and me. "Jimmy Fong is a bad man."

I looked at Stanley, who grinned. I looked at Leon Chow, who sat there trying to look serious. "You think?"

"You cannot let him know I talked to you."

"I personally guarantee it."

"You promise to protect me?"

"Cross my heart." I used my right index finger to emphasize the point.

"Mr. Lee gambles very much and needs to borrow money from Jimmy Fong's boss to pay debts."

I looked at Stanley and rolled my eyes. "Old news, Leon. Tell us something we don't know."

"I think maybe Jimmy Fong came to collect, and Mr. Lee had no money."

"Goddamn, Leon, but you're like my personal encyclopedia, aren't you?"

He wrinkled his brow to look confused, but I figured he was quicker on the uptake than he wanted us to believe—so did Stanley. "This guy is jerking us around, boss. Let's charge him and put him in the sheriff's jail overnight and arraign his ass in the morning." That comment seemed to create the desired effect. Leon sat upright and looked more alert. "I am telling you what I know. No bullshit—is all true."

"Perhaps true, Leon, but not complete. Tell us *all* you know. And do it now."

"I think maybe Jimmy Fong cut off Mr. Lee's finger to scare him into paying back money."

"Now why didn't I think of that?" I said sarcastically.

Stan the bad cop took another shot. "Maybe he'd get serious about telling the truth if I beat his head against the concrete wall in the cell block." Stanley is six-foot-four and built like a professional wrestler. Leon's eyes bugged out after hearing the sergeant's suggestion.

"Couldn't hurt," I said. "Well, bad choice of words, huh? But I'm not cleaning up any blood."

"I'll let Leon clean up his own mess...if he's still conscious."

Leon's head shifted between Stan and me so fast I thought it might break loose and spin three-hundred-and-sixty degrees.

"Please, I am telling you what I know. I worked at cash register when someone cut off Mr. Lee's finger. You saw me."

I knew that to be true since I had been standing less than six feet from him. But it was no time to let the pressure slacken. "Last chance, Leon. Five people from the restaurant were in the kitchen when Mr. Lee lost his finger. What do they say? They saw it happen. What did Jimmy Fong say?"

"Okay, okay. They say Jimmy Fong cut off finger. Mr. Lee owes fifty large to Martin Kee in Atlanta. Mr. Lee missed deadline to pay."

"Thank you. That wasn't hard, was it?"

Leon shook his head.

"Did Fong threaten to kill Mr. Lee if he didn't pay?"

"I do not know," Leon said. "No one said."

"Why kill a restaurant owner who owes you money?" Stan asked. I shrugged. "Dead men don't pay debts."

"Mr. Lee does not own restaurant," Leon said. "Mrs. Lee owns. Mrs. Lee is real boss."

Leon Chow hadn't told us anything we didn't already surmise except who owned the business, and he did confirm our suspicions, so we released him with a warning that if his information led us into a brick wall, we'd charge him with all possible offenses. The next morning, I called Rosie Kwan in Atlanta and asked her to pick up Jimmy Fong and hold him for questioning.

Rosie was enough to restore a cynical cop's faith in the FBI. She and her band of merry men scooped up young Fong less than a day after I called.

I never thought tough guy Jimmy Fong would break down under questioning and confess to hanging Jerome Lee, but I didn't envision my parade getting rained upon so soon.

Less than an hour after Fong landed in FBI custody, his lawyer showed up to officially state that his client invoked his right to remain silent. Fong's mouthpiece further stomped on my theory that Fong might be my killer by providing a rather nifty alibi, one supported by Fong's photograph appearing in a Duluth, Georgia weekly Asian newspaper. At the time Jerome Lee died, Fong had accompanied Martin Kee and two other members of the chopstick mafia to the opening of a new Chinese restaurant.

So, I went back to looking for revelations in my fortune cookies. "Leon Chow said Agnes Lee was the real owner of the Magic Panda," I told Bettye. "See if you can locate the county business license application. The certificate hanging on the restaurant wall just says owned and operated by East Asia Food Preparation, Inc."

"I can do that," she said.

"And while your fingers are flying over the computer keys, see what her financials say and if Jerome had a healthy life insurance policy on his head. Agnes needs fifty grand to pay hubby's debts."

"Is Agnes officially a suspect now?"

"Sure, why not."

———

Bettye's data search gave me exactly what I wanted to see. Agnes Lee, nee Yang, was named as principal owner of the restaurant, and Jerome had a $500 thousand policy issued with Agnes as beneficiary. But so did she; not an uncommon thing for business partners to do.

Then my hopes for a quick clearance were dashed when the writing agent told Bettye suicide would negate a death benefit payment. And I had learned that Agnes was in the restaurant when Jerome died.

I felt as if I was floating dead in the water. My most obvious suspects dropped to less than prime. The fingerprints Shuman and Sparks had collected still weren't back from the AFIS search, and time was marching on.

So, I called my wife.

"Okay, I'll do it," I said.

"What are you talking about?"

"If I must, I'll play mah-jongg. But I have to speak with Margaret and George Wing. Maybe they'll know something that will help me find Jerome Lee's killer."

"You're certain he was murdered?"

"No, but..."

"Fine. I'll arrange it. What's the worst that can happen? You'll learn nothing, but you get a home-cooked Chinese meal, and you'll play a few games of mah-jongg. When are you available?"

"I'll change my schedule to accommodate them."

"I'll call you back."

———

THAT NIGHT, I LEARNED MARGARET WAS EXCITED ABOUT HER favorite guest paying them a visit. I wondered if she liked me because I'm so charming or because I'm the only one who's ever gobbled up a dozen of her spring rolls and still had room to consume a large meal. Nonetheless, women who like to cook seem to love me. They may not know what I look like, but they remember the cannibal who went crazy over their food.

At 11:15 the next day, I prepared to leave the PD.

"Hey, Betts," I said, "I'm going to interview a couple and see if they can help with the Jerome Lee case."

"Okey dokey, sugar. I'll keep the home fires burnin'."

"These are nice people who'll feed me, but they may insist that I act sociable and play mah-jongg with them."

"Is Kate going with you?"

"She is. Kate has no problem with the mah-jongg angle, but I do. If I'm not back by two o'clock, call my cell phone and fake an emergency."

"I've never lied so much until I met you."

"You're a good woman."

"I know."

—————

AFTER MARGARET PLACED A PLATTER HOLDING NO LESS THAN thirty-six spring rolls on the table, George began carrying in the entrees—chicken with broccoli, sub gum chow mei fun, sticky rice wrapped in banana leaves, garlic shrimp with vegetables, pork dumplings, and home-style tofu, made extra spicy for Samo, the oriental gourmet.

Glad I ate a small breakfast, and foreseeing no need for a dinner after a lunch like this, I took full advantage of Margaret and George's hospitality. And I'm sure I perpetuated my reputation as the only round-eye who could eat more than everyone who attended last year's annual Sibu food festival.

"Do you guys know Agnes and Jerome Lee?" I asked while spooning two dumplings onto my plate.

"Yes," Margaret said. "They are friends of George's brother from Atlanta."

That surprised me. "The Lees lived in Atlanta? Did they own a restaurant there?"

"No," George said. "They work in big dim sum palace. Jerome was cook and Agnes hostess."

"So when they opened the Magic Panda, your brother told you his friends came to your town?"

"Yes," he said. "We go to meet them, wish good luck and also play mah-jongg."

"Where did you play?" Kate asked.

"At first, their home," Margaret said. "But when restaurant open, we play there."

"How often did you see them?" I asked, bit off half a spring roll, and using my chopsticks, added hot pepper sauce to the remainder.

"Only play mah-jongg three, maybe four time," Margaret said. "Jerome want to play for too much money."

"He is big time gambler," George said. "But not big winner."

"Mah-jongg is fun, right, Kate?" Margaret said. "But when bets too big, not fun anymore."

"I don't like to play for money," Kate said.

Margaret continued, and I ate the second half of that spring roll. "My sister-in-law lose three thousand in one night. She crazy."

"US dollars?" I almost choked on a spicy shrimp. Margaret nodded and opened a bundle of sticky rice.

"I think in Atlanta," George said, "Jerome lose more—plenty times."

"How many people played at the Magic Panda?"

"Maybe four, five tables, four people each game." Margaret said.

"Do you know men named Jimmy Fong or Martin Kee?" They both made faces. George blew out a long breath. "Everybody know," he said. "Bad men. They never play when we there. If they come, we would leave."

"Who were the players?"

"Agnes invite friends," he said. "And maybe three, four restaurant workers. And her nephew. He was always player."

George turned his attention on his plate and dug into a mound of rice noodles with his chopsticks.

"Who is the nephew?" I asked.

Margaret spoke with a mouthful of broccoli and pointed at me with her chopsticks for emphasis. "Gilbert Yang. Young man who work in restaurant. Nice boy, but also big gambler like Jerome."

"Were the bets very large? Did anyone lose three thousand in a night here?"

"No," Margaret said. "Restaurant workers not have much money. But Jerome and friends bet on other things?"

"Like what?" Kate asked.

"Anything. Everything," George said. "Jerome once bet me it would rain next day."

"Who won?" I asked.

"George." Margaret smiled. "He win ten dollar."

"So, you would say Jerome was addicted to gambling?"

"Yes, addicted," George said, nodding enthusiastically. "Bet on everything. Stupid things. One time, Gilbert was clearing food and plates from table, and Jerome point at bottle of soy sauce. He say to other man with him, 'I bet you Gilbert can drink whole bottle of soy'."

"Other man put hundred dollar bill on table," Margaret said and popped another floret of broccoli into her mouth.

"And Gilbert say, 'No, no, no,'" George added. "But Jerome, he say, 'You drink!' It was big bottle." He too jabbed his chopsticks in the air to emphasize his point.

"Did the kid drink the soy sauce?"

"Yes," George said. "But he get sick. Run into kitchen, throw up."

"Did Jerome always pick on Gilbert?"

"Yes, all the time. Jerome give Gilbert hard time," George said.

"Gilbert very angry after that," Margaret added. "He was shamed in front of girlfriend."

They were introducing a cast of thousands, and I was getting confused. "What girlfriend?"

"Gilbert want to marry waitress at Magic Panda," Margaret said, like that was common knowledge to everyone in the county but me.

"Jeez, I'm starting to lose track here." I downed an entire spring roll and waited for a new remark.

"Why does Jerome pick on Gilbert?" Kate asked.

Margaret, probably the better of the two at keeping track of all this intrigue,

answered. "Gilbert is Agnes nephew. Her father ask Agnes to sponsor Gilbert and give him a job in America. Jerome not happy about that."

"Why?"

"Because they not sponsor any of Jerome family. Only Agnes family."

I repeated myself. "Why?"

"Agnes father very rich man in Sibu. Agnes brother, Gilbert father, also rich. He own three, maybe four big fishing boat. They want Gilbert come to America and go to school."

"Did Agnes's father arrange for Martin Kee to help the Lees open a restaurant?"

"He ask big man in Sibu. Then big man *tell* Martin Kee. Is no other way," George said.

"What did Gilbert do in Malaysia?"

"He work on father's boats."

––––––

At 2:30, after only three mah-jongg games, I strolled back into the PD. Without even a moment to fondly remember the amount of excellent food I consumed, Bettye began questioning me.

"Enjoy your lunch, darlin'?"

"You can't believe. George Wing is a great cook. And Margaret's spring rolls are to die for."

"Sounds good. Eat much?"

"Don't remind me. I'll be surprised if my size thirty-two pants ever fit again."

"Well, before you loosen your britches and take a nap, call Dr. Mo. He's got some results for ya."

"I'm in gastric distress, and you put me to work."

"That's why you get the big bucks, Sammy."

———

"MORRIS, I HOPE THIS IS GOOD. YOU'RE INTERRUPTING MY DIGESTIVE process."

"Get yourself a Bromo-Seltzer, Samilah. I'm going to throw a monkey wrench at you."

"Just what I need."

"Your Mr. Jerome Lee died from a broken neck, but that wasn't his first injury on his day of demise."

"From mah-jongg to soy sauce to swan tattoos, this business hasn't been easy. Tell me more."

"I thought the knot business with the rabbit and the tree sounded strange, but you're not making any sense, boychek. By the way, my mother used to play mah-jongg. I was fifteen before I learned the game wasn't invented by a Jew."

"Oy, Morris, explain what happened to my victim."

"He was hit in the head. Rather forcefully, I'd say, but there was no blood. Something blunt and solid caused damage to the left temple—a rather sensitive spot. I wouldn't be surprised if the blow rendered him unconscious. If not, he certainly would have been quite woozy."

"Is 'woozy' a technical term, Doctor?"

"Nice talking with you, Samilah. Call me some day for another chat."

———

AT 3:30 WHEN STAN ROSE CAME TO WORK, I ASKED HIM TO DRAG IN Leon Chow for another round of questioning.

A half hour later, Stanley ushered Leon into the squad room where I was waiting. Leon almost smiled. I didn't.

"Cuff him to the desk," I said.

Leon looked more shocked than a cheerleader who didn't have a date for the prom.

"Why are you doing this?" he asked.

"You gave us worthless information. Now you're under arrest."

"You can't."

"Watch me."

"Please. I helped you."

"You told us nothing. I need more information. Good information."

"What can I say?"

"Tell me about Gilbert Yang."

Leon looked surprised at that question. "I work with him."

"I hear he gambles a lot, and Mr. Lee gave him a hard time."

"Mr. Lee did not like him."

"Why is Gilbert working in the restaurant and not going to college?"

Leon shook his head. "College? Gilbert never finished school."

Conflicting information. Not exactly what Margaret Wing heard. "Are you close friends with Gilbert?"

He shrugged. "We live in same house."

"I heard Gilbert worked on his father's fishing boats. How long?"

"Not sure. He did not talk about Malaysia."

I slammed my fist on the desk. Leon jumped. Stanley grinned. "Goddamnit. I don't want to hear, 'I don't know.' Tell me about Gilbert Yang, or you're going to jail. If he isn't going to college, why did he come to America? Certainly not to become a bus boy. His father is wealthy."

Leon hung his head and jiggled the pair of handcuffs attaching him to a three-inch steel ring fastened to a three-hundred-pound metal desk. "Gilbert's father *was* wealthy. Now owes too much money to triad. Gambles too much. Is big loser at cock fights."

"What does that have to do with Gilbert?"

"Gilbert worked on boats only sometime. Most time he work for triad—or used to. Ah Long gang, I think, or maybe Wah Kee."

"You said used to. I thought that was a lifelong job."

"Yes, but when Gilbert's father late paying debts, gang members visit—broke arm once."

"And Gilbert felt bad about that?"

"Yes. He want to quit triad, only leader say no."

"That doesn't sound good," Stan said.

"Was bad." Leon showed us a serious frown. "Mr. Yang had to sell one boat to pay debt and then ask leader to release Gilbert from gang."

"Just like that?"

"No. Gilbert's father pay big bribe—and promise Gilbert leave Malaysia."

"Exiled?"

"What?" Leon didn't seem to understand.

"Gilbert can never go home."

"Never."

"What if he does?"

Leon drew a finger across his throat and stuck out his tongue. I got the picture.

———

I waited until 2:00 p.m. the next day before going to the Magic Panda. The lunch crowd had thinned out to only a half dozen patrons.

A pretty young waitress whose name tag read Elizabeth asked me, "How many?"

"I want to see Gilbert Yang. I'm not eating."

She frowned and looked as if she wasn't sure what to do next. Then I saw a young man wearing a black shirt and pants set a stack of clean plates on the end of a buffet island.

"Excuse me." I left Elizabeth and walked toward the young man. Being a trained investigator with superior powers of deduction, I knew I found my subject. His name tag said, "Gilbert."

I put my hand on his shoulder. "I'm a police officer. I'd like you to come with me."

His face dropped. So did his shoulders, almost like a great weight had been removed. But he said and did nothing.

"Is Mrs. Lee in the kitchen?" He nodded. "Have the waitress tell Mrs. Lee you have to leave. Don't make trouble."

He shook his head. "No trouble."

When we reached the cash register, Elizabeth stood wide-eyed, with her mouth open. Gilbert rattled off a few sentences in Chinese and then nodded to me. "Okay to go now."

———

ONLY GILBERT AND I SAT IN THE SQUAD ROOM. ME ON THE CHAIR I had turned around, resting my forearms on the back, and he with his hands in his lap and his head hanging low. I let him feel the silence for a long moment.

He finally lifted his head and stared at me. "I knew you would come."

Gilbert was a handsome kid with broad shoulders, no more than five-five, but powerfully built. He looked like a gymnast.

"You have something to tell me?" I said.

He nodded slowly. "Is better this way. I am failure. I can offer Elizabeth nothing."

"She's the girl you want to marry?"

"Yes."

"Roll up your sleeves."

"What?"

I pointed to my shirtsleeves. "Roll them up. I want to see your arms." As Gilbert pushed up his right sleeve, he exposed a swan flying across a muscular forearm.

"You were a member of a Sibu triad?"

"Yes, since I was fifteen."

"But you quit?"

"Yes, but not easy."

"So I hear. You caused your family many problems." He hung his head. "And when you got here, your uncle Jerome caused you problems."

Gilbert nodded. "Yes, many. He did not like me."

"He embarrassed you in front of other people."

"Yes, and he do much more."

"Tell me."

He took a long moment and a few deep breaths before starting. "If I lose at mah-jongg and need money to pay, he lend me, but make me pay back much more. He take most of my salary for debt and food and room."

"So he made a profit from you and used it to pay his debts to Martin Kee?"

"He owes much money."

"What else did he do?"

"One time, he make me drink whole bottle of soy sauce in front of mah-jongg people. He bet man I could drink it all. I knew if I didn't, he would do something bad—maybe to Elizabeth. I drank, but got sick. Ran to kitchen and throw up."

"You lost face. I understand."

"Yes, but that was not worst thing."

"I'm listening."

"He know I love Elizabeth, and we want to marry. When he learn this, he start to pay attention to her—touch her—say things—more than he do to other girls. He was dirty man."

I let out a little air. "He disrespected you and molested your girl. That's not good."

"Yes, I hate him for it. Then I write to father and ask if he can send me money to get married. He say yes. I ask if he can help us get better job, in Atlanta maybe. He say he can try—pay somebody for job. Then I could leave Magic Panda. Elizabeth and I get new jobs, new life."

I shrugged. "Sounds like a good idea."

"Then one night after mah-jongg, before locking restaurant, Jerome say, 'You think you know Elizabeth enough to marry her?' I say, 'Yes, of course.' Then he say, 'I bet you one-hundred dollar she is not virgin.' I say 'no bet', and he laugh and say, 'Maybe I check her anyway.'"

"Jerome sounds like a cruel man."

Gilbert's eyes opened wide. "Yes, very cruel, very bad."

But not as bad as Jimmy Fong or your old triad associates.

"And you went to see him at his home?" I asked.

He nodded slowly. "Yes."

We were at a point where that pesky Constitution began to get in the way of my progress. "You don't have to tell me more," I said. "If you want, you can say nothing. Understand?" Not exactly a precise Miranda warning, but I think he got the point.

"I understand. But you already know, and I must end this."

Lucky me. "Tell me what happened."

"I leave restaurant and find Jerome home alone. I tell him he must stop shaming me. But he only laughs. I knock him down and tell him he must write apology for everyone to see that he is sorry for shaming me. He laugh again, but I bend his arm. You understand?"

He attempted to show me he meant a hammerlock. "I understand. Finish your story."

"When I hurt arm so bad, he agrees and writes paper for me. When I take note and start to leave, he laugh again and says, 'Before you marry that girl, I'll be the one who makes sure she is not a virgin,' Then he tells me to get out."

"And you got mad and...?"

"I hit him."

"With what?"

"I pick up brass Foo dog and hit his head."

"You knocked him out?"

"He did not move. I thought he was dead."

"And you wanted to make it look like Jerome took his own life?"

"Yes. I would leave note. Maybe my aunt would think he meant he shamed her by so much gambling. Jimmy Fong cut off finger, and everybody knows why. Jerome was also shamed."

"Where did you get the rope?"

"Garage."

"You carried him upstairs?"

"Yes."

"You're a strong man."

"Yes. Jerome was not big."

"But he wasn't dead yet."

"He wake up when I put rope around head."

"But you dropped him off the balcony anyway?"

"Yes."

"You learned to tie a bowline when you worked on your father's boat?"

"Bow-lin?"

Obviously, sailors from Sibu use a different name.

"The knot you tied to make the noose around Jerome's neck."

He nodded. "Ah, yes."

"My people checked the living room for evidence, and they found no traces of Jerome's hair or skin on the one Foo dog still here. They usually come in pairs. Do you have the other?"

"I took it. I have it still."

"Your room?"

"Yes."

"Your aunt would have known one Foo dog was missing."

"Yes, I think so."

"She knew you killed Jerome, and she protected you?"

"I think maybe."

"She didn't care?"

"She would not."

"Why?"

"She dislike Jerome. Too much gambling, drinking, no money. He shame her by touching waitresses. Agnes and Jerome was arranged marriage. She never love him."

"Interesting. You know I have to charge you with killing Jerome Lee."

"Yes, it does not matter."

"Will Agnes help you pay for a lawyer?"

"My grandfather will say she must. She has obligation."

"Good." I took a business card from my wallet and handed it to Gilbert Yang. "Call a Mr. Costello. He's expensive but very good."

———

KATE, BETTYE AND I SAT IN THE BACK ROOM OF WAH LUM. I FILLED them in on all the intricacies of the case while picking at a plateful of Hunan chicken with chopsticks.

"Different way of life, isn't it?" Bettye suggested.

"Not really," I said. "No one likes to get humiliated in front of other people, and when some slob messes with your best girl, a guy sees red."

"Gilbert Yang came from a violent background," Kate said.

"Yeah, but so did the Hatfields and McCoys," I said. "In the big scheme of things, what Gilbert did wasn't overly brutal, just very stupid. And stupidity knows no national boundaries nor is limited to a specific ethnicity. There are morons all over the world just waiting to violate the law. That's why the lovely Mrs. Lambert and I have a job."

"I guess when you look back into history, the same thing has happened over and over," Bettye said between bites of sweet and sour pork.

"Gave Shakespeare inspiration to write *Romeo and Juliet.*"

"Right," Kate added. "Everyone has a creepy uncle somewhere."

THE END

ALVIS IS IN THE BUILDING

LIKE MOST MUNICIPALITIES, PROSPECT, TENNESSEE NEEDED MONEY. If the council voted to raise taxes, they feared a general insurrection. So, the Prospect Police Department was asked to bring in revenue through fines.

That's how Sergeant Stan Rose and I found ourselves standing at a DUI checkpoint on McTeer's Station Pike one balmy evening in May. PO Jamey Hawkins sat in his vehicle, prepared to transport drunk drivers to headquarters or pursue anyone who failed to stop at Stan's request.

There hadn't been much traffic, but it was still early, and I hoped we'd get some action. Then Stanley drew my attention.

"What the hell is that?" Stan said, holding up his right hand, making a policeman's universal signal to stop. A six-cell flashlight dangled from his left hand, illuminating the blacktop in front of him.

I stepped next to Stanley as a candy-apple-red Cadillac with a sparkling, white convertible top rolled to a stop a few feet in front of us.

I answered his question. "Looks like a '59 Caddy with Louisiana plates."

"Those fins would make the Batmobile jealous, and there's enough chrome to blind me."

"Hell of a boat."

"Let's see who's driving."

Stan moved to the driver's side, I took the right and shone my flashlight into the car. Two black men sat in the front. The driver cranked down his window. The passenger looked at me and put his hands on the dashboard as if he'd been trained to do so. I spun my finger in the air, indicating I wanted his window down.

The driver, a large man with a shaved head and sport jacket almost matching the color of his car, spoke to Stanley. "Hello, my brother. How y'all this fine evenin'?"

Stan took a moment to reply. "Don't remember seeing you at the last family reunion, so I guess I'm not your brother."

"No offense, officer. I jus' meant ... Well, y'all know what I meant. What can I do for ya?"

"I'd like to see your driver's license, registration and proof of insurance."

"I do somethin' wrong, suh?"

"Not yet. This is a DUI checkpoint. Have you been drinking tonight?"

The driver fumbled opening his lap belt and pulled a wallet from his back pocket. "Drinkin'? No, suh, ain't touched a drop. Swear ta Jesus." He handed a driver's license to Stanley and turned to the man in the passenger seat. "Spider, git me that envelope from the glove box wit the regstaration and in-surance card."

I drew the Smith & Wesson from its holster and pointed my light at the glove compartment. "Do it slowly, Spider. I get jumpy at night."

Spider stopped cold, waited a moment and turned to look at me. "Yessuh. Movin' nice an' slow, suh. Donchew worry." Spider handed the driver a tattered white envelope. He in turn gave everything to Stanley.

Stan looked over the three documents. "Princeton LaShott?"

"Yes, suh. That's me. Princeton 'Cannonball' LaShott."

"You're a long way from New Iberia."

"Yes, suh. Been a long drive."

I bent down and scanned the interior with my light. Spotless, white leather seats matched the top. There wasn't a speck of dust or piece of trash to be seen.

"Nice wheels, Mr. LaShott," I said. "Own it long?"

"Thank ya, suh. Yes, suh, 'bout ten year now. She's a honey, ain't she?"

"She is. Spider, why don't you dig out some ID, so we can get acquainted?"

He wasn't wearing a seat belt, so fishing out his wallet looked easy. He handed me another Louisiana license. I matched the photo to Spider's face. He was as thin as a fishing pole and had café au lait skin, short hair with a part razor-cut into the side, and a pencil line mustache.

"Cordell Vinson," I said. "And you're also from New Iberia."

"Uh, yes, suh." He looked at my jeans and windbreaker. "Or should I call y'all dechecktive?"

"I'm not a detective, Mr. Vinson. I'm the police chief. You don't have to go beyond 'sir.' What are you gentlemen doing in Prospect?"

The driver turned and ducked down to make eye contact with me. "We's lookin' for Tommy Crowe's Smoky Mountain Billiard Club, suh."

"You're on the right road. Going there tonight?"

"No, suh. Lookin' ta stay the night at the Foothills View Mo-tel. Got us a reservation."

"Easy to find," I said. "About a half mile from here, on the right. You'll see the sign."

"Thank ya, suh."

"You're welcome. Now, give us a minute to check if you two gentlemen are wanted by any jurisdiction between here and Louisiana, and we'll wish you good night."

Spider nodded quickly, and Cannonball said, "Yes, suh. Take y'all's time."

I met Stanley in front of the Caddy and walked to his police car.

"Princeton 'Cannonball' LaShott and Cordell 'Spider' Vinson going to Prospect's own little pool hall. Son of a gun."

"You know these guys?" Stan asked.

"I know a couple of hustlers when I see them."

Neither man was wanted for anything in the US or by INTERPOL. We thanked them for their cooperation, and they continued down the road to find their motel rooms.

After they left, we spent an otherwise uneventful night looking for drunks.

———

THE NEXT DAY AT AROUND 11 A.M., I DROVE FROM THE MUNICIPAL building to Tommy Crowe's Billiard Club. I spent a few minutes in the parking lot looking at an all black, 1967 Pontiac GTO with Kentucky plates and a pimped-out Dodge pickup from Georgia. I jotted down the numbers before walking inside.

Tommy's pool hall was a private club where he could legally serve liquor and food as well as allow patrons to wager on their billiard games.

I moseyed up to the bar and received a cordial greeting from the owner. "Mornin', Chief. To what do I owe the pleasure of your visit?"

Tommy Crowe would never see sixty again, and he'd lived in so many places that I could hear no discernible regional accent. He'd been a professional pool player since he left a small Indiana police department a little too corrupt for his comfort. He was a trim, good-looking guy with a full head of white hair and a likable face.

"You've got some line of shit, Tommy. I'm just paying a friendly visit." I took a moment to look around the wide-open room. "You got a big match coming up?"

"Why do you ask?"

The question was an answer in itself.

"Last night I met two hustlers named Cannonball and Spider from Louisiana. It's before noon, and you've got a couple of slick vehicles from out of state in the lot. My po-leece training and acute powers of observation make me think the heavies are assembling."

He laughed silently. "Yeah, we've got a few people coming to run the balls. Not a big crowd, but a few good players."

"You promoting a tournament?"

"Hosting. Banjo Bobby Scott's got the book on this. He'd like me to play the winner."

"Why do I know that name?"

"Bobby's been around the circuit. He's a fair player, but not great. Won't make any money playing the pros. So, he took up matchmaking—holding the book, as we call it. You might remember him from that oldies station in Knoxville that went out of business. He's a disc jockey. Works for a country-and-western station now. Not sure which one."

"Will he be taking bets on this contest?"

"He'll make a few side bets, but nothing illegal. I won't allow that. He doesn't operate as a bookie, if that's what you're asking."

That was exactly what I meant. "Okay."

"When he organizes a match, the invited players agree to pay him twenty percent of what they win—which could be considerable. He collects a commission for services rendered. Any member can play and make legal bets because this is a private club."

"See that," I said. "Put an ex-cop in business and he'll make money and keep things legal."

Tommy smiled. "I try."

"I'll bet you do."

"Why don't you come around? Shoot a game or two. Like many of the members, you won't win a game, but you can say you played someone like the big man himself. Cannonball LaShott is like the black Minnesota Fats. These hustlers love to tell war stories about who they played."

"LaShott is that good?"

"He's the man to beat. I figure that's who I'll be playing before it's all over."

"You going to win?"

"Sure hope so. Or my checkbook will be a little thinner."

"Maybe I'll come and watch."

"You're always welcome. As the talent rolls in, they'll start playing the elimination rounds, so to speak. We'll get to see who's good. That's how they come up with the odds. Tonight, there'll be some serious pool played. Some of these wannabe players will ask for a game against a pro if they're feeling froggy. These guys will lose some serious money."

"Sounds complicated."

"Not really. Once the competition dwindles, the field narrows, and there's a winner I get to play."

"I wish you luck."

———

As I left the pool hall, an orange Datsun Z-240 pulled into the parking lot. That baby had more coats of wax than Joan Rivers had face-lifts. Sunlight made it shine like the gold tooth I saw when the driver smiled.

"Nice car," I said. "You don't see many of these. What year? '69, '70?"

"Nineteen and seventy-two." He spoke with a local accent. "I only drive it occasionally. Y'all like old cars."

"I've got a '67 Healey 3000 about as minty as this."

"Who-ee, I'll bet that's worth a perty penny."

Mr. Datsun looked to be in his late-forties, lean and medium height, with long sideburns that extended far below his narrow-brimmed fedora. "I know you from somewhere." I said. "Live around here?"

"I live up ta North Knoxville, and yessir, I believe ya do. Y'all questioned me 'bout a gun I done sold last year or thereabouts."

"Sure. Your name's Alvis. Help me out with the last."

"Seebold. Alvis Seebold."

"The diesel mechanic."

"Yessir, y'all got a good memory."

"Now you're a pool player?"

"Have been fer years. Yessir, I like shootin' guns and pool."

———

"STANLEY, THIS IS MY LAST NIGHT WORKING UNCOMPENSATED overtime. Tomorrow is Sunday, and there won't be a creature stirring. I'll trust you and the guys to keep Prospect safe for democracy."

"I've got a feeling we're gonna catch us a few drunken fools tonight."

"Hope so. It'll give the mayor a sense of accomplishment if we drum up customers for the magistrate."

As I finished my thought, a pair of headlights popped over the rise, less than a hundred yards down the road.

"Looks like a fish chasing the lure," Stan said.

I reached into the cab of his cruiser and flipped on the flashing roof lights. Stan signaled for the car to stop. He met the driver and asked for identification.

"Something wrong, Sergeant?"

"This is a DUI checkpoint, sir. Have you been drinking tonight?"

"No," the driver said, "just a little hospice work. I'm the rector at St. Paul's Episcopal. One of the parishioners is dying."

Stan quickly looked over the paperwork and turned his flashlight toward the driver. A white clerical collar sparkled like the North Star.

"Sorry to trouble you, Father." He returned the man's documents.

"Thank you, Sarge." The priest smiled and drove off.

"One of the biggest drunks I ever knew was the priest at St. Martha's back in New York," I said. "Father Fergus liked to sample the sacramental hooch."

"You better hope *He* isn't listening. He is and you're goin' straight to hell."

I laughed, and the radio squawked. "Dispatch to five-three-five and one other Prospect unit for a DOA in the county's area. Sixteen-fifty-five McTeer's Station Pike. Complainant Puryear says possible ten-five."

I grabbed the microphone. "This is Prospect-one. I'm with five-thirty-five. We'll respond with unit five-twelve."

"Ten-four...Prospect-one. Advise the status of your call."

"Yeah, ten-four." I slammed the mic back onto the dashboard.

"A possible homicide a hundred yards outside our jurisdiction, and there are no county cars available. Did the radio sound that busy to you?"

Stan shook his head. "Not to me." Jamey Hawkins got out of his car and walked over.

"Any call at that cathouse and the deputies run like rabbits," I said. "No one wants to find the local politicians in a compromising position."

"Look on the bright side, boss," Jamey said. "You get to see the foxy redhead who runs that whorehouse—and word is she's got the hots for you."

"I can hardly wait. Either of you believe Chastity Puryear wouldn't recognize a homicide if she saw one. Possible ten-five, my ass. She wants a few minutes to clear out some customers before we arrive."

———

STAN, JAMEY AND I PULLED UP IN FRONT OF A HOT PILLOW JOINT called the Frenchman's Holler Social Club. Only three cars sat in the parking lot. Six young women, some wearing trench coats and others with peignoirs wrapped around them, stood on the covered porch near the entrance of a large antebellum farmhouse. Three men and a woman stood near the red Cadillac Stanley and I saw the other night.

We walked slowly toward the car and stopped a few feet short of a large, black man slumped down below the tail fin of the old car.

Stan approached the body and laid two fingers over the carotid artery. He glanced back and shook his head. Cannonball LaShott's sports jacket hung open, allowing us to see the large splotch of blood that formed on his chest and spread down his pale, yellow shirt and onto his black trousers. I joined Stanley and looked at the two wounds.

"Looks like a knife," I said. "The one in his belly was probably the first. The other looks like it hit the heart or damn close. That one did him in." Both cops nodded.

"Robbery?' I asked.

Stan checked the body. "Still wearing an Omega watch, a heavy gold ring with a diamond big enough to choke a small dog, and his wallet is there."

The good-looking redhead Hawkins had mentioned walked up next to us. "Hello, Chassy," I said. "These officers will speak with the three men. You tell me what happened."

Stan and Jamey separated the men. I asked the six women to go inside and wait. Then I wrapped a hand gently around her upper arm and led Chastity Puryear toward a quiet spot. Her smile could have lit up one of the limestone caverns found throughout East Tennessee. "It's been a while, Sam."

Chastity had crossed the fifty-year line, but looked ten years younger. Long hair the color of polished rust hung below her shoulders. Her face could make Helen of Troy jealous, and any young woman would envy her figure.

"It has, and seems like we always meet under less than social circumstances."

"It doesn't have to be like that, ya know." She spoke with a soft Smoky Mountain accent.

I returned her smile. "I appreciate the offer, but let's clear this murder first. Then we'll see."

"You lie with the best of 'em, Sam Jenkins."

"Comes with my po-leece training."

She touched my upper arm. "What can I tell you, sugar?"

"For starters, the names of the other customers who didn't wait for us to get here."

"Other customers?"

"Don't."

She shrugged. "I didn't want a bunch of po-leece cars pullin' up with their lights and sirens goin b'fore a few gentlemen could leave ... unmolested, I guess you'd say."

"I understand, but need a list of names."

"Promise to be discreet?"

"No reason to ruin someone's life if he's not directly involved."

"Thank you, sir."

I nodded. "What happened?"

"I was inside when someone came back in sayin' the big man's been killed. That's all I know. Then things got sort of excitin'."

"Who found the body?"

"I called it in."

Vague, but I let it go. "Get the girls together, and ask them to have their IDs handy. When I finish with these three gentlemen, I'll find you."

"I'll get everythin' you need, darlin'." In the light from a front window, her green eyes twinkled. "But don't let me catch you *socializing* with one of these young girls and not me."

I laughed. "Never happen. I'm totally professional."

She gave me a sexy chuckle. "I know and can't understand why."

I joined the three men who stood between Stan Rose and Jamey Hawkins. Two looked familiar.

"Spider?" I said.

"Yes, suh, Cordell Vinson, suh."

I looked at a second, older black man. "What's your name?"

"Calvin Woodvine, suh. An' like I tol' these gennelmens, from Jackson, Mississippi." He was almost as big and almost as dark-skinned as Cannonball, with a deep voice that made Robert Goulet sound like a soprano.

"What brings you to this neighborhood, Mr. Woodvine?"

"Billiards, suh. I play professional billiards."

I turned to a thin white man. "And what are you doing here, Alvis?" Alvis Seebold's little fedora looked like something he bought at one of Frank Sinatra's yard sales. He used two fingers to push it back a few inches off his forehead.

"Well, sir, this is a mighty sad time fer our friend Mr. Cannonball here, but truth be told, Chief, I come ta enjoy a sociable drink and the company of a lady friend a'fore goin' back ta Knoxville fer the night."

I shook my head. "Got all the information you need from these men, Sergeant?" Stanley nodded and looked less than enthused with his results.

"May I assume no one provided you with any material information?"

"Nothing to help you identify the killer."

———

AN HOUR LATER, WE FINISHED INTERVIEWING THE SIX LADIES-OF-THE-evening employed by the Frenchman's Holler Social Club. A phone call to my wife, explaining why I was spending my evening with a beautiful madam and her good-looking hookers, wasn't as difficult to pull off as one might expect.

The list of patrons who bugged out prior to my arrival didn't surprise me: two county commissioners, a deputy chief from a nearby police department and two Japanese businessmen visiting an auto parts manufacturer. I expected three of those five to blush when I questioned them.

After cutting the six hookers and three pool sharks loose, Jamey Hawkins went off duty, and Stanley, Chastity and I sat in the living room.

"Can I get you gentlemen something to drink?" she asked. "I'll be pourin' myself a Southern Comfort on the rocks." Stan looked at me, waiting for a response. "Give the young man whatever he wants," I said. "He's had a tough night."

"Canadian Club and Coke, please," Stan said.

Chastity turned on the charm. "Certainly, Sergeant. Sounds like you've got a sweet tooth."

Stanley took advantage of the opening to do his act. "Yes, ma'am, us people o' color sho likes 'r sweets."

I doubted she knew how to interpret that, so I intervened. "Pay no attention to my Uncle Remus. Occasionally, he likes to mess with us white folks."

Stanley flashed his pearly whites at her and spoke in a normal voice. "I meant no offense. Just a little cop humor."

"You two certainly are different than most of the local officers I've met."

"We come from different worlds," I said. "Could I trouble you for whatever single-malt you've got? Just add a splash of water."

"'Course you can, darlin'." She went on to name five.

"A better selection than most gin mills," I said. "Royal Lochnagar, please. That's hard to find."

She provided another high wattage smile. "Be my pleasure."

Moments later, Chastity returned from behind an eight-foot, mahogany bar at the opposite end of the room with a tray and three drinks in crystal glasses. She handed me the scotch first.

"Thanks," I said. "If I've never said it before, you've got a beautiful place here. Some of this furniture is spectacular."

"Thank ya, Sam. Much of it is original to the house, and a few pieces even came generations ago with my ancestor Barton Puryear."

"That's interesting."

Chastity's eyes twinkled as she sipped her drink.

"Another interesting thing," I said. "I didn't see a bouncer here tonight. Where might he be?"

"Sam, sweetie, this is not a common gin mill, as you'd call it. I do not employ bouncers. I have security consultants."

I chuckled. "Who was tonight's consultant, and why did he leave?"

She fluttered her eyelashes and peeked at me over the rim of her glass. "I know y'all are an understandin' man, Sam, so I need ya to be a little ... understandin' here."

She proceeded to explain that bouncer Farley Gayton, a former college lineman who lost his scholarship because of a DUI arrest during football season, had an outstanding bench warrant hanging over his head in Hamilton County, stemming from a bar fight in Chattanooga.

"May I assume he found the body?"

"He did."

"Can you contact Farley?" I asked.

"I believe I could."

"Tell him I'm more interested in what he saw here than his beef with the court in Chattanooga."

"I could do that."

"I'd appreciate it. And by the way, this is excellent whisky."

––––––––––

TOMMY CROWE OPENED THE BILLIARD CLUB AT ELEVEN SUNDAY morning. I walked in thirty minutes later.

"Hear about what happened to your man Cannonball last night?" I asked.

"Yeah, it was all over the news at eleven. Damn shame. He was a good guy."

I nodded. "Anything happen here—a fight, argument, something that would connect to the murder?"

"No fights or arguments. Just a surprising loss to that sandbagger from Knoxville."

"What's the sandbagger's name?"

"You know him. Alvis Seebold, the dipshit."

"Sounds like Alvis is on your shit list?"

"Not because he beat Cannonball, but the way he did it."

"So, skinny Alvis beat the big favorite?"

"Remember I called him a sandbagger?"

"Yeah."

"When he started playing, Seebold looked like he knew what he was doing, but made mistakes, lost more games than he won and didn't seem like a threat to anyone. Then he asked Cannonball for a game."

"Was Alvis entitled to play him after doing poorly in the elimination rounds?"

"Tournament structure isn't that tight. Anyone can ask a big winner for a game, especially if they offer a bet."

"What was the wager that enticed Cannonball to play a no-threat guy like Alvis?"

"Everything Seebold had—seven thousand dollars."

"Anyone taking side bets at big odds?"

"Always. Guys won't pass up the possibility of an upset. But I don't know where the action was."

"I'm surprised someone didn't kill Alvis because of his sandbag act."

"Me, too. You should have seen him play against LaShott. The man had a golden stick."

"And today you play Alvis for the title? Or will you postpone the game?"

Tommy shook his head. "Can't. Today's the day."

"Gonna beat him?"

He shrugged. "I've beaten better players, but Alvis had his shit together last night."

"What's the action going to be?"

"Cannonball would have made it ten thousand. But now Alvis has fourteen grand in his pocket and may be feeling hot. If he's got the balls, he might bet the farm."

"Can you cover that?"

"Got no choice, do I?"

"Any other games before the big one?"

"Anyone can challenge Alvis. Some will, but after the way he played against Cannonball, I doubt any of the big guns will lay down much cash until they see how he can really play—consistently, without sandbagging."

I raised my eyebrows. "This puts you in an awkward position."

"Sort of."

"You'd rather play LaShott. Did you get pissed when he lost to an unknown?"

"What are you asking?"

"In a roundabout way, where were you last night?"

He pulled a face. "Here until after midnight. You really think I killed the man?"

"Probably not, but I like to ask pertinent questions."

"Thanks a lot." He tossed a white bar towel at a laundry basket and missed by a foot.

"Suppose Alvis beats you. What does that do to Banjo Bob's commission?"

"If a non-invited player wins, it's customary to toss the promoter a tip to stay in his good graces and look toward him inviting you somewhere else. But Alvis won't pay anything close to the twenty percent LaShott or I would."

"Tough break."

———

TOMMY'S GRILL MAN MADE ME A GREASY CHEESEBURGER THAT I washed down with a draught of Yuengling while I waited to see who showed up.

By 12:15, a half-dozen players arrived before Alvis Seebold swaggered in. No one paid him any attention, much less the respect due a man who unseated the king. I guess no one liked a sandbagger, but it didn't seem to trouble Alvis.

"Hey, gennelmens," he said. "Y'alls doin' aw right t'day?" Any eyes that turned toward Alvis quickly returned to the cue balls or other objects upon which they'd been focused prior to his arrival.

Alvis stood a few feet within the room looking the picture of an Appalachian gentleman. His tight Levis were pressed and crisp, and the modern cowboy shirt he wore—one with real mother-of-pearl snaps—had been fabricated from plaid cotton so brightly colored, I needed sunglasses to look at him. His Rat Pack fedora sat atop his head at a jaunty angle.

When Alvis spotted me sitting at the bar, he bent his knees, slapped his palms together and pointed at me with an index finger.

"Hey, Chief, you doin' aw right t'day? Come ta see some pro-fessional pool playin'?"

Tommy Crowe didn't allow me to comment before he tightened Alvis up. "Mr. Seebold, I'd appreciate it if you showed a little respect. Many of us lost a friend last night."

Alvis canned the smile. "My apologies, Tommy." He moved toward the bar. "I meant no disrespect. No, sir, surely did not. Mr. Cannonball was a fine pool player. His passin' is a tragic loss."

Tommy nodded and finished drying a twelve-ounce beer mug. Alvis laid his elbows on the bar and set his cowboy boot on the brass rail with a loud scrape.

"Afternoon, Alvis," I said. "How's it feel to be yesterday's big winner?"

He smiled, but not enough to show he'd gone back to his happy mood. "Jest fine, sir. Real fine. I was right lucky yesterday."

"And today you play Tommy?"

"Yessir, and that ain't gonna be easy. I'm commencin' to get my game plan in place as we speak." He wrinkled his nose like someone planning his strategy. "Hey, can I buy ya another beer?"

"No, thanks. I'm good."

"Well, y'all whistle when ya ready."

I smiled and took a sip of the amber lager. "You gonna bet the farm against Tommy?" Tommy stood a few yards away, but the question drew his attention.

"Ain't decided yet," Alvis said. "If I'm feelin' real good, mebbe. Or I might could tuck away a little cash fer another day. Know what I'm sayin'?"

I nodded and drained the Yuengling. Just then, the door opened, let in a blast of sunlight, and, as in a western movie, all eyes turned to see who stepped into the saloon.

A thin, middle-aged man, no more than five-six stood still letting his eyes adjust to the darker environment. He had narrow shoulders, a receding hairline that he covered by carefully combing his hair, which he wore over his ears, probably the same as he did in the 1970s. His powder-blue shirt looked a size too small, and his designer jeans might have been something Jordache sold him forty years ago. He walked to the bar and took a spot to my left, away from Alvis.

Tommy Crowe started walking over. "Whaddayasay, Bobby?"

The man nodded and maintained a solemn expression. "Tommy." He didn't acknowledge Alvis or me.

I waited a few seconds and cleared my throat to get Tommy Crowe's attention. He raised his eyebrows. "Oh, uh, Bobby, this is Sam Jenkins, police chief here in Prospect. He's investigating Cannonball LaShott's murder. Chief, Bobby Scott."

Scott stuck a right hand in my direction. "Good to meet you."

I shook his hand. "I understand you arranged for LaShott to play pool here."

He nodded as I spoke.

"Do you know if he had any problems with anyone, something where an argument could have escalated into murder?"

Scott stopped nodding and turned on a few carefully executed facial gestures I took to represent his version of method acting. He wrinkled his brow, narrowed his eyes and then did a funny thing with his mouth. "I didn't know him that well. Followed his career and reputation—he was one hell of a pool player. I wanted to organize a tournament and bring talent and money into the area. I figured others would follow if they heard Cannonball was coming."

His voice sounded bigger than what should come from his body. He enunciated carefully and exaggerated key words whenever possible. It all seemed a bit phony.

"So nothing you knew from prior association or anything you saw since he arrived in Prospect would lead you to believe someone had a beef with Cannonball?"

"Can't think of anything."

"After the final game last night, where did you go?"

"Straight home to Knoxville. I saw my chance for a big commission cut in half. I needed a drink and wanted to be alone."

"Thanks for your time."

I tossed more money than necessary onto the bar to cover my lunch tab, said a universal good-bye to anyone in close proximity and left the club.

In the parking lot, I stopped to look over Alvis's Z-240 and a pristine, banana-yellow Triumph TR-6 parked in a shady spot with the top down. The black upholstery looked showroom new and smelled like fine English leather. A Nardi wood-rimmed steering wheel and shift knob added class to the cockpit, and Michelin redline tires put a little icing on the cake. *These pool sharks like their retro automobiles.* I jotted down the plate number to see who owned the snazzy wheels.

———

It only took three minutes to drive from the pool hall to the Foothills View Motel and park my car near the office. The weather had been perfect. The pine pollen disappeared a week earlier. A Canadian front dipped into the south, bringing cool temperatures and clear skies. The air smelled clean.

I picked up a key for Princeton LaShott's room and learned where to find Spider Vinson and Calvin Woodvine. All three stops took me to the second floor wing that paralleled the road.

Crime scene investigators searched Cannonball's room on the night of his murder, but I've got this thing about snooping. I've always thought a detective can't connect with his victim if he never feels their presence, sees how they lived, what made them tick or just rummages through their belongings.

I found a small collection of clothing and an expensive two-piece pool cue in a travel case covered with alligator leather, but couldn't locate anything that resembled a clue. I found nothing hidden in the toilet tank, between the mattress and box spring, behind the furniture or taped to the backs or bottoms of the dresser drawers. Cannonball seemed like a straightforward guy who wore expensive underwear and bought fifty-dollar shirts.

After looking under the bed, I stood up as someone knocked gingerly on the door. I opened it to find Calvin standing behind Spider.

"Gentlemen," I said. "You looking for me?"

Spider Vinson answered. "Yes, suh, I need ta ax ya somethin'."

"Sure."

"Beins that I was Cannonball's good friend, suh, I was wonderin' if I ... If y'all could give me his pool cue? He once said if anythin' happened ta him, he'd like me ta have it."

I raised my eyebrows. "I'm sorry, Mr. Vinson, but I can't do that. I'm conducting a homicide investigation, and when it's completed, I'll release Cannonball's belongings to his next of kin." His face dropped—more than if I told him James Brown couldn't sing.

"Look, Spider, It's not that I don't believe you, but his estate has to distribute the property, not me."

Spider nodded, but looked disappointed. "Yes, suh, I unnerstand. Jus' wish I could have that pool cue."

"I'll bet Mrs. LaShott will give it to you."

"Mebbe she will." He was about to leave when he turned back and asked, "Then I s'ppose I ain't gonna drive his Caddy back ta Loosiana?"

"I'm afraid not."

"Aw, man, how's I gonna git home ta New Iberia?"

"The airport's a few miles away, and there's a bus station in Knoxville."

Calvin Woodvine saved him from making a decision. "I'll take ya far as Jackson, Spider. Then y'all can catch a bus rest o' the way. Won't be a long ride."

"Thank ya, man." Spider turned to leave.

"You gentlemen playing more pool before you leave Prospect?" I asked.

"Not me," Calvin said. "Ain't in the mood. B'sides, I cain't stand playing with no sandbaggin' son-of-a-bitch."

"I guess Alvis is no one's favorite today."

"No, suh, he ain't," Calvin said.

"How about you, Spider? You going to try and get even?"

He shrugged. "Mebbe. I kinda wanted ta play that ol' boy usin' Cannonball's cue."

"Can't help with that," I said. "But if you play, good luck."

Spider nodded. "Thank ya, suh."

"Oh, one more thing," I said. "Mr. Woodvine, what car do you drive?"

He looked surprised. "That black DeVille down below." He jerked a thumb toward the parking area. "One wit the Mi'sippi tags."

"Thanks," I said.

They left; I picked up a few things and locked Cannonball's room.

———

I GASSED MY CAR AT THE CITY PUMPS AND OPENED THE PD, WHICH IS normally closed on Sundays. Walking through the parking lot, I juggled Princeton LaShott's suitcase, pool cue and a half-empty bottle of Wild Turkey. Once inside, I locked everything in the evidence closet.

Like LaShott's motel room, his '59 Caddy had been thoroughly searched, vacuumed and visually scoured by two top-notch evidence technicians, but I wanted to look again. I probably wouldn't find anything of substantive value, but I love old cars.

With the keys, I walked across the blacktop to the city garage where, in a pinch, one of the bays doubled as our impound lot.

As I raised the overhead door, sunlight bounced off the metallic-red paint. I couldn't find a scratch on the body, and the white vinyl top appeared spotless. After circumnavigating the car, I couldn't help thinking the Widow LaShott could auction that boat for a small fortune.

I opened the door and slid into the driver's seat. The leather smelled good, as only the interior of a vintage car can. Everything looked orderly. Even the glove box lacked the clutter and junk present in most vehicles.

I spent thirty minutes searching under the hood, in the trunk and anywhere a clue could be hiding. I had a great time fondling the Caddy, but found nothing of investigative value.

Back in my office, I took Cannonball's gator-hide case from the evidence locker, thinking I may as well check out his one-of-a-kind pool stick and see if I could tell the difference between it and any other cue.

But I never got to admire the woodwork. Instead, I got hung up on the carrying case. I'm not a fan of alligators, but the mellow shine on the textured, honey-colored leather and the superior workmanship made me think it must have cost more than a full set of American Tourister's finest.

As I gave the case a thorough look, I noticed something didn't jibe. The lower half—the part where the cue halves rested—looked too shallow. I've seen plenty of briefcases with false bottoms. Some are well-constructed, and others are amateur attempts to fool someone. This could have been the finest piece of work I'd ever examined. By tapping the floor of the case, I heard a muffled hollow sound. I looked carefully, but couldn't find a way to lift the bottom. No buttons on the inner or outer sides. No tabs to lift, nothing apparent—a real Chinese puzzle. As I ran my fingers over the green felt lining, I found two indentations in the lower corners. When I pressed down, something clicked, and the case floor moved slightly upward, as if I'd triggered a spring-loaded device.

I hate trick boxes, trap doors, secret panels or anything that could be booby-trapped. No one wants a secret compartment that an interloper can breach. If the owner has either a sense of humor or a mean streak, they may want he-who-violates-his-hidey-hole to never forget the experience. Was there a failsafe button that only Cannonball knew about? Or was it straightforward? I doubted that he rigged his case with an explosive or poison darts. Maybe my knowledge of James Bond clouded my reason. Perhaps a rubber snake might jump out, or a canister would release a puff of smoke; and in life, Cannonball would have laughed his ass off.

I said, "What the hell," stood aside and lifted the inner bottom.

Taking only a second to realize nothing sinister would happen, I saw why the hollow sound was muffled. Foam lining covered the top and bottom of the compartment, except for three five-by-seven-inch recesses. Manila envelopes occupied two of the three spots.

————

THE FIRST ENVELOPE PROVED TO BE A MINOR DISAPPOINTMENT. TEN crisp pieces of green paper showing Ben Franklin's headshot. A grand of sequentially numbered bills isn't something you see every day, but I wasn't looking at a sack of rare, twenty-dollar gold pieces either. A simple phone call would tell me where these bills originated and if they had any history.

The second envelope looked more interesting and opened a few possibilities for an astute homicide investigator to explore. Cannonball had hidden away twenty professionally taken, mildly pornographic photos of an attractive, black woman who appeared to be in her mid-thirties.

I wondered if Mrs. Cannonball had visited her neighborhood boudoir photographer and presented these to hubby before his trip. Did Cannonball have a mistress who worked as a risqué model, or was she someone else's wife? Did an irate husband find out about the pictures and follow him to Prospect? There were more possibilities, but I stopped wasting time. I went looking for an informant to provide the skinny on Cannonball's sexy friend.

I drove back to the motel looking for Spider Vinson, but had no luck. At Tommy Crowe's club, I hit pay dirt. Spider was shucking and jiving his way through a game of 8-ball with a lanky, young guy from Maynardville. I sat at the bar noticing Spider's lack of sorrow over the demise of his comrade. When Spider finished trouncing the kid and collected a fistful of cash, he stepped up to the bar and asked for a double shot of Wild Turkey.

"Having a good day, Spider?"

"Yes, suh, I damn near ran that table three times."

"Good for you." Tommy dropped off Spider's bourbon and asked if I wanted anything. I waved him off. "Spider, I need your help." He gave me a glance and frowned. "Yes, suh, wit what?"

"I'm going to show you a photo. You ID the woman."

Spider slurped down a ration of bourbon and nodded. I chose a conservative shot that provided a good look at her face, but showed a lot more than the average mug shot. I laid a folder on the bar. "Do this discreetly, partner. The picture is on the personal side."

Spider frowned as he opened the cover.

"Who is she?"

His eyes widened. "Cannonball's girlfriend."

"He pay for her affection?"

"Don't know. Too late to ax him."

I wasn't satisfied with the answer. "Is she a pro or a real girlfriend?"

"You mean, do she do tricks?"

"Yes. Have you ever paid her for sex?"

"Mebbe once or twice."

"Can I assume she is not Mrs. LaShott."

"Naw, her name Jolie Dupree, a dancer from Lafayette."

"Dancer and hooker?"

"Not so much a hooker. Sometimes, if she like you and she need cash. Ya unnerstand what I'm sayin'?"

"Pretty clean and healthy-looking for a hooker."

"Jolie ain't got ta do many tricks. She make plenty dancin'. And she do lots o' modelin'. Big money for pitchers like these. Been in a couple o' flicks, too." He took a long pull on his whiskey.

"Skin flicks?"

"Yes, suh."

"Can I assume Mrs. Cannonball does not know about Ms. Dupree?"

"Don't think so."

"She have a steady man who would object to her and Cannonball getting it on?"

"Jolie? No way."

"This photo give you any ideas about who killed Cannonball?"

Spider drained half the contents of his glass and shook his head. "No, suh, cain't think o' nobody."

————

NO ONE KNEW SQUAT. BUT OUR VISITOR FROM LOUISIANA OBVIOUSLY had pissed off someone enough to stab him to death.

The Cajun detective I spoke with at the Iberia Parish Sheriff's Office found nothing but a couple of traffic violations on LaShott and one domestic disturbance between Mr. and Mrs. Spider more than ten years ago.

The answer would come from Prospect, but from whom?

————

AT EIGHT O'CLOCK SUNDAY EVENING, KATE AND I SAT DOWN TO watch a period British drama on PBS. She sat next to me on the love seat sipping the remainder of a Portuguese vinho verde we drank with dinner, and I jiggled two cubes floating in a couple ounces of Famous Grouse.

Just as a dashing young cavalry officer cantered to a stop a few yards from where three sisters in Empire dresses sat picnicking, the phone rang.

A county sergeant named Hugh Bledsoe said my presence was requested at the French Holler Social Club.

Kate complained. I put on a pair of sneakers, took a gulp of Listerine to hide the scotch on my breath and headed toward the best little whorehouse in Blount County.

Hugh Bledsoe met me in the parking lot. His car and two other county units were parked near the house, not far from Calvin Woodvine's black Caddy and Alvis's orange Z.

"Sorry 'bout this, Chief," he said, "but the victim and Miss Chastity asked me to call ya. Said this may have somethin' ta do with the homicide y'all caught the other day."

He had explained this recent incident when we spoke on the phone.

"You arrest the assailant yet?"

"No, sir. Vic wanted ta talk with you a'fore signin' a complaint."

I shook my head. "Why me?"

Bledsoe laughed.

"Okay, let's re-interview the complainant," I said.

"He's settin' in the kitchen. Miss Chastity he'ped clean him up."

I found Alvis Seebold sitting at a table across from Chastity Puryear. He held a glass between his hands. It smelled like bourbon. A county deputy I didn't know leaned against the sink cabinet. I nodded to the cop.

"Chastity, sweetheart, you keep calling me to sort out your problems and I'll wanna go on the payroll."

She smiled like an old girlfriend. "Sammy, darlin', I think we could arrange somethin'.'"

She wore a sleeveless, pale orange dress that complimented her russet hair. The top had a scoop neck and low back and clung to her figure like Glad Wrap. The straight skirt cascaded over her hips almost to the floor and had a slit up the side half way to the ceiling.

Chastity stood, took a cordial glass from a wall cabinet and filled it from a bottle of apricot brandy that sat on the counter. She turned, caught me looking and flashed a smile that made me forget what I wanted to ask Alvis.

"Sam, would you like something?" she asked.

My answer contained a double meaning. "No, thanks." Then, being a world-class detective, I quickly regrouped.

"Alvis, that's quite a fat lip you've got. What happened?"

"Chief, I 'preciate ya comin' out on this, but I strongly suspect y'all may git the clue ya need ta solve Mr. Cannonball's murder."

I wondered when Alvis became an expert on criminal investigations. "Can I assume you came back to Ms. Puryear's establishment to ... have a drink with a lady friend before going home to Knoxville?"

"Uh, yessir, somethin' like that."

"And our friend Cordell Vinson decided to assault you?"

"He did."

"For no reason? Just out of the blue?"

"Fer no *good* reason, that's fer damn sure."

I pulled up a chair and sat. "Tell me."

"As y'all know, I done beat Cannonball outta seven thousand dollars."

I nodded. Chastity's eyes got a little wider.

"Well, sir, unbeknownst ta me, Mr. Cannonball didn't have the money ta cover his bet. He borrowed it from Mr. Vinson. Accordin' ta Spider, Cannonball's granddaughter took real sick and he, Cannonball that is, had ta leave his daughter, who ain't married, with cash ta cover the doctor bills."

Alvis moved a plastic bag full of ice around on his sore lip.

"And because you won all the cash from Cannonball, Spider decided to punch you out?" That didn't sound kosher.

"Well, sorta."

"Let's cut to the bone, Alvis. What was Spider's complaint?"

"He accused me o' cheatin' and said 'cause three thousand o' what I won was his money, I oughta give it back."

"Everyone says you spent the day sandbagging and then found your expertise when Cannonball agreed to play you. In normal billiards is that considered cheating?"

"Nosir, ya calls it strategy."

"When Spider asked for the cash, what did you say?"

"I done tol' him ta piss off—'cuse me, Miss Chastity."

Chastity dipped her head an inch to acknowledge the apology. "Certainly, Mr. Seebold."

"And Spider, who'd been drinking, was a little short on patience, hauled off and clocked you?"

"About the size of it."

"And what makes this the clue to solve a murder?"

Alvis rolled his eyes. "'Cause most likely ol' Spider done tol' Mr. Cannonball he wasn't anticipatin' losin' his money in a match against the likes o' me." Alvis spoke as if he was helping an obtuse child grasp a simple concept. "An' Mr. Cannonball, he says, 'Ain't nothin' I kin do 'bout it.' And as we may assume, Spider, who's got hisse'f an uncontrollable temper, jest pulled out a knife and kilt his friend."

I shook my head. "Alvis, that might be a stretch of the imagination."

Alvis smiled.

The cop smirked.

Chastity frowned.

"One problem," I said. "Spider was otherwise disposed when we assume Cannonball was murdered. A young lady will verify that."

Alvis's face dropped. "Oh."

I shrugged. "Anything's possible. I'll talk to him and the girl again. But if his alibi is solid, do you want to charge him with assault? It's only a misdemeanor."

Alvis spent a long moment pondering the question. "Havin' another player locked up ain't good fer the reputation. Nosir. You tell'im I won that money fair an' square. He ain't gettin' nothin' from me 'cept if he wins it the same way. If he's okay with that, I'll let him slide on the assault."

I found Spider Vinson handcuffed and sitting on an unmade bed in an unoccupied room, guarded by a deputy big enough to bite the wheels off a commercial tractor. I pulled up an armchair and sat.

Spider wore black slacks, a white dress shirt with the top four buttons open and the sleeves turned up on his thin forearms. He was sweating and looked as if he consumed more than his share of liquor. From four feet away, his breath reeked of sour mash, and he smelled like the dumpster behind a testosterone factory.

"Howdy, Spider." He raised cloudy, bloodshot eyes toward me and nodded. "You might have put yourself in a jackpot tonight, partner. Let's hear your story."

Spider added nothing to what I already knew. I questioned him in detail about the granddaughter's health problems, but he couldn't get specific. With a thousand dollars of hidden money, I wondered if Cannonball was scamming his friend, wasn't sure about his ability to beat Tommy Crowe or just wanted to gamble with someone else's money.

What if Spider learned about the scam and confronted Cannonball? I knew Spider had anger management problems and was only half the big man's size. Could he have slipped outside and used a knife?

A lot of ifs. And I couldn't shake the question of Tommy having a reason to kill his biggest rival. I'd investigate Crowe's financials to see if he couldn't afford to lose ten thousand bucks.

Spider's alibi held, and Alvis Seebold decided not to press the assault issue. That made my new problem simple—cut everyone loose. On my way to the kitchen to speak with Chastity on another matter, I found Jamey Hawkins standing in the living room with Hugh Bledsoe.

"Came to see the ladies?" I asked.

"Figured I'd see if you needed help."

"Thanks, but I'm only going to chase the complainant out of here and speak to Chastity. I think we're done—unless you've got something more, Sarge."

"No, sir," Bledsoe said. "Situation resolved."

Bledsoe and his deputies left. Alvis wanted another drink and promised to behave, and I didn't care what Spider Vinson did because Calvin Woodvine was driving and looked sober.

Chastity placed a hand on my arm and smiled. "I really need ta thank y'all for comin' here, Sam, and Officer..." she looked at Jamey's name tag. "Hawkins. Can I get you boys somethin' ta drink?"

"No, thanks," I said, "but let's sit down and talk about the favor you were going to do for me."

"Oh, and what was that again?"

"Locate your bouncer, Farley Whatshisname—the guy with the bench warrant."

"Farley Gayton. Yes, I was, wasn't I?"

"And where is Farley?"

"Hmm, I s'pose I should call him."

"A good start."

When Farley answered, Chastity handed me the phone. "We need to talk about the night a man was killed outside Chastity's place."

"I know," he said, "And right after that you gonna arrest me?"

"Not necessarily. But I'll help you. If you don't answer the warrant sooner or later, you'll get dragged out of bed when a zealous cop finds you."

"I suppose."

"Come into Prospect PD tomorrow morning. I'll see what I can do."

"I'll tell ya right now, I didn't see no murder."

"Okay, you're not a witness, but you may have seen something I'll consider important. Let me decide how much you know."

"If you say so."

"In case you get lost, give me your number and address."

He did.

"What time tomorrow?"

"Nine thirty, and be there. You don't want me to be the guy who hunts you down to execute that warrant."

————

FARLEY GAYTON LOOKED THE PART OF A BOUNCER OR BODYGUARD. A couple inches over six feet, he weighed in at a solid two twenty. He was a good-looking kid with short, brown hair and a once-broken nose that gave him rugged character. He'd fit nicely into any sleazy joint between Tennessee and Las Vegas.

Farley took a seat in one of my guest chairs and looked like he trusted me as much as a brown recluse spider.

He broke the ice. "No handcuffs?"

"That bench warrant doesn't interest me. When we finish, I'll have someone call the court and see what we can arrange."

He nodded, but didn't look at ease. "You split just after Chastity called 9-1-1?"

He nodded again. A man of few words.

"Did you hustle a few VIPs out of the house?"

"Yeah. Miss Chastity thought they'd get embarrassed."

"Was each man in a room?"

"Uh-huh."

"Could they have made a trip outside at about the time the black guy got killed?"

He cracked a smile for the first time. "Not the way I found them."

"How often do you make a trip outside to check the grounds?"

"Depends. I don't watch a clock. Don't set a pattern."

"Tell me about the trips you made that night."

"Not much to tell you don't already know."

"Did the victim go outside at all?"

"Matter of fact he did. I saw him go outside for a smoke. Chastity don't allow smokin' in the house."

"A non-smoking whorehouse. Good idea." He didn't pick up on my sarcasm.

"Law says ya can't smoke in a public place, right?"

"It's a private club, but I'd make the same rule."

"Sure."

Farley didn't seem enthused about helping with my investigation.

"Did you see the victim go back inside?"

He tilted his head like a light bulb just went on. "Actually, no. I saw him smokin', but after I took a turn around the grounds, he wasn't out front anymore."

"And not inside?"

"Nope. The next time I saw him, he was next to that old convertible he drove."

"So, you found the body?"

"Uh-huh."

"And who did you tell?"

"The boss."

"And she called 9-1-1?"

"Right."

"So, sometime between when Cannonball lit up and you found his body, someone in the lot killed him."

"I guess so."

"Can you match each of the cars in the lot with the people using the club?"

"I usually count cars. Yeah, I guess so."

"One car for each patron?"

"No. The two county commissioners drove together. So did the two Japs. We were two cars shy."

"Aha! Now we're getting somewhere."

He looked surprised. "Aha?"

"It's what detectives say when they see a breakthrough. Two of the pool players drove together. We've got an extra car."

"Hmmm."

"Let's make a list of cars and drivers. Work with the regulars first."

"Okay. The one commissioner drove a Chevy SUV—a blue one. The police chief had a white unmarked Ford—a big one like yours. The Jap businessmen had a rental car—silver Buick. Then the four pool players, at least I thought all four drove alone, all had old stuff—flashy, restored cars. The black caddy wasn't restored or that old—ten, twelve years maybe, but clean. You know about the red convertible. Then there was a bright orange sports car—a fastback. And then another sports car—a two-seater, yellow with a black top."

———

I ASKED BETTYE LAMBERT TO CALL A JUDGE'S CLERK AT THE Hamilton County Court and see what kind of good deal she could arrange for Farley Gayton.

As she attempted to work her magic, I headed to the billiard club, but arrived too early to find it open. I saw Tommy's pickup parked on the side of the building, so I pounded on the door like a hungry bill collector.

"Yeah, yeah, keep your shirt on. I'm coming." Tommy opened the front door carrying a push broom. "Chrissakes, you make enough noise."

"You didn't think it was someone selling Girl Scout cookies?"

"At a pool hall?"

"Congratulations, I hear you beat Alvis."

"News travels fast. Wasn't an easy game. He's pretty good for a guy with grease under his fingernails."

I thought if we stood in the sunshine any longer I'd get a tan. "Can we go inside, or are you going to sweep the steps?"

He stepped aside. "Come in. Can I get you a beer?"

I looked at my watch. "It's only ten-thirty—too early even for me."

"What's up?"

"Did Banjo Bob watch the big match?"

"Sure."

We each sat on a barstool. "Did he collect his twenty percent?"

"Not yet."

"Why didn't you pay him?"

"Alvis didn't have cash with him. Said it was in the motel safe."

"You believed him?"

"Sure. Some guys don't like to carry big wads around. People have been known to get mugged in a parking lot. And he invited me to come along if I thought he'd skip."

"Did you?"

"No need. A guy who plays that well wouldn't welch on seven-K. He'd never get another game if he did."

"Has he paid you yet?"

"Sure. Dropped off the money and said he was heading to a cat house. The two black guys liked that idea and followed."

"When do you square up with Bob?"

"Today, I suppose."

"So, he collects fourteen hundred for his troubles?"

"That's only part of what he'll get. Remember I said each player in his book agrees to pay a commission? He invited Calvin Woodvine, Spider Vinson and a guy from Kentucky named Denver Corum. Calvin won a lot. The other two won more than enough to cover expenses and still go home happy. Bobby will do okay."

"But he missed out on the expected two grand from Cannonball."

"It's not only two large he's out. Cannonball was the big name coming to town—the guy who'd draw a crowd. Bobby probably fronted him some expense money for gas, motels and incidentals. Cannonball is a celebrity. If you want to pull him in, you've got to make it worthwhile."

"You think Cannonball losing to Alvis was more than a big letdown for Banjo Bob?"

"About cut his profit in half." He shrugged. "But shit happens."

"Is Bob hurting for cash?"

"Ask him."

"Can you get him here to collect what you owe? I need to clear up a few details."

Tommy gave me a look that said he didn't believe my intent. "I can try. Why do I think this won't be Bobby's best day?"

"Tell him you've got a few errands to run and want to pay up before you leave the club."

"Uh-oh."

———

FORTY-FIVE MINUTES LATER, BOBBY SCOTT WALKED INTO THE POOL hall. He looked a little pale and nervous and sat next to me at the bar.

"Pay day?" I asked.

He nodded.

"Congratulations. You organized an exciting tournament."

He didn't smile. "No one saw that upset coming."

I drank beer, and he ordered a sweet Rob Roy.

"Shame about Cannonball LaShott," I said.

"Yeah, he was a good man."

Maybe it was my imagination, but I thought I noticed him tense up. He took a healthy sip of his drink.

"You driving the TR-6 today?"

"It's all I've got."

"Mind if I take a look?"

"I don't mind. Let's finish our drinks first."

I downed the last of mine. "Bring yours outside."

"Is it legal to drink off premises?"

I chuckled and dismounted the bar stool. "I know a cop."

He followed me, and I wondered how I could look inside his glove box without a warrant. I needed the knife that stabbed LaShott, and that was a great place to start. Of course, if he tossed the murder weapon in the river, my only suspect would go free.

Mother Nature was still cooperating with us mortals. A bright sun peeked from between a few puffy, white clouds. A temperate breeze rustled the leaves at a comfortable five miles per hour. Perfect weather to drive a vintage sports car with the top down.

Bob's yellow Triumph sat under the old maple on the west side of the lot. The convertible top had been tucked back, and a tonneau cover kept any dust from invading the cockpit. I helped him unsnap the cover and admired the interior.

"I owned a TR-4 once," I said. "I'll bet your six cylinders add a lot of pep."

"I love this thing. But that Austin-Healey I hear you've got is a nice car, too."

"It is. Mind if I sit?"

"Help yourself."

Sitting in the driver's seat put me within arm's length of the glove box, but I still hadn't thought of a way to legally look inside.

I ran my hand over the polished wood rim of the steering wheel. "I love these Nardi wheels."

"What have you got in the Healey?"

"An old Derrington. They don't make them anymore."

A casual glance to the left solved my investigative dilemma. Tucked into the driver's door map pocket was a modern version of a classic Italian stiletto. This one came equipped with a metal clip to keep the knife from sliding into a pants pocket or, in this case, out of grasp at the bottom of the map pouch.

I pulled it out and pushed a button just below the hilt. The spring-loaded blade swung out smartly and locked open.

Scott looked concerned.

"Switch blades and knives more than four inches long aren't legal in Tennessee," I said. "This is both."

"Uh, I carry a lot of cash at times. I just bought it for protection."

"Sounds like a reason for the sheriff to approve a handgun permit, but not to carry one of these."

"Oh, for chrissakes." That came out shaky, not belligerent.

"Look, there's a bill in the state Senate to repeal that law, but as of today, this is an illegal weapon."

His face dropped.

"I'm not going to arrest you, but I have to confiscate the knife. If the law passes, you can have it back."

He shrugged. "Okay."

"Follow me to the PD. I'll give you a receipt."

He downed the remainder of his Rob Roy and set the glass on the root of the big maple.

IN MY OFFICE, I HAD ONE CHANCE TO GET THE REACTION I WANTED from Banjo Bob. I sat behind my desk, snapped open the switchblade and started my act.

"You cut yourself with this?"

"No, why?" He looked apprehensive.

"Looks like blood under the cross guard."

"Don't think so. Probably dirt."

"I've been a cop a long time. I know blood when I see it. If not yours, whose?"

"I don't know what you're talking about."

The pitch of his voice changed. Perhaps he forgot his disc jockey training. I cranked up the drama a little. "Wait a minute. Things are coming together now. I'm going to send this to the TBI lab and have it compared to Cannonball's blood. He was stabbed with a thin bladed knife."

"That's ridiculous. I didn't kill anyone."

I smiled. "Then you've got nothing to worry about. But if the blood matches and those state cops want to make a quick collar, you're toast. They won't let you write a statement telling your side of the story. They lock you up and recommend no bail for murderers."

"Look, I'm telling you—."

I didn't let him finish. "I'm beginning to understand everything. That's why your car was seen at the whorehouse Saturday night."

"I wasn't—"

"Yes, you were. The bouncer saw the TR-6. Stop lying. LaShott lost to that doofus Alvis Seebold and stiffed you out of two grand. I'll bet you advanced him expense money and only wanted reimbursement, right?"

He looked down and shook his head.

"Stop lying, or I'll hand you off to those TBI agents. Hey, this isn't so bad. I can envision what happened. You followed him, asked for your money, and Cannonball refused. He was a huge guy, and you're not. You insisted, and he pushed back. You felt threatened, scared. Anyone would. You used the knife to defend yourself, right?"

He kept shaking his head. I didn't want to give him time to think. "If you tell the truth, I'll give you an opportunity to tell your story—anyway you want. Put it in writing. Get out in front of this. Don't let a pair of state cops railroad you into a premeditated murder charge. Admit what happened. Judges love that."

He took a deep breath and looked up. "Hypothetically, what could happen if someone defended himself against a big guy like LaShott?" His disc jockey voice had come back to life. He was trying to act himself into a reasonable compromise.

"Depends on how convincing you sound to a jury. If they believe you acted in self-defense, you could walk. Cannonball wasn't robbed. It looked like a crime of extreme emotion. With me, you're talking about manslaughter, not capital murder. These state cops like to ask for the death penalty."

"Death penalty? Are you kidding?"

He didn't see me smiling. "Once I turn things over to the TBI, you're not my concern. But if you want to trust me and cooperate, I'll talk to the

DA and say you took responsibility for your actions. You were a standup guy and deserve consideration."

He remained silent for a long moment, but I interrupted his thought process with a little more pressure.

"Yes or no? If you walk out of here, I'm sending the knife to the lab. You can't wash blood away. Scientific tests are definitive."

"Do I need a lawyer?"

"Up to you. While you're dealing with an attorney, the TBI will be comparing blood and DNA. But you have that right." I dropped the knife into a manila envelope.

"Hang on now. I got your word that you'll talk to the DA and get me a deal?"

"I'll talk to the chief assistant. She'll talk to you about a deal."

He thought for a few moments. "I can write what I want?"

"It's your statement."

He nodded slowly. "I hope you're not bullshittin' me."

"You write. I'll talk to the DA."

———

According to Banjo Bob's statement, things happened much as I suggested. Perhaps they did, but I'd let the forensics speak for themselves.

I invited Tommy Crowe to sit in on the explanation I gave Bettye Lambert and Stan Rose the next afternoon.

"Bob freely admitted all that to you?" Tommy sounded doubtful.

"He's got this way of getting into a guilty man's head," Stanley said. "I've never seen him beat anyone, but he can scare these people half to death."

"We've been thinking of lending him to Guantanamo Bay to interrogate terrorists," Bettye said.

"I'll only go if you come to put sunscreen on my nose."

She smiled and then stuck out her tongue like a little kid.

"Now that Bob is out of the picture, who's going to pick up the book on these local matches?" I asked.

"I could take over," Tommy said. "It's not a hard job, and I know all the players."

"Who are you going to invite?"

165

"Since he can't sandbag us any more, Alvis Seebold is a good place to start."

"It's a shame someone had to die, but Alvis emerged from the rubble. Think he'll ever be good enough to beat you?"

"Anything's possible. I'm not getting any younger."

"Then someday, Alvis may be king."

THE END

GRACELAND ON WHEELS

GARLAND HUMPHRIES AWOKE WITH A BUCKET OF COMPOSTED COW manure in his mouth—or so he thought. When he raised his head, bolts of lightning flashed before his eyes, and a mule kicked him in the forehead. Using the strength of three men to open his eyelids, Garland saw dried vomit on his white jumpsuit. Fearing what it would cost to clean the sequined leather garment, he began to shake his head and received another kick from that troublesome mule.

The smell of his breath reminded him of the stench in a cesspool. He needed to wash the putrid taste from his mouth and gingerly attempted to sit up. Swinging his legs off the wide mattress felt like he just cleared a high hurdle. But when he stood, an image of the Milky Way covered his field of vision and caused him to sit quickly.

Garland sucked in a large volume of air, attempting to stop the spinning sensation, and after a few seconds, he again tried to stand. That time he made it. In a few moments, a flicker of confidence radiated from his head, through his body and down into his legs. He took a step, then another and felt the all too familiar sensation of his brain being too big for his skull. He decided to look for a bottle of aspirin, but really wanted a glass of Jack Daniels to clear his head.

When he reached the doorway of the bedroom in his big RV, he looked down the narrow hallway toward the little kitchen, the dining and sitting areas and finally the driver's and passenger's seats and the door. The hall between him and the wide-open spaces looked like a tunnel, with walls no farther apart than the width of his shoulders. The kitchen was no more than fifteen feet away, but it seemed like a hundred yards, and he began to feel claustrophobic. The sides of the tunnel began to pulsate. Garland saw stars again. Bile collected in his mouth, and nausea overtook him. Garland Humphries needed a toilet or a bucket—fast. He ricocheted off the walls and the first door he found opened into the combination toilet closet and shower. Garland dropped to his knees, hugged the commode and lost the contents of his stomach in two great heaves.

Unable to move for what seemed like an eternity, he mustered the strength to push himself upright, turn and use the sink as a crutch. He scooped up hands full of water to rinse his mouth and splash on his cheeks. When he stood, Garland couldn't focus on the pathetic drunk staring back at him from the small mirror and opened the medicine cabinet looking for a bottle of mouthwash. The childproof cap caused major problems, but finally he took a drink, rinsed and spat into the sink. That accomplished, he grabbed a bottle of aspirin, cursed the cap, opened it with his teeth and swallowed half a dozen.

Leaving the toilet and sink as they were, Garland moved toward the door of the RV and opened a portal to fresh air and the outside world. As most drunks would, he exaggerated a careful descent of the two steps and, without falling, found himself on solid ground. The noise of the slamming door erupted inside his head.

"Hello, Garland. Y'all don't look so good."

Humphries couldn't see who had spoken, tried to look through the foggy darkness, but only saw a shadow approaching. It was the last thing he ever saw.

———

By anyone's standards, Crystal Creek is a proper little river. But it's not as big as the Little River into which it empties near the site of the old Cherokee town of Ellejoy, a place now an agricultural research center for the University of Tennessee.

Jackie Shuman and I were fishing a deep pool on an outside bend of Crystal Creek. He with a float and fly attached to an ultra-light, spinning rig and me with a rubber bug called a Trout Magnet attached to a small jig head.

"Why don't you git yerse'f some new fishin' gear?" he asked.

"This works. Why replace it?"

"Must be fifty years old. Part with some o' yer New York po-leece pension and git you a new rod and reel."

"It's almost sixty, and I like this one."

I retrieved the lure and cast it upstream, watching the red and white bobber move with the current as I cranked the handle on my Orvis reel. Then I snagged something; I assumed a submerged log because it wasn't fighting, just dead weight.

"Goddamnit." I felt the drag slip as I turned the reel handle. I raised the tip of my seven-foot rod, and something white broke the creek's rippling surface about twenty yards away in a spot of bright sunlight.

"What in hell you got hooked to?" Jackie said.

"Can't see with the glare, but it weighs a ton." In a few seconds, it came closer, the current pushing it toward the bank where we stood.

"Good thing you're usin' a rod big enough ta catch a tuna," Jackie said.

I drew the object closer to the shore. My eyes popped. "I'll be damned. Looks like I hooked Elvis Presley."

———————

WHEN HE'S NOT FISHING, JACKIE SHUMAN WORKS AS A CRIME SCENE investigator for the Blount County Sheriff. I'm the police chief in the small city of Prospect, Tennessee.

Two Prospect cops, Junior Huskey and Vernon Hobbs, responded to my call as did Deputy Medical Examiner Morris Rappaport and his assistant Earl Ogle.

"Not much fer us ta do here, boss," Junior said. "Man ain't got no ID on him, and who knows where he fell inta the creek?"

"I believe I seen this ol' boy around some," Vernon said. "If he ain't drivin' a big RV, he's got him a bright blue Cadillac convertible. Sometimes he's towin' the Caddy behind the RV."

"I seen him over ta Pigeon Forge," Earl said. "He works them music halls."

"Remember his name?" I asked.

"Naw. There's more guys impersonatin' Elvis over there than ya kin shake a stick at."

"Which music hall did you go to?"

"Big one near the Titanic Museum."

"How many of us can say we've investigated the death of an Elvis impersonator?" Morris asked.

"The big question, Doctor, is how did he get here?" I said. "Few people take a swim in a sequined, white leather jump suit."

Morris pointed to a hole in the chest of the bloodstained suit and lowered the zipper for a closer look. "Obviously he argued with a gunman and lost. You thought maybe someone made him walk the plank?"

"We've had a rash of pirate sightings lately."

"They need comedians in the Catskills, Sam, not the Smokies."

"Looks like a .38 or 9 mil," Jackie said.

"I'll let you know at the post," Morris said.

"I'll be there with bells on," I said and pinched my nose.

"I hate them things," Jackie said. "Stink always gets ta me."

"Vern," I said, "put out an alarm for Mr. Presley's RV and Caddy. Let's see if he was parked near the creek or if this was a dump job."

Vernon shifted the toothpick from the right side of his mouth to the left. "Okey dokey."

"Junior, go into the office, and start calling the shows in Pigeon Forge. See if you can get a name for this guy. I'll be there after the doctor packs it in."

"You got it, Sam." Junior and Vernon hit the road.

"So, who caught the biggest fish?" Morris asked as he and Earl puttered around the body. I smiled.

Jackie sighed. "I cain't believe this man uses a rod and reel almost sixty years old, heavy enough ta land a whale and he gits more'n me."

"Experience counts," I said.

"Good," Morris said. "Then with your experience, you just might catch the killer."

———

Jackie followed me to Prospect PD where I called in

Sergeant Bettye Lambert on her Sunday off to handle the computer work. Junior was busy on the phone in the squad room.

"The sheriff going to pay you overtime for this?" I asked Jackie.

"You kiddin'? I'm jest interested and bein' nosey."

Junior walked up to the front desk smiling. "Garland Humphries," he said.

"Sounds like a good old American name," I said.

"The place Earl mentioned knew our vic and told me about him."

I sat in Bettye's swivel chair, and the other two pulled over a pair of guest seats.

"Enlighten us," I said.

"They say he's been doin' this Elvis thing fer years all over the country. Won a few awards at Elvis impersonator contests, too."

"They have Elvis contests?" Jackie said. "Lord have mercy."

"Made some records," Junior added. "And even a couple music videos."

"I guess he's famous to some people," I said.

"Must be," Junior said. "Their payroll records show he's born on September 9, 1956, but got no fixed address."

"Say again?"

"Yep. Got no home address. Lives outta his RV. All mail and official bidness goes to a talent agent name o' Arnold Posner from Knoxville. How's that fer quick work?"

"Bulldog Drummond, eat your heart out."

"Who?"

"Never mind."

As Junior sat there beaming, Bettye Lambert walked in wearing a pair of tight blue jeans and a pink T-shirt with the wording 'World's Best Mom' printed across the front.

"Hello, gentlemen," she said. "It's too beautiful a day to get murdered. What have we got?"

I told her and added, "By the way, is that true?"

"What?"

"Are you the world's best mom?"

"'Course I am, darlin'. Also, the world's best desk sergeant and best partner you occasionally take out on the road to help you play detective."

"Wow. Not only beautiful, but modest." I stood up. "Here, have a seat.

I need you to be the best computer cop in Tennessee. See what you can find on Garland Humphries."

Bettye fired up the computer. I called in two off-duty cops to assist Junior and Jackie searching the banks of Crystal Creek for traces of Garland's car or motor home. And then I called the number Junior had gotten for Arnold Posner. Only Arnold was neither in his office nor answering the home number listed in the Knoxville white pages.

I walked out and sat next to Bettye. She turned away from the computer keyboard and looked at me, her hazel eyes peeking over a pair of little granny glasses.

"Whaddaya know, Blondie?"

"That's Sergeant Blondie to you, troublemaker."

"Of course. So, what's the scoop?"

"Some good information from the Department of Safety. I ran Garland's name for a driver's license and vehicle ownership and got three hits. His middle name is Jake. The address on file is in care of Posner and a Knoxville address. The RV tag is KING-1 and the Cadillac is KING-2."

"Excellent."

She smiled. "Then I did a group search on the name Humphries and found not only Garland Jake, but a Jake Garland who lives in the Cold Springs section of Prospect. I figured that was no coincidence and called the house and spoke with Jake's wife. She says Jake is Garland's older brother and owns Safe Place Mini Storage out on McTeer's Station Pike over in Walland." She handed me a slip of paper with an address and phone number.

"Is Jake working today?"

"Went in after church to do paperwork. I called, and he's waitin' for ya."

"Did you break the news?"

"He took it pretty hard."

"Let's hope he didn't shoot his kid brother."

———

SAFE PLACE MINI STORAGE LOOKED MUCH LIKE ANY SIMILAR facility except everything was painted in UT colors. White, cement block buildings with bright-orange doors sat at the end of a long driveway preceded by a boat and RV storage yard fenced off with eight-foot chain-link. I found Jake Humphries, a stocky man with a graying crew cut, dressed in his Sunday-go-to-meetin' clothes.

"Sorry for your loss, Mr. Humphries."

He shook his head. "Garland never hurt nobody. Who'd wanna do this?"

"Too early to say. We haven't found either his car or RV yet. And we're looking for a possible spot where someone might have killed him."

"I kin he'p with some o' that. His car's in the storage bay he keeps here. Number six-two-six, all the way in the back. Building behind the wide gravel strip. That's where people garage their ve-hickles."

He handed me a key, and I walked to the rear of the property. When I raised the overhead steel door, I found a restored turquoise 1956 Cadillac convertible, which I later learned was a duplicate of the car sitting on a platform outside the building at Graceland that houses Elvis's car collection. The thirty-foot long, climate-controlled garage also held shelves full of Garland's belongings, clothes racks with spare jumpsuits and even a flashy red cape and a few suits and sports jackets in the styles of the 1960s and '70s. Even creepier were the life-sized cardboard likenesses of Elvis collected from theaters and clubs around the country. I spent almost an hour poking around, but found nothing of investigative value.

I handed the key back to Jake. "I'm going to put a police seal on the door and keep it there until the investigation is over."

He nodded. "Anythin' you need."

"Any idea where Garland was staying or parking his RV?"

"No, sir, sorry. We don't always see each other when he switches ve-hickles or uses the storage spot. He's got him a key ta the gate fer the RV lot, so he don't need ta come when I'm here."

"Does he have a wife or girlfriend or anyone who keeps tabs on him?"

"He's been divorced twice. Last marriage ended 'bout fifteen years ago. He's had a few local girlfriends, but no one special, I don't guess. Always met girls when he travelled, but he never mentioned no one steady. He got him an agent in Knoxville you might could check with. And there's A.R. Chalmers, his bidness manager. They's been friends since hi-skoo."

Jake provided a few phone numbers for me to try.

"I HAVE A PILE OF INFO FOR YOU, DARLIN'," BETTYE SAID.

"Good, I found nothing at the storage place, but have phone numbers for you to call."

"Okey dokey, but you know what?" She showed a mischievous smile. I shrugged and lifted my hands to my sides.

"Garland Humphries was born on the same day that Elvis made his first appearance on the Ed Sullivan Show. I've heard about that, but never saw it."

"Fascinating. I watched that show as a kid. Never saw the big deal in Elvis."

"Sam Jenkins, that's blasphemy."

"They used to call him Elvis the pelvis. Gyrating to your music was radical back then."

"Elvis Presley is an American hero." She sounded disappointed in me.

I didn't want to disagree, so I changed the subject. "Did Arnold Posner return my call?"

"He did and said he'll be home all afternoon. Here's his address. It's different from what's in the phonebook." She handed me a slip of paper.

"Thanks. Call him back and say I'm on the way."

"It's almost one o'clock. Want lunch first?"

"Sure, I'm always hungry."

"If you call for Chinese, I'll make us tea."

"Good idea. You want the usual?"

"That'll be fine."

Fifteen minutes later, a kid named David from Wah Lum's delivered an order of steamed vegetables for Bettye and Hunan Chicken and vegetables, white rice and two spring rolls for me. After fortifying myself, I headed to a townhouse complex off Gallaher View Road in Knoxville.

Arnold Posner looked around sixty, was short and a few pounds overweight and as hairless as a ball bearing. Large tortoise shell glasses rested on a hooked nose you could use to open beer bottles.

At his invitation, I sat on a modern sofa covered in shiny, striped fabric. Mr. Posner didn't offer me a drink.

"This is a shock," he said, pulled a six-inch cigar from an aluminum tube and lit up. Posner blew smoke upward, and I envisioned getting a headache in minutes.

"Who would kill Garland?" he asked. "Was it a mugging? Kids? What?"

"That's what I'm trying to find out." I wanted to smack him for smoking. "What can you tell me about him?"

He shrugged. "What's to tell about an Elvis impersonator? For twenty years almost, I've represented him. I get him gigs, and he goes—most of the time. He drinks too much. He's embarrassed me a few times by missing dates, but not that often. That's not to say I don't get other complaints. Sometimes he shows up so plotzed they have to carry him on stage. But he delivers the goods, and the people love him—people our age, people who remember the real Elvis. Garland is second best." He puffed and blew more smoke into the atmosphere. "Actually, I hear he's still very good. I haven't listened to him in years. Other than that..." He shrugged again and let his thought trail off.

"I found him dead this morning, wearing his white leather jumpsuit. I assume even an Elvis impersonator doesn't go around the house or run errands wearing a getup like that. Is he mentally unstable, or did he have a job on Saturday?"

Posner bent at the waist and tapped an inch of cigar ash into a ceramic tray on the cocktail table that stood between us. "He appeared at the antique tractor and engine festival they hold at the school each year."

"Heritage High School?"

"Right, I also booked Marla Owenby for the event. You know her?"

"Don't think so."

"An almost pretty blonde with a guitarist who looks like Stephen King."

The description rang a bell. "Okay, I think I've seen them somewhere."

"Anyway, it was a good day for me. Maybe not for Garland, but..." Posner trailed off again and puffed on his stogie.

"Know anything about his private life? Anything that could provide a hint about why this happened?"

Arnold blew three smoke rings toward the ceiling, the bastard. I started feeling pain over my eyes. He took a long moment to think.

"Garland thinks he's still thirty years old. He thinks he can work and party twenty hours a day. Besides the booze, there's the occasional woman. And he likes to talk about them, I'll have you know. He thinks he's a tough guy. And he tells me about that, too. If someone heckles him during the show, he talks back. It's gotten him a few pokes in the nose.

"Look," he continued, "I spent twenty years working for an agency in New York before going off on my own and then coming down here. I've seen his kind many times. They're good, but never really make it big. You know what I mean by big?"

I nodded. "Sure. Real Elvis big."

"Even half that big would be good for Garland." After another blast of pollution from his burning phallic symbol, Posner added, "I like you, so lemme give you a little tip. You need to talk with that putz, A.R. Chalmers. He calls himself Garland's business manager. Ha! Some business manager. They went to school together, and Chalmers gives him bad advice on the stock market—things he hears about on television, I think. For years they've been friends, but like cats and dogs, they fight."

———

I DIDN'T GET BACK TO THE CAR BEFORE MY CELL PHONE SOUNDED off.

"Junior and Jackie found the RV," Bettye said.

"That was quick."

"Vern and the two boys you called in covered the roads near Crystal Creek. Jackie borrowed his cousin's canoe, and he and Junior started way upstream. They got lucky."

"Cool. Now we've got a marine bureau. Give me a location."

"Know where Creek Side Farm is on Turtle Trace Road?"

"Sure."

"Across from the big house is Baxter's Ferry Lane. Take it to the end. The owner bush-hawged about a hundred yards of ground and rents it to campers. The RV's white and blue. It's the only one there."

"Thank you, ma'am."

"And if you need to call the boys, use the radio. Junior's got his portable. They can't get cell reception there."

"I'll find them."

———

FORTY MINUTES LATER, I TURNED ONTO BAXTER'S FERRY LANE AND drove on gravel through heavy brush until I reached a clearing roughly the size of a football field, situated half way to where the lane rejoined the main blacktop road.

A white, county crime scene SUV was parked near the big motor home. Junior, Jackie and two deputies stood in the shade next to a wide swell in the creek where a hundred years ago, an old codger named James Baxter ran a ferry barge to the opposite bank.

"You called in the cavalry," I said.

"Figgered you'd want the scene worked over," Jackie said, "so I called Neal and Cobb. They already checked for tire tracks and footprints and latents on the door."

I said hello to crime scene investigators Neal Brickman and Cobb Rankin. "Find anything?"

"Looks like someone mighta pulled outta here pretty quick," Neal said. "Accordin' ta the guy who owns the farm, your vic is the only one usin' the area right now."

Brickman was wiry with thinning, reddish hair. He and Rankin wore white polo shirts with an embroidered badge on the breast and black tactical pants.

"We got shots o' the wide RV tires and somethin' wide, but not as big," Cobb said. "Figger a pickup or SUV. We'll let ya know exactly what when we match up the tread with our files."

He looked almost twice Brickman's weight, had thick, but short, brown hair and a small, military mustache.

"Anybody from the house hear a shot?"

"Farmer says no, but his two dogs started barkin' like crazy a little after eight o'clock last night," Junior said.

"Anything else I need to know?"

Junior smiled like a kid who just peeked into the girl's locker room. "Yes, sir, jest over yonder is where the killer or killers drug him to the creek and threw 'im in."

"Now that you've done all this, I feel unnecessary. Want to go out and find the killer...or killers?" I said, mocking Junior.

"I wouldn't mind taggin' along."

"Me, too," Jackie said.

"Our lieutenant ain't that liberal with overtime," Neal said. "When we finish up here, we'll wish y'all good luck."

"Go inside yet?" I asked.

Cobb answered. "Gotta pop the tumblers for ya. Musta locked when the ol' boy come out here. He have any keys on him?"

"Had nothing in his pockets," I said. "Go ahead, and open up."

Cobb took an auto body dent remover from the crime scene vehicle and screwed it into the knob of the RV's door. With one sharp yank of the weighted sliding handle, the cylinder broke free, and the door opened.

I pulled on a pair of latex gloves. "Okay, give me a minute to snoop around, and then you crack evidence technicians can take over."

———

THE MOTOR HOME SMELLED AS SOUR AS THE ALLEY BEHIND A SLEAZY gin mill, but otherwise it seemed orderly and ornate for an RV—more like a rolling whorehouse. Everything was white—shag carpets, leather seats and other upholstery, walls, Formica cabinets, ceiling.

There's not a lot of unused wall space in a well-equipped recreational vehicle. Here, every available spot held framed photographs of Elvis, Priscilla, Lisa Marie, the Graceland mansion...all in matching red frames. A corny portrait of Elvis, painted on black velvet, hung in a place of honor behind one of the dinette seats. On another wall over the dinette table, a series of three shelves held a TV, video player and a VHS collection of Elvis movies. I wondered how many times a person could watch *Speedway* before going insane.

I left the sitting area and kitchen. Nothing there looked out of place, and there were certainly no signs of a struggle. I looked into the washroom and recoiled slightly from an intense pungent smell. Someone, I assumed Garland, had lost their cookies in the bowl. The medicine cabinet door hung slightly ajar and uncapped bottles of Scope and Bayer aspirin stood next to the basin on the small vanity counter.

A queen-sized bed occupied most of the rear bedroom, as well as a built-in closet and chest of drawers. Framed record album jackets covered the walls—none were by the Beach Boys. A key ring, some change, a gaudy, gold-colored wristwatch, a cell phone and a wallet containing forty-six dollars and all the usuals lay on a tiny nightstand next to an equally small lamp. The unmade bed upheld the tradition of the place and smelled like it had been last occupied by a drunk.

I checked all the drawers and found a pearl-handled, nickel-plated Colt

Detective Special, loaded with six rounds of round nose .38 special cartridges lying on top of Garland's undershorts in the top one. I saw nothing remarkable in the closet and walked out, leaving the RV to the two crime scene technicians.

————

I ARRANGED FOR A COP WITH A LONG BED PICKUP TO TAKE JUNIOR, Jackie and the canoe to their vehicles. I headed back to the PD to see what progress Bettye had made.

"I found two A.R. Chalmers for ya, darlin'," she said. "I figured Andrew Reed Chalmers from White Bluff in middle Tennessee wasn't our man."

I nodded, waiting for the punch line.

"But how about Arvil Rex Chalmers with a 1956 DOB and Wildwood address?"

I shook my head. "Arvil Rex? Why don't you people name your children Vito or Carmine?"

Bettye smiled. "Sammy, you sound like a fish outta water."

I shrugged. "At least *your* kids have normal names. Anyone call about the autopsy schedule?"

"Doctor Mo says be there at eight-thirty on Monday. Garland Humphries is on the top of his list."

"Buzz Jackie Shuman for me. He's got to attend, too."

"Already left word with his wife."

"Remind me to buy you flowers on Valentine's Day."

"You always do."

"Got anything more to do here?"

"Waitin' for the financials on Humphries to come back, but they're not workin' on Sunday. Other than that, I'm finished."

"The crime scene guys will take hours to process the scene, write up a report and print the pictures. Someone will probably deliver the package tomorrow and the results of the fingerprint search after that. Let's go home."

"I'm right behind you."

————

I'VE ATTENDED MORE AUTOPSIES THAN SPORTS FANS ATTEND HOME games. They're one of the necessary evils set upon the shoulders of those who investigate suspicious deaths. If a pathologist recovers a crucial piece of evidence from a body, it's incumbent upon those who first encounter the victim to be present and help the prosecutor maintain a chain of evidence.

Morris Rappaport and Earl Ogle were dressed in sage-green hospital scrubs, aprons and wore protective face shields. Jackie Shuman and I draped throwaway paper suits over our street clothes to keep from contaminating the corpse and to insure no stray bodily fluids splashed on our duds.

We found Garland Humphries laid out on a stainless-steel table under the bright lights of the postmortem operating room. Autopsies are interesting and educational, but the gory details are disgusting.

Dr. Rappaport extracted a semi-jacketed, hollow-point bullet from Garland's chest. The conical shaped projectile that entered the body behaved as the manufacturer intended, so what Morris dropped into a small jar looked more like a metal mushroom.

"Looks like a .357 or hot .38," Earl said as he screwed a lid on the jar.

"Be my guess," Jackie added.

"I'll weigh it up," Earl said, "but I'm thinkin' 158 grains."

"Sounds about right," I said.

"Our Mr. Humphries must have feared getting old," Mo said.

"How so?" I asked.

"I see evidence of three cosmetic surgeries. Look here. See the tiny incision scar eliminating the baggy eyelids? Then the general face lift scar here behind the ears?" He pointed to each with the back end of his scalpel. "And I'm thinking liposuction on the abdomen."

"He was an entertainer," I said. "I guess it goes with the job."

"Maybe. We all get old and want to look young. Or maybe he wanted to stay attractive to the ladies."

"Don't we all?"

Morris laughed. "I see nothing to indicate that the bullet wasn't the only contributing factor in his death, except maybe a liver that's scarred like the sole of your shoe. I say with confidence, the man was an alcoholic with cirrhosis just around the corner."

"Nothing sinister that I have to worry about like mysterious needle marks, blowgun darts or poison symptoms?"

"You read too many comic books, Sam. I'll fax you my report as soon as possible."

"You're a sweetheart, Morris. Thanks for the sideshow."

———

Bettye greeted me with a message from Mrs. Jake Humphries and a page full of information about Arvil Rex Chalmers. I took everything into my office, hung up my sport jacket, but didn't get a chance to sit before my intercom buzzed.

"There's a Mr. Luther H. Gillis here to see you," she said.

"What's the H stand for?"

"What?"

"Never mind. What's he want?"

"He's a private detective."

"We have private detectives in Prospect?"

"From Knoxville."

"Back to my second question. What's he want?"

"It's about the Garland Humphries murder."

"He knows who did it?"

She didn't answer. "Go right in, Mr. Gillis. First door on your left."

I hung up, sat down and watched a middle-aged guy with a pear-shaped body, a wide face with a furrowed brow, a wrinkled, seersucker suit and a straw fedora step through my doorway.

He halted six inches from my desk and stuck out a hand. "Looter H. Gillis, private cop. Nice ta meet ya."

I stood and shook his hand. "Sam Jenkins, police chief. My pleasure."

He sat in the armchair a foot to his right. "You're not from around here are ya...originally, I mean."

"No, I'm not," I said. "You don't sound like a local either."

"Saint Louie. I spent five years with SLPD before I set up my own shop. Couple years ago, I got tired o' the cold winters up there and moved my operation down here."

"Uh-huh. What can I do for you, Mr. Gillis?"

"I hear you were a dick lieutenant up in New York."

"Guilty. Who told you that?"

"I got my informants. I get around. Hear things. Remember."

I felt like we were filming a remake of a second-rate George Raft movie. Against my better judgment, I smiled. "How can I help you?"

"Gimme everything you got on the Garland Humphries hit."

"I beg your pardon?"

"I been retained ta find his killer. I need your forensics reports, autopsy results, field reports—the whole nine yards."

"By whom have you been retained?"

"That's confidential."

That was the straw that broke the camel's back. I stood up. "Take a hike, Mr. Gillis."

He looked surprised. "What?"

"You heard me. Scram. Split. Beat it."

"You can't—"

"The hell I can't. I'm not one of your informants. I've got an open homicide, and my investigation's confidential. Capiche?"

"Yeah, yeah, I get it. You got no use for PIs." He remained seated in the guest chair I didn't invite him to use. I looked him in the eye. He pushed the fedora back a couple of inches. Defiant bastard.

"Tell me who hired you and I might give you something."

He snorted silently and began nodding. "So that's the way it's gonna be, huh?"

"Are you from outer space? I have no obligation to provide you with information. Why am I even explaining this? Get out."

"All right, all right. Don't get your shorts in an uproar, big guy." He rearranged himself in the chair. "Humphries' business manager hired me to find the killer."

"You mean Arlo Rex Whatshisname?"

"Arvil Rex Chalmers. Yeah, that's the guy."

Luther H. Gillis could create a headache almost as quickly as Arnold Posner's Cuban cigar. I touched my forehead with both hands and shook my head.

"You okay, big guy? Somethin' wrong?"

"Why did he hire you?"

Luther paused, perhaps trying to think up a clever answer. "He went to school with my secretary. They go to the same church. She asked me to help him out."

"That's interesting," I said. "I was just going to speak with Mr. Chalmers. So far he's the closest thing I've got to a suspect."

"Arvil? A suspect? That's crazy. I talked to him. He's a wimp."

"Mr. Gillis, how many homicides did you investigate in...*Saint Louie?*"

"Hey, look." He sounded offended. "I'm just tryin' ta make a livin' here. And because this Arvil character is Blanche's friend, I'm on the case. You're lookin' at him for this thing, okay, but I still think you're crazy."

I took a few seconds to digest that. "Go back to your client, and tell him we need to talk. After I hear what he has to say, I may give you something to work on. Maybe. Are we clear on that?"

"Yeah, sure, big guy, I know how it works. Everything's copacetic. I scratch your back. You scratch mine. I'll tell him. Never let it be said, Looter H. Gillis don't cooperate with the law. How soon you want him here?"

I felt like we were in a time warp ... characters in a 1940's film. "Have him call me. We'll make a date."

Luther stood up. "Okay, you got it." He pointed at me with his index finger. "I'll be back." He turned and left.

I followed him to the lobby where, without looking back, he told Bettye, "Sweetheart, I'll see you and the big guy again."

Luther disappeared, and Bettye looked at me over the tops of her glasses. "He's like something out of a black-and-white movie."

I let Bogie answer for me. "You got that right, doll-face, a hardboiled gumshoe, and he's on the case."

She chuckled. "I'll bet he is. By the way, a deputy just delivered the crime scene reports and photos, and Neal Brickman called to say he'll let you know about the fingerprints as soon as AFIS gets back to him."

She handed me the opened envelope. "I looked at the pictures," she said. "Do you know that motor home is furnished just like the livin' room at Graceland?"

"I've never been to Graceland."

"How long have you lived in Tennessee?"

"You know perfectly well how long I've lived here. Why would I go to Graceland?"

"That's un-American."

"Pfui. We've got a murdered Elvis impersonator and now a version of Graceland on wheels. Why did I come to work today?"

"So you can talk to Mrs. Humphries. She called again. Says she has a question and maybe something important to tell you."

"Good. I'll call. She can't be more annoying than Luther H. Gillis."

———

THE PHONE AT SAFE PLACE MINI STORAGE RANG FOUR TIMES BEFORE a female answered.

"May I speak to Mrs. Humphries, please?"

"This is Fern Humphries."

"Sam Jenkins, Prospect PD. Sergeant Lambert said you called."

"Yes, sir. Jake told me you said Garland hadn't been robbed, is that correct?"

"It didn't appear so, but he had nothing on his person when I found him. Why do you ask?"

"Well, uh, I'd like ta know if you have things like his watch and pieces of other reproduction Elvis jewelry?"

"We inventoried a wristwatch plus cash and a few other personal things that I saw in the RV. What kind of jewelry are you talking about?"

"Garland bought pieces of gold jewelry worth a fortune, and I believe as next o' kin, my husband is entitled ta all that."

I wasn't sure whether I smelled a scam or a new avenue of investigation. "Mrs. Humphries, I don't know what anyone is entitled to at this point. We're trying to find a will filed with the state. If Garland had one, all those questions will be answered. If not, his estate will have to be probated."

"Chief, Jake has provided Garland with an expensive storage facility for his property and that god-awful-lookin' Cadillac o' his fer years at no more than the cost of climate control. I'm here ta tell ya he's entitled ta all that stupid jewelry and everythin' else Garland owned."

And I thought Luther Gillis was going to be a problem.

"That may be so. Perhaps Garland left everything to your husband. I don't know yet. But settling estates is none of my business. Do you know if Garland made a will?"

"I have no ideal."

"Can you give me a description of the jewelry?"

"A gold cross on a chain, a stupid-lookin' wristwatch and a couple o' rings. All gaudy, but expensive. Real gold. Do you know the price of gold today?"

"Not exactly. If your husband can give me a better description of the jewelry—something I can send to pawn shops and dealers who buy estate jewelry, it would be helpful."

She huffed. "Well, I'll ask him. But don't hold your breath."

She hung up. I took a bottle of Advil from my desk drawer and shook out a half dozen.

———

THE CRIME SCENE REPORTS TOLD ME LITTLE MORE THAN I ALREADY knew, except that the unaccounted for tire track was made by a relatively new Cooper Discover H/T radial, size P235/75R15, something probably used on an older model pickup or large SUV. That narrowed my possibilities down to about one fourth of the 124,000 people who lived in Blount County. Perhaps the fingerprint search would turn up more helpful information.

———

BEFORE I COULD PULL OUT THE BOTTLE OF SCOTCH I KEEP IN MY bottom desk drawer and attempt to take the edge off a frustrating morning, Bettye walked in smiling.

"As you might say, Sammy darlin', the plot thickens."

"Tell me you've got something good."

"How about Garland Humphries's will?"

"Okay."

"The county clerk's secretary is faxin' us a copy, but basically, it says he's leavin' his Cadillac to the Smoky Mountain Celebrity Motor Museum in Pigeon Forge."

"That'll make his sister-in-law happy."

"And the proceeds from the sale of his RV and all personal property are to be donated evenly between the Elvis Presley Memorial Trauma Center in Memphis, and to buy peanut butter and distribute it to all the charity food banks in Tennessee."

"Peanut butter?"

"You heard me. It was one of The King's favorite foods."

"No relatives or friends are mentioned?"

"None."

I shook my head.

"But while I was doin' more checkin' on your Mr. A.R. Chalmers, I learned that besides havin' an absolutely horrible credit ratin', he took out a $500,000 life insurance policy on Garland Humphries."

"Is A.R. the beneficiary, or are we buying more peanut butter?"

"A.R. is sole beneficiary."

"Hell, that's convenient. Would he happen to own an older pickup or large SUV?"

"How about a '96 Lincoln Town Car?"

"I'll see what size tires that uses."

"I thought you might."

———

LUTHER GILLIS RETURNED UNANNOUNCED JUST BEFORE I LEFT FOR A lunch at Howell's Pub. Interrupting my routine annoyed me, but when he dragged Arvil Chalmers into my office, I forgave him.

Chalmers was a short number, no more than five-six, with dark hair combed into a pompadour and slicked back on the sides. Judging from his cheap, gray suit, it looked like he just returned from a Caribbean cruise—stowed away under the cover of a musty lifeboat. He had ferret-like teeth and puffy cheeks. When he spoke, he reminded me of a middle-aged chipmunk.

"I understand you're now a wealthy man, Mr. Chalmers," I said.

"Me?"

"You're beneficiary of a half million because of Garland Humphries' demise."

"I can explain that."

"Please do."

He shot a quick look at Luther who shrugged. "Garland and I've been makin' the premiums together, sharin' the cost, so ta speak."

"Why would he do that?"

"Oh, right, well, 'cause I only git half the money."

"You plan on putting a check for a quarter mil in Garland's coffin?"

"Huh?"

Luther chuckled. "Good one, big guy. Let the little feller explain."

"Mr. Chalmers," I said, "it's your dime."

"Huh?"

Luther shook his head and looked impatient. "Tell him the arrangement."

"Garland said he'd pay half if I sent half the money to his daughter, 'case he died."

"Is this in writing anywhere?"

"Writin'?"

"Who else knows about this besides you?"

"Well, uh, he signed the policy application when I took it."

"The insurance agent can verify this?"

"I guess."

"Tell me about his daughter. Where is she?"

"Lives up in Strawberry Plains. Got her two kids, a boy and girl. She ain't married now, so Garland sent her money, when he could, to he'p bring up the kids. He wanted the insurance money to provide fer their education."

"Be sure to give Sergeant Lambert a name and number for your agent on your way out."

"Yes, sir."

"Why did he agree for you to take out a policy on his life?"

"'Cause I been workin' as his bidness manager lots without gittin' paid. I mean I git paid some, but not a lot."

"You're losing me. I don't understand the whole arrangement."

"We's been friends a long time, and I liked Garland. Liked hangin' out with him. Liked goin' places with him. I didn't mind he'pin' him out some with his financials."

"What's with the policy?"

"I looked at it as an investment. It's with a good company, and I could always turn it in fer the cash value."

"Why didn't Garland buy his own policy for the kids?"

"Was cheaper this way. One half-million dollar policy is cheaper than two quarter-million ones."

"When you're not working for Garland, what do you do?"

"I'm a bookkeeper at Denso, that big Japanese company in Murr-vull."

"Uh-huh."

"Then durin' tax season, I work part-time fer Liberty Tax."

I nodded. "What exactly did you do for Garland?"

"He'p manage his money."

"You get a good return for his bucks?"

"Well, uh, as ya know, the market's been up and down lately."

"I've been told that you and Garland were known to fight often. What's that all about?"

"Who told you that? Oh, I know. Arnold Posner."

I didn't confirm his suspicions, so he continued.

"Well, most o' the time it's about Garland's drinkin'. The man's killin' himse'f. I mean, was. Then sometimes it was about not makin' much money on investments. But that ain't my fault."

"Garland's sister-in-law alleges that there's a sizeable fortune in gold Elvis jewelry that's unaccounted for. Know anything about that?"

A big smile crossed A.R.'s face. "Now, that's one o' the good investments I recommended. I found the people makin' the reproductions, and Garland bought those pieces when gold was down. You know what the price was jest the other day?"

"No, but can you provide a good description to send to pawn shops and estate jewelry dealers?"

"I kin do better than that. I'll show you a website. Each piece is handmade from the original in the Graceland collection and comes with a letter of authenticity. All gen-u-ine reproductions of somethin' worn by Elvis himse'f. They's special order only."

I turned to my computer and clicked on the browser. "Come over here, and pull up the website."

A.R. spent a few moments getting to the site and the catalog pages. "See here?" he said. "That's the watch."

I thought it had a zip code and not a price. "We've got the watch in property. What's next?"

He switched to another page. "Here ya go. See this here lion's head ring? That's one piece. Look at those ruby eyes."

"Yeah, it's not *too* gaudy."

"Now look here. This filigree cross... Elvis always wore one. So did Garland. They's both God-fearin' men. It got nine sapphires in it."

"Okay. Is there more?"

He scrolled down the page. "And the TCB ring—one of Elvis's favorites. We was in the Heartbreak Hotel when I heard they was makin' these. I told Garland ta hurry, and he picked it up at the introductory price. Look what they's goin' fer now."

"There's really a Heartbreak Hotel?" I asked.

A.R. frowned as if he was looking at a fairly stupid child. "O' course, on Elvis Presley Boulevard in Memphis."

"I should have known. What's TCB mean?"

Now he looked at me as if I suggested they bulldoze Graceland and put up a parking lot. "Takin' Care O' Bidness. It's what Elvis called his band."

"I knew that."

Luther snorted.

"I'll have the sergeant copy these pictures and send them to the county's lost property squad. They'll get copies to all the dealers and brokers here and in the surrounding counties."

"I hope it he'ps. I wouldn't mind getin' my hands on those myse'f. Garland did say he'd like me ta have them, case anythin' happened ta him."

"You'll have to wrestle Fern Humphries for them. She's pretty hot on the gold herself."

"I never liked her," A.R. said.

When he got settled back in one of the guest chairs, I changed the subject. "What size tires do you use on your Lincoln?"

"Do what?"

Luther interceded on his client's behalf. "How many people know what size tires are on their car, big guy? Give the little feller a break."

"You have the car here?"

"Yeah," Luther said. "He drove. It's out in the lot."

"Good. We'll look. Now tell me where you were between six and midnight Saturday."

"Uh, I was home. Right, I was at home."

"With anyone?"

"I ain't married right now."

"Alone and no one can verify that?"

"Mebbe a neighbor seen my car."

"Maybe. I'll check that. You and Garland getting along okay last couple days?"

"Yeah, fine. Like I said, we's been friends since...shoot, I guess, since the '70s."

"Even though your financial advice caused him to lose money?"

"Garland didn't hold nuthin' against me."

"Okay, let's look at your Town Car."

Arvil's Goodyear P215/70R15 tires were remotely in the ballpark, but not wide enough and with a less aggressive tread. As we stood in the parking lot, Luther asked, "You got any suspects yet?"

"Yeah, him." I pointed at A.R.

"The little feller didn't kill a fly."

"Perhaps."

"You gonna give me any names when you get 'em?"

"I'll have the sergeant email your friend, Blanche the secretary, any press releases we send out."

"Email? That sergeant don't have a phone? Blanche don't use a computer."

"And people call me a dinosaur."

He shook his head. "I'll start checkin' all the pawn shops between here and Chattanooga."

"That's a big job, Luther."

"It's what I do, big guy."

"I'll have someone hit the two in Prospect."

"Thanks a bunch."

———

LATER THAT AFTERNOON, JACKIE SHUMAN CALLED. "NEAL GAVE ME the results from AFIS when they came in 'bout a half hour ago. We got us a hit on one o' the latents."

"Give Neal a cigar."

"Ever hear of an ol' boy name o' Wilfred Partridge? Goes by the nickname o' Dub."

"Haven't had the pleasure."

"Ain't been caught doin' nuthin' illegal in the last few years, but he was a bad one in his younger days. Couple o' stolen cars, burglaries, petty larcenies, minor drug involvement. Got convictions fer about half the arrests and some hard time, but never more than ninety days at a shot."

"Anything suggest he'd escalate to murder? He known to do any meth or something else that would send him over the top?"

"No, but he needs ta explain why he was messin' with Garland Humphries's RV."

"May I assume you'd like to be here when I question him?"

"How'd ya guess?"

"Square it with your boss, and I'll see if I can find him this afternoon."

———

BETTYE PUT HER COMPUTER IN OVERDRIVE AND FOUND PARTRIDGE registered as the owner of Dub's Auto Detail Shop, a business located behind his single-wide in a semi-residential area off Gateway Road. We found Dub power washing a black four-door pickup. He switched off the machine; I identified myself and introduced Jackie.

"What can I do fer you gennelmens?" Dub asked.

From Department of Safety driver's license information, I knew he was thirty-one years old and five-eight. What we saw was a medium-size specimen with a dark, grown-out crew cut who hadn't shaved in about a week. He wore the ubiquitous summer uniform adopted by the male residents of the Smokies: a T-shirt and blue jeans.

"We've got a lot to talk about, Mr. Partridge," I said. "For starters, where's your 1992 Ford pickup?"

The question was redundant since we saw it parked next to the mobile home less than a hundred feet away.

"My truck?"

Jackie began walking toward a shiny red F-150.

"I just love people who answer a question with a question. We're getting off on the wrong foot, Dub. Let's try again, or should we plan on taking you in with a stop at the emergency room to get you fixed up?"

"Do what?"

"Start making sense, or I'll start getting physical. Understand?"

He raised his hands in surrender. "Don't go gettin' excited. What ya need ta know?"

"Let's try this one. Why would I find your fingerprints on a motor home owned by a guy named Garland Humphries?"

"I do work fer Garland."

"Sam," Jackie yelled, "Truck's got Cooper tires with about forty thousand miles o' tread left."

"When did you see Garland last," I asked Dub.

"Seen him singin' at the big show and tractor pull Saturday."

"That's it?"

"Yes, sir."

"Then why did we find your tire tracks at a spot along Crystal Creek where Garland parked his RV?"

"Must be some mistake."

"Wrong answer, Dub. Time for you to go to Prospect PD and us to impound your truck."

"Impound my truck? How's I supposed ta git around?"

"If you don't stop dodging the truth, we can find accommodations for you at the county lockup. That way you'll never miss your vehicle."

"Hang on now! I ain't done nuthin'."

Jackie joined us just as my cell phone sounded off. "Sam," Bettye said, "Your friend Luther H. Gillis called to say he's found a piece of Garland Humphries' jewelry. He's at Autry's Square Deal Pawn shop. It's in a strip mall on 411 just south of where 129 turns east toward Houston's Station."

"He give you a phone number?" She gave it to me. "Send a car to Dub Partridge's place. Jackie is bringing Dub in for questioning. And get a CSI unit to check over Dub's truck and impound it if they find evidence it was at the murder scene."

Partridge overheard me on the phone and spoke up. "Murder? I ain't got nuthin' ta do with no murder."

"We'll see," I said.

Ten minutes later, PO Will Sparks showed up in his Prospect PD cruiser. He and Jackie waited for the crime scene investigators, and I went to find Luther.

––––––––

AUTRY'S PAWN SHOP AND THE OTHER STORES IN THE LITTLE STRIP mall had seen better days. The blacktop parking lot was cracked and patched and home to a few funky-looking vehicles. The pawn broker shared a common building with an appliance repair shop, a biker's clothing store, a used auto parts dealer and a country diner that hadn't had its windows washed since the Nixon administration. For some reason, I assumed the maroon 1979 Mercury Marquis parked outside the pawn shop belonged to Luther Gillis. I opened the front door.

"Whattaya say, big guy?" Luther didn't wait for an answer. "This here's Lester Autry. And this," a gold filigree cross on a chain dangled from his fingers, "looks like one of the pieces once owned by our Mr. Garland Humphries."

I palmed the cross and counted nine sapphire blue stones set into the filigree. "Looks like it, Luther. Where'd you get it, Mr. Autry?"

Lester was a small, middle-aged geezer with salt-and-pepper hair on the sides and a patch of shiny skull on top. His pursed lips and tiny mustache made him look like a water rat.

"Came in this mornin'. My brother Chester booked it. Here's the ticket."

He pushed an eight-and-a-half-by-eleven form toward me. "Chester bought it for scrap value," he said.

The seller, twenty-nine-year-old Marbeline Silas, lived in the Fort Gamble section of Maryville, just outside the Prospect city line. She used her driver's license and debit card for identification.

Chester Autry came out from the back room to give a description of Ms. Silas. Chester looked like a younger version of Lester without the pencil mustache, but with a pair of bifocals. I gave them a receipt for the cross and walked out with Luther.

"Okay, big guy, you ready for us to scoop up this Marbeline dame?"

"What do you mean 'us', Luther?"

"I found the cross. You can't cut me out now."

"Let's make sure it's the right piece of jewelry first. Find your man Chalmers, and bring him to Prospect PD."

———

THINGS BEGAN MOVING QUICKLY.

Dub Partridge sat in the squad room, not yet arrested. We talked about how he cleaned Garland's RV inside and out on a regular basis as well as detail and wax the '56 Caddy. Other than that, he wouldn't go for spit.

Neal Brickman called with news that the tires on Dub's pickup matched the tread found at the murder site, and they took minute dirt samples from the frame and wheel wells for the lab to match with the soil along the banks of Crystal Creek. But we'd have to wait for the test results to see if the particular characteristics of Dub's tires matched exactly and if the soil test came back positive.

Luther dragged A.R. Chalmers to Prospect where he positively identified the cross, based on a unique clasp on the chain.

Betty found Marbeline Silas through Social Security records, working at a beauty shop in Maryville.

Dub, the small time ex-con, thought he'd be slick by requesting a public defender. So, he cooled his heels while Jackie and I drove to Maryville. Luther objected when I said he couldn't go, but he and Chalmers stayed at the PD waiting for new information.

———

Iola's Styling Barn and Tanning Salon was a cottage industry, full-service beauty shop built into a pre-fab corrugated aluminum building on a back street in the Eagleton section of Maryville. As soon as Marbeline tucked her current customer under a cone-shaped dryer, we conversed.

I thought the soft approach might be best. "You're implicated in the murder of one Garland Humphries, Ms. Silas. Before we slap on the cuffs, I'll allow you to explain why you had property belonging to the deceased."

"Who the hell is Garland Whatshisface? And what property am I supposed to have?"

"Unless I get some good answers, I'm charging you with a robbery-homicide. You sold a gold cross this morning. It was the victim's property."

"I sold that cross, but I *do not* know what the hell you are talkin' about. Jesus have mercy!"

Marbeline had straight, shoe-polish-black hair and a sharply contrasting pallor. A Prince Valiant haircut did nothing to improve her looks.

"Where'd you get this?" I dangled the cross in front of her.

"Dub Partridge gave it to me."

"Go on."

"I seen him Sunday. Came over ta say he loved me." She expelled a large quantity of air. "And the butthole gives me a murdered man's cross? Lord have mercy."

"Why did you sell it?"

"Just 'cause I had sex with Dub, don't mean I love him. I need money more than I need a gold cross."

"Why pick Autry's Pawn Shop? They're not the closest."

"I called around. They offered the best price on gold."

Jackie talked her through writing a statement, and I left her with a message. "Stick around, Ms. Silas. I'll want to talk to you again."

"Don't you worry, sugar. I ain't plannin' on protectin' Dub Partridge."

———

I DID THE DANGLING CROSS ACT AGAIN IN FRONT OF DUB PARTRIDGE and his legal aid attorney. "You've got one minute to explain this."

"Don't respond to that, Mr. Partridge," lawyer Hadley Billings said.

"How many homicide suspects have you defended, Mr. Billings?" I asked.

He got a sheepish look on his face. "I, uh..."

"I thought so."

"Got yourself a real winner here, Dub. Don't say anything. Just listen. Marbeline gave us a statement. The cross came from you. You took it from Humphries's body. Your vehicle was at the murder scene. Your prints were on the door of the victim's RV. Guess who's under arrest and getting a one-way ticket to a lethal injection? Sayonara, dipshit. Jackie, lock him up."

Jackie Shuman pulled a pair of cuffs from a pouch on his gun belt.

"Whoa!" Partridge sounded shocked. "I dint kill nobody."

"But you were there. You had the victim's property. You have one chance to save yourself. Who did it?"

Billings jumped in. "What will you do for Mr. Partridge if he cooperates?"

"Tell the DA he played ball. Then you two can work out a deal I won't oppose. If he just took the cross from the body, I'd suggest one count of grand larceny and let him slide on the felony murder."

Those two mumbled behind Billings' hand for what seemed like a long time. Then Hadley Billings nodded, and Partridge spoke.

"Eddy Ray Guerrier."

"How'd he kill Garland?"

"One shot. I thought he was only goin' ta rob Garland. I didn't even know the damn gun was loaded."

"Sure you didn't." I tossed a lined pad and pen at Partridge. "Write it up. Counselor, give him some advice."

EDDY RAY GUERRIER BELONGED TO BLOUNT COUNTY'S CLOSEST thing to an organized crime family. They really weren't that organized in the traditional sense, but they—the brothers, sisters, cousins, aunts, uncles and the patriarch himself, big Aldus Guerrier, a displaced Cajun, spent their days shoplifting, stealing cars, selling drugs, doing strong-arm robberies and a myriad of other offenses that made them the darlings of most cops in three counties.

Jackie and I found Eddy Ray under the hood of an old, black Trans Am that looked more like a spacecraft than an automobile. He was about six-one and a lean piece of meat with wavy brown hair that almost reached his shoulders. A good-looking kid of thirty-three, Guerrier spent fourteen of those years incarcerated for everything from minor juvenile crimes to a more recent series of armed robberies for which he did five years. To any cop, Eddy Ray would have looked dangerous—like an alligator who left the swamp for a stroll through a civilized neighborhood full of toy poodles.

We transported him back to the PD, while Will Sparks stayed behind to guard the car and the travel trailer Guerrier lived in at the Off-Broadway Mobile Home Park.

Eddy Ray never said a word, but sat in the back seat grinning like the village idiot—or a fox.

"LOOK, DUB," I SAID. "I'VE GOT EDDY RAY WARMING THE BENCH IN one of our D cells, but I can't keep him forever."

"Why? I told ya..."

"Ask Mr. Billings. I can't convict him on the uncorroborated testimony of his accomplice—an upstanding chap like you. I need physical evidence linking him to the murder. I want the gun and the two rings he took from Garland."

"Man, you're gonna git me kilt. Y'all have any idea what kind o' family that ol' boy comes from?"

"Sure, the coon-ass version of Murder Incorporated. So what? If I tell the chief ADA you gave me a name and nothing else, she'll laugh me out of the Justice Center, and you'll be back facing robbery and murder charges. That sound right to you, Counselor?"

"He's right, Mr. Partridge," Hadley Billings said. "You've got to provide information that convicts Guerrier, not just a tip."

"Je-sus Lord! How long y'all think I'm gonna last inside when Eddy Ray's old man puts the word out on me?"

"You've been in the county lockup a few times. How long do you think you'd last in the state slammer unless you roll over and be someone's punk?"

Dub opened his mouth, but nothing came out.

"Can you arrange for protection? A new identity maybe?" Billings asked.

I figured he'd been watching too many gangster movies on his off time, but didn't want to rain on his parade. "I'll do what I can. So will the ADA. She's tough, but not totally unsympathetic. She'll do the right thing."

"You've got no choice, Dub," Billings said.

Partridge took a long moment to respond. "I ain't sure about the rings. Mebbe he already sold them. He's a spooky bastard. Paranoid like. He got him this big .357 revolver he keeps in a holster screwed to the side rail o' his bed. He brags about it. Thinks he's slick 'cause he's ready ta take ya on twenty-four-seven.

"You think he might keep the rings in the car?" I asked.

"Mebbe. I seen him keep a big wad o' cash in the console. He might keep the rings there 'til he sells 'em. But, ya know, he jest might keep that lion ring fer hisse'f. Sick bastard...he liked them red eyes."

———

WITH DUB PARTRIDGE'S INFORMATION AND KNOWLEDGE OF THE GUN and the rings Guerrier kept, I obtained a search warrant for the Trans Am and the trailer home.

I arranged for two more Prospect cops to provide backup, and Jackie called in two county crime scene investigators for photos and forensic work after the search.

Everything seemed peachy on our way to Guerrier's trailer until Will Sparks called in a 10-1—officer needs assistance—urgently.

Big Aldus Guerrier and four other clan miscreants somehow got wind of Eddy Ray's problem and decided to scare off the cop left to guard the objects of our search.

Luckily, the two additional cars I sent to assist arrived before the five Cajun morons could get physical with Will. Within moments, two state troopers, three deputies and the chief of Rockford PD arrived and added to the officers who now outnumbered the Guerriers.

Dub Partridge's information turned out to be golden. It didn't take me two minutes before I found a Colt Python just where he predicted it would be. The rings were another story. It took us an hour to find them hidden in a mayonnaise jar in the refrigerator.

———

EDDY RAY WAS A COOL CUSTOMER. I ASKED QUESTIONS, AND HE JUST grinned. Anyone who knows me would understand that I badly wanted to wipe the smirk off his face—even go a little further and save the county the expense of a trial. But I behaved like the consummate professional and simply processed his arrest for murder and robbery, possession of a deadly weapon with intent to use it during the commission of a felony and possession of stolen property. If I could have squeezed in passing on the right, I would have done so.

Eddy Ray helped me fill in the blanks on his arrest report, but he admitted and said nothing more except, "Y'all can tell Dub Partridge and his black-haired bitch of a whore that they're dead. And they can count on it."

———

TWO DAYS LATER, BETTYE AND I WERE SITTING IN MY OFFICE EATING Chinese takeout when Luther H. Gillis and his secretary walked into the lobby. PO Joey Gillespie, who was filling in for Bettye at the desk, buzzed my intercom, but Luther didn't wait to be announced.

"Hi ya, big guy." He touched the brim of his fedora. "Hello, Blondie. He treatin' you right?"

"Hello, Mr. Gillis," Bettye said and turned her attention to the woman who stood next to him, a middle-aged blonde who looked like she should be named Blanche.

Luther," I said, "introduce us to the young lady."

"Oh, yeah, I forgot my manners. This is Blanche. Blanche, say hello to the sergeant and the big guy."

Blanche did.

I stood and shook her hand. "Hi, I'm Sam Jenkins."

Bettye did the same. "I'm Bettye Lambert." She cleared away her vegetables and my home-style tofu, and I pulled a couple of chairs into place, so our guests could sit.

"This thing finally wrapped up?" Luther asked.

I nodded. "Partridge got his sweetheart deal, and Guerrier copped a plea to robbery and manslaughter one—a lot better than he deserved, but I can envision a few people showing up in fifteen years to oppose his parole application."

"One thing I don't get," Luther said. "Why? I mean why shoot that poor slob for a couple pieces o' gold?"

"Far as I can tell, Eddy Ray Guerrier is just plain evil. Partridge said that he and Eddy Ray went to the tractor show where he introduced Eddy Ray to Humphries. Guerrier spotted all the bling Garland was wearing and got ideas. And Partridge was no saint during this operation. He told his partner that Garland would probably get smashed later that night, and if Guerrier wanted the jewelry, he could just knock on the door of the RV and take it."

"But stealing wasn't enough for Guerrier," Bettye said. "He didn't want to leave a witness—drunk or not."

Luther shook his head. "Hell of a thing."

"You've got that right," I said. "Guerrier took the rings, and Dub got the cross, but little went according to plan. Garland was totally sloshed and locked himself out of the RV. Guerrier's shot roused a couple of dogs at the farmhouse across the road, and Partridge panicked. Guerrier would have broken into the RV, but Dub fired up his truck and Eddy Ray didn't want to get left behind. End of story."

Luther stood up and offered a right hand. "Well, big guy, it's been fun.

Anytime you need help with another case you can't handle, just gimme a call. I'm in the Yellow Pages."

I shook his hand but didn't answer. I caught a look from Bettye. She was giving me the evil eye, and her quick nod told me she expected me to be nice.

So, I acted nice. "Thanks, Luther. I couldn't have done it without you. Glad you found the cross." Blanche beamed. It was easy to see she was more than a secretary to Luther.

"Any time, big guy."

Luther turned slightly and stuck out an elbow under which Blanche tucked an arm. "Come on, Blanche. Let's blow this joint."

When they cleared the doorway, I shook my head. Bettye put a hand on my arm and kissed my cheek. "Big guy," she said, "you're an ol' pussy cat."

The End

If you enjoyed *The Great Smoky Mountain Bank Job and Other Sam Jenkins Mysteries* and would like a free copy of the award winning *A New Prospect*, simply go to
http://waynezurl.authorreach.com

Don't miss out on your next favorite book!

Join the Melange Books mailing list at
www.melange-books.com/mail.html

Perks include:

- First peeks at upcoming releases.
- Exclusive giveaways.
- News of book sales and freebies right in your inbox.
- And more!

ABOUT THE AUTHOR

Wayne Zurl grew up on Long Island and retired after twenty years with the Suffolk County Police Department, one of the largest municipal law enforcement agencies in New York and the nation. For thirteen of those years he served as a section commander, supervising investigators. He is a graduate of SUNY, Empire State College and  served on active duty in the US Army during the Vietnam War and later in the reserves. Zurl left New York to live in the foothills of the Great Smoky Mountains of Tennessee with his wife, Barbara.

Zurl has won Eric Hoffer and Indie Book Awards, and was named a finalist for a Montaigne Medal and First Horizon Book Award. He has written seven novels and more than twenty novelettes in the Sam Jenkins mystery series.

www.waynezurlbooks.net
www.facebook.com/waynezurl
www.twitter.com/waynezurl

ALSO BY WAYNE ZURL

A New Prospect

A Leprechaun's Lament

Heroes and Lovers

Pigeon River Blues

A Touch of Morning Calm

A Can of Worms

Honor Among Thieves

From New York to the Smokies: A Collection of Sam Jenkins Mysteries

Murder in Knoxville and Other Sam Jenkins Mysteries

The Great Smoky Mountain Bank Job and Other Sam Jenkins Mysteries

Graceland on Wheels and More Sam Jenkins Mysteries

Coming 2018 ...

A Bleak Prospect